Oil Change:

(A Nina Bannister Mystery)

by

T'Gracie and Joe Reese

For information, email **Cozy Cat Press**, cozycatpress@aol.com or visit our website at: www.cozycatpress.com

COZY CAT
PRESS

ISBN: 978-1-939816-45-0

Printed in the United States of America

Cover design by Karri Klawiter
http://artbykarri.com/cover-art/e-book-print-cover-art-design

1 2 3 4 5 6 7 8 9 10

To University of Louisiana-Lafayette friends and colleagues.
Thanks for the memories: Geaux Cajuns!

PROLOGUE: UNDERNEATH

Water had gotten into the cement tank, and some of the cement had solidified. The cement tank looks like a farm silo and sits in one of the rig's legs. It was his job to be lowered down into the tank and chip away the hardened cement.

Cement irritates sensitive skin, nostrils, and lungs.

He worked with a small hammer and chisel. The fragments of cement went into a wicker basket, which was pulled to the top, then dumped overboard.

Chip. Chip.

He tried not to think that the platform was ten miles from shore; that today was his last day, that he was getting out of it; or that the leg of the platform extended down more than a mile into the water, and that he was now an extra sixty-three feet beneath the ocean's surface.

Chip. Chip.

Fragments into the basket, swinging there beside him held to the rung of the ladder.

Absurdly the basket reminded him of Easter egg hunts.

There was no technology involved here, no high speed compressor pumps, no state of the art machinery.

Water had gotten into the cement. Fragments of cement had hardened and had to be removed.

Sounds surrounded him. Dull roaring of engines, circulating vents of air, creaking of the aluminum joints that held the ladder together.

What if the ladder collapsed?

He tried not to think of that.

Better to think of the money he was going to be paid.

That he was going to take, and escape with.

And he *was* going to escape. There were warnings that one could not do that.

But he had figured out a way to do it. And with money.

A great deal of money indeed.

There were stories, of course, about The Tool Master, and about what he would do if he learned...

But he would not learn.

Tomorrow: the helicopter, shore, and then somewhere else.

First New Orleans, then London.

He would not be found in London.

There he could disappear.

And drink. Drink a great deal, because out here there was no drinking.

Chip. Chip.

Basket almost full now, no eggs, no green and red and banded and speckled and children all around, shrieking and running through the cool wet lawn.

How long ago since he had been a child?

He was not a child now.

He was, indeed, very far from being a child now.

The cement was chipped away now, revealing bare patches on the side of the well.

He took two five-inch square packets from the pocket of his orange jump suit.

Very carefully he taped them to the well wall.

Five minutes later, he was climbing out into the sunlight.

And he was squinting through sweat-filmed eyes at the thunderheads, out there, farther at sea, vast pink and purple popcorn balls, with tracings of lightning illuminating the guts of them, dark inky guts of them, the lightning writing its name inside them and then evaporating, disappearing, forgetting where it had been or what it had written.

He was outside.

And a mile under water, sixty-three feet under the mud that was the bottom of the ocean...

...he had left something underneath.

CHAPTER ONE: WHAT SHE FOUND IN THE
DRAINAGE CANAL

The thunderstorm that appeared huge, menacing,
inspirational, colorful, fantastically colored, and deadly as
the sea itself to workers on the offshore oil rig Aquatica—
owned and operated by Louisiana Petroleum Ltd—was
hardly visible at daybreak to the citizens of Bay St. Lucy.
Those of them who were awake at five thirty a.m. saw
nothing monstrous at all, but simply a twin of the rising
sun, a silver-dome-topped peach curve that could have
been old sol reflected in morning haze, just as well as it
could have been what Keats called a 'huge, cloudy
symbol,' and what Nina Bannister, ex-English teacher of
thirty years, would have recognized as the inspiration for
what seemed ninety percent of all romantic poetry.

"Oh my God," she wheezed.

Then she stopped running.

Or rather she stopped doing whatever it was that she
had been doing, because 'running' would have been
putting it a bit dramatically, overstating to a ludicrous
degree what it actually was.

What she had been doing did not even properly arrive at
the status of 'jogging,' and was actually no more than
advanced walking with one's weight distributed in such a
way as to make falling forward and scraping one's face
across three feet of red clay track a distinct and frightening
possibility.

"Oh my God."

She was bending double now, hands pressing in hard on
whatever part of the body that was just above the hip
bones, and bits of dizziness alternating through her brain
with equally disturbing bits of 'lightness of the head,'

while she cursed herself for having taken no real exercise at all for the previous five months.

Five months?

Well, ten months actually.

Ten months?

Oh the hell with it. Who knew how long had it been since she had taken any real exercise?

The job of high school principal had taken its toll, both on her free time (she had none) and on her willingness to do anything other than deal with myriads of school problems, eat (too much) and sleep (too little).

But that was done now.

Now she was the proprietor of Elementals: Treasures from the Earth and Sea, responsible only to Margot Gavin, who would be a far easier boss to work for than the school board had been.

Breaths were coming a bit easier now, so she could straighten up and begin to enjoy both the morning and Gerard Park.

Neither was hard to do.

The morning was like a jewel, and, yes, what was indeed so rare as a day in June? And not just any morning in June: June first, the first exquisite real day of summer, with acacias all in bloom and sea birds floating like shards of whole cloth above evergreens and magnolias that dotted the town's landscape; and smells of Flowering Judas bushes mixing gleefully with all the aromas of coffee and pastry and kilns and sea air and ocean spray…

…and then there was the park.

Bay St. Lucy was a village of parks.

Its white sand beach was a park in and of itself, of course, and its little doll house downtown could have been considered a park—bright blue clapboard houses set off under palm trees and crumbling sidewalks bordering red brick streets—but there were other parks, each of them possessed of a certain kind of charm.

McKenzie Park had a duck pond. Stonewall Jackson Park had the bandstand where, in only a few days, the Bay

St. Lucy Brass Band would begin its Summer and Sousa
series. Kimmel Park had perhaps the region's most
complete   jungle   gym/   seesaw/   swing   set/
giantplasticbrightyellowtubething.

And here, surrounding her as she began walking as a
warm up to one more attempt at near-jogging, was Gerard
Park, which had a bit of everything.

It had the running track, which outlined the boundaries
of a giant amoeba, if amoeba-boundaries were comprised
of red clay bitlets that sounded scratchy when one's not
new but not very often used either Nikes scraped across
them. It had copses of willows that bent soothingly over
the gazebos that were circular white porches without
houses attached to them. It had a creek running through it
to no purpose, with no particular destination, and only the
rumor of a current that bubbled along over flat rocks and
small frogs, luring very young children and picnicking
lovers and wild-eyed poets and Nina to sit upon its banks
and submerge their bare feet.

And it had that quality of timelessness that all real parks
possess, the soft breath emanating from all its elements, all
its minnows and palm fronds and shadows and arches and
groves and brickwork—emanating from all these rags and
bones of the universe, whispering:

"We were and will be, just like you weren't and won't
be. So just enjoy, and the hell with it."

Or something like that.

She was beside the giant maple tree now. Two
cardinals, the bright red male and his much more modestly
dressed spouse—one would assume they were married, but
these days, these days, these younger birds, these younger
birds, where did they get their values?—were chasing each
other through the branches, upon which a black squirrel sat
and yammered at them, probably realizing that they were
up to no good and were on drugs.

"Hey Nina!"

"Nina!"

These voices came from two other cardinals, who differed from the first two only in that the female was dressed more brightly than the male, that they were flying on the track and not in the trees, that they were oblivious to the squirrel, and that they were humans.

"Hey you two!"

They were moving with such effortless grace and such deceptive speed that her greeting, which had begun with every intention of being a shout, had whimpered down to little more than an everyday utterance by the time it had reached its exclamation point, which really, given the fact that they were now no more than a few feet away from her, did not deserve to be much more than a period.

"John and Helen Giusti! My favorite runners!"

There were those exclamation points again. But they were probably all right, and even justified, given the exclamationness of these two perfect people, these late-in-their twenties still newly marrieds, these ex stars of the Broadway stage and Mississippi gridiron, these earths, these realms, these Englands, these Giustis.

Who were standing still now, and smiling at Nina just as broadly as she was beaming back at them.

This was possibly because they were by nature happy people, in the first glorious months of their marriage.

Or it might have been because they were just enjoying the morning.

Or it might have been because Nina was one of those people that all humans in Bay St. Lucy seemed to like, and they were humans in Bay St. Lucy.

Or it might have been because they were out here on the running track in Gerard Park, not in the laundry room of the state prison, where Helen might well have been had Nina not solved the murder of her ex-husband.

"We haven't seen you out here!"

"I know," she nodded, still a bit out of breath. "My first time in more months than I want to think about. Do you guys come out and run every morning?"

And, of course, the answer was bound to be 'yes we do,' which was absurd, because—well, there it was, wasn't it? Absurd because those people who did not need to run did so constantly and those who desperately needed to run did so with the frequency of Christmas, Valentine's Day, or Halloween, that is, once a year.

"We try to," said Helen, smiling as she said the words, her dark eyes sparkling, her lilting actress's voice spreading like honey over the park and causing all the small animals to swoon like Disney characters.

"John has to open 'The Pelican Skeleton' at six thirty; vets have tough hours. I've been helping out at Bagatelli's bakery—you know I've always loved that place—but bakers' hours aren't the easiest things to deal with either. Nina, have you heard from Margot?"

Nina nodded, trying not to be openly envious of Helen's superbly sculpted abs, or the fact that she could run in a two piece red bikini-like thing—as opposed to Nina's floppy sweater—or the fact that she could run at all.

She failed at not being openly envious of all these things but answered anyway.

"Got a call from her yesterday. She and Goldmann are back at The Candles. First guests are arriving next week. The week long honeymoon in Chicago is over."

John shook his head. He was not as magnificent or radiant or red or sculpted or hauntingly beautiful or darkly mysterious as his wife but as men went he wasn't bad, and he looked like he still could start at fullback for the Bay St. Lucy Mariners.

"Who would want to honeymoon in Chicago?" he asked.

There was silence in the park.

No one knew.

Nina gave, finally, the best answer she could come up with.

"Well. They're Chicagoans."

"That," said John, seemingly trying but not succeeding in making his head stop shaking, "should be reason enough."

"I know. I know. I told Margot the two of them ought to go to Bimini or Tahini or one of those 'ini' places with umbrella drinks. But they were having none of it. Anyway, she said she was already missing Bay St. Lucy."

"Serves her right," said John, "for leaving. By the way, when are you bringing Furl by for his vaccinations?"

She paused.

This was an area of some disagreement between her and her cat.

"We talked about it last night. I told him I felt it would be in his own best interests. I described, with some graphic detail, some of the diseases a cat his age could get if he neglected preventive health care. I emphasized that going in the cat carrier wasn't as bad as he seemed to want to believe, and told him that it was really pretty silly—demeaning actually—to have to use a plumber's helper to force him down into it, especially since last time he chewed a big gap out of the plumber's helper and now it's lost its vacuum seal thing so it isn't really much of a helper. To the plumber, I mean."

"How did Furl react?"

"He jumped up on the kitchen table and left a little turd there."

"So he was against the idea?"

"That's the way I interpreted it."

"Still…"

"I know, I know. We'll be there."

There was silence for a time, and Nina regretted, almost immediately, having mentioned the turd on her kitchen table.

Still, John had asked, and if he as a veterinarian could not handle such matters…

"You have to come out for dinner!" he said, brightly, proving that he could indeed handle such matters.

Nina reacted exactly the same way she always did when invited out for dinner:

"When?"

John and Helen looked at each other, communicated symbiotically, and chimed in harmony:

"This Friday!"

Nina answered, also in harmony:

"Good."

John nodded:

"We'll be leaving town at about five thirty to drive home. Why don't we just pick you up at your place?"

"Excellent!" answered Nina, who was not certain which she most looked forward to: the ten mile drive, most of which skirted the beach and the rest of which wound through dark and hauntingly beautiful pine forests; or the house itself, set on poles far out into the ocean and glimmering like a jewel on moonlit nights; or whatever feast the Giustis would make for her; or just being with John and Helen for an evening, listening to Helen reminisce about life on the stage in New York, or to John talk about the strange and wondrous sea creatures one could spy from the deck.

"That's done then," she said, adding: "But only on the condition that I can have you two out the following weekend."

Their HAPPYCOUPLESYMBIOTISM remained in force, and they both nodded and agreed simultaneously.

So that was it then.

There were a few more words of near-perfunctory pre-parting, a few words of actual parting, mutual shouts over the shoulder after having parted, and then Nina was by herself again, panting, wheezing, and sighing as her mental speedometer approached two m.p.h.

The creek was on her left now, and there, ten feet ahead, was the small Ichabod Crane bridge that crossed it and behind which the Headless Horseman could not have hidden because it was too small.

Eight feet ahead.

Pant pant…

Shuffle shuffle.

Six feet ahead.

She was really moving now.

So what, she asked herself as the small red clouds of clay particles rose around her ankles, *could she feed the Giustis?*

Fish of some kind, certainly.

She would go out into the surf and cast for whitefish.

Which she would broil on the charcoal grill that sat beneath her bungalow.

Two feet, one foot, and there…was….that…

…little bridge.

Many parts of her body were beginning to hurt now. Her knees, her ankles, the small of her back, her shoulders…

Who had created the myth that exercise was good for the body? But no…when one thought about it, that statement was not a myth at all, since myths were simply fanciful albeit unprovable tales that masked elemental truths: why the sun moved from east to west, why evil existed, etc. No, the statement "Exercise is good for the body," was simply a lie. It expressed no elemental truths at all; it simply deceived ordinary people into thinking that stretching or pulling or heaving or panting or sprinting or doing any other completely unnatural activity meant primarily to be done by children on playgrounds would lessen rather than augment pain and would make blissful inertia somehow more exalted than it would have been anyway.

The bridge was behind her now.

This meant that the full mile had been done, and that the only landmark to fix one's eyes on was the blessed Vespa, her little blue cycle that sat waiting for her, chained to a gleaming aluminum bike rack, its handle bars and central headlight forming a smiling face that seemed to be saying, in the language of putt-putt, "Come ye back ye weary runner, come ye back to Mandalay!'

Which was 'Vespa' spelled backwards.

She attained the rack, slowed her speed from 2 to 1 m.p.h., stopped so that the world would stop also, and bent over the lock.

There, in the distance, were John and Helen, already at the other end of the track, their radiant smiles boring a little tunnel of light and happiness some few feet in front of their gazelle-like strides.

She unlocked the chain, slipped it rattling into the compartment that had been made for it, and straddled the cycle.

Vrrooom.

Two of the geese stepped back as the engine started.

The others continued to stare.

The entire contingent of geese followed her, though, as she guided the Vespa onto a serpentine concrete walkway that bisected Gerard Park and led to the three apartment complexes that sat neighboring it.

She increased speed slightly; the geese gave up and watched.

Now the apartment buildings—which were the ugliest structures in Bay St. Lucy—surrounded her.

The thrill of high speed—for she was making over nine miles an hour now—exhilarated her as she wove her way past ponderous and identical green doorways, all of them staring implacably into the street, all of them protecting the fascinating secrets of people so magical and creative that they would choose to live in such surroundings.

After a time, Colonial Gardens Estates was behind her and she was entering a deserted area; nothing but weeds and scrub trees to her right.

The great coulee that formed an intercoastal waterway and canal loomed before her. She approached it, then turned sharply right, and soon was driving beside it.

This coulee formed one of the only distinctive features of "the wasteland," as Bay St. Lucyans rather derisively called the area. It was in fact a kind of drainage canal, lined with concrete walls which formed a flat-bottomed

"V" shape that led from road level down to a stream of filth and refuse that eddied along thirty or so feet below. The liquid in the bottom was curiously clear, or at least translucent enough so that an observer sitting on a small toy-like motor bike apparatus—much like the Vespa—could peer into it and see schools of ponderous black carp grazing like cattle at the drainage vents that fed the waterway.

The innocuous gray walls of the thing stretched before her.

Breakfast.

BREAKFAST!

What could she have for breakfast?

She had done her penance, lived through The Ordeal of the Jog, suffered the pain, and lost perhaps some percentage of a pound, which she could now enjoy putting on again in any number of ways. There was normal old dry stick-in-the mouth oatmeal and brown sugar breakfast, but that been the stuff of a previous life, school day stuff. No more of that for her. She was an artisan now, the operator of a small shop that sold Ramoula Peters seascapes and Hummels by Bridgewater and clay pots by Emil Lanning and Sons.

She deserved something better.

Bagatelli's?

The shop was only a half-mile away, toward the center of town. Perhaps Helen would even have arrived by the time her puttering blue cycle could transverse the distance.

She could get a small basket of croissants, a cup of cappuccino to go, or a bear claw, or...

These reveries were interrupted by the sight of something ahead of her, something down there, in the bottom of the coulee.

What was that?

From some distance it appeared to be a red tarpaulin that had been cast aside and had floated down into the water.

But now, as she approached, she saw that it had a form.

No, that was not a tarpaulin; it was a jacket, and those were red running pants.

It was a corpse.

CHAPTER TWO: CADDIE DIDN'T SMELL LIKE LEAVES ANYMORE

Her cell phone, she could remember thinking, was the same color as the sky.

Strange that she had never noticed that before. Both were light blue. The sky was larger, of course, and on some summer mornings it was the largest thing in the world, because it arched over and covered everything in the world; while her little phone was the size of a toad frog, a plastic toad frog with numbered keys in it that looked out at you when you flipped it open.

Scroll down. Down a bit more.

There was the number.

How unfortunate that this particular number happened to be third in the list of places she most often called. One would have hoped a child, or a husband, or a best friend...

...but there it was, and into that her life had somehow transformed itself.

Press the green button.

Look at the weeds and blighted trees while some kind of wave, some kind of acoustical disturbance shudders its way through the warm air of Bay St. Lucy and inexplicably makes its presence known in a dingy office tucked into the entrails of the village.

Look at the Vespa beside you.

Don't look at the coulee, never look down into the coulee, not ever again, not at the whirling eddies of garbage and refuse, or at the fat sluggish carp bodies with their thick lips sucking air from the fumes just above water level.

Just look at the deserted vacant lot while the phone rings at the other end.

One ring.

Two rings.

"Hello, sheriff's office."

"Moon?"

"Yes, this is Moon Rivard."

"This is Nina Bannister."

"Oh, how are you this fine morning, Ms. Bannister?"

And for a second she did not know what to say. Certainly not:

'Fine and you?'

Because of course she wasn't fine.

"Moon, I think something terrible has happened."

Another pause, this time coming from the phone, which sat open in her palm as quiet and implacable as the sky, and, like that other elemental entity—for if phones and skies are not elemental, then what things are?—unmottled by clouds.

"Ms. Bannister?"

"Yes."

"Are you all right?"

"I'm all right."

"Are you sure?"

"Yes."

"Where are you, Ma'am?"

"Do you know the coulee that runs behind those deserted lots on the south side of town?"

"I do."

"I'm there. Down in the water, there's…"

The voice at the other end interrupted her.

"I'll be there in two minutes."

And he was.

Other things were too, of course. Two ambulances. Three patrol cars. After a short time, she simply lost count, and lost all focus. She could only think about finding a place to sit down, but, of course, there was no place to sit down, and so she simply wandered about, watching the flashing lights, listening to the sirens, and reflecting on the fact that certain events made other events impossible. She was going to go to Bagatelli's, then home, then to Elementals. She was going to eat pastry, then drink coffee or tea. She was going to unlock the shop, get some receipts in order, open several packages that had arrived the other day from potters and clay makers whose work she and Margot sold on consignment.

Now it made no sense to do any of those things.

Somehow a surrealistic mental picture formed itself in her mind. She was walking into Bagatelli's, smiling at Helen Giusti, who had just arrived there from running— and she was saying, 'I'd like two cinnamon croissants, I've just discovered a corpse, floating face down in the old coulee on the other side of town and maybe you could throw in a prune Danish and three scones.'

No. That was impossible.

So was motoring home, climbing the stairs, unlocking the front door, taking off her sweatshirt, and starting the coffee maker. So was sliding open the glass door and making her way out onto the deck to peer at the morning sun-sparkle on the incoming waves. So was waving good morning to the porpoises, and planning her day.

She couldn't do those things.

It wouldn't be fair to whatever was down there below her, the thing that had been wrapped in yellow plastic and was being cantilevered up the slippery concrete banks— slippery-brown from a small shower that had hit Bay St. Lucy an hour before dawn—by several paramedics, or policemen, or whatever other uniformed people seemed to be used to doing this kind of thing.

"Ms. Bannister?"

Well, here was something to do, anyway.

Perhaps the only thing to do.

"Yes, Moon."

She could talk to Moon Rivard.

Which she did, after he, a tree branch-thick forearm wrapped consolingly behind her back, had led her to his squad car and seated her in the front seat.

People kept coming and going.

The radio on the dashboard kept squawking and rattling with a static that sounded like gravel was being poured on the car's hood.

"Are you all right, Ma'am?"

Strange. It seemed that she was always being asked that.

Yes, I'm just very good.

No, I'm not at my best right now.

'For the essentials,' Sherwood Anderson had written, 'of what use is language?'

And this—aha, the corpse was coming up out of the coulee now and the gurney was being trundled over to an ambulance—this, yes, was one of the essentials.

She could still remember the look of the thing, its long hair matted and floating like fair Ophelia in her stream.

The bright red jacket bloated and quivering in soft, filmy current, while carp nibbled the neck.

"I'm all right."

This was not an outright lie. It was just a useless and irrelevant thing that circumstances were forcing her to say.

"Can you tell me about what happened?"

She shook her head:

"Nothing. Nothing happened, Moon. I can't tell you anything."

"You didn't see anyone?"

"No."

"Not even anybody coming out of or going into the apartments back there?"

"No."

"What were you doing out here?"

"I had come to run."

"Where?"

"Over in Gerard Park."

"When did you get there?"

"About forty five minutes ago."

"Anybody else in the park?"

"Helen and John Giusti."

"Do you know if they're there now?"

"I don't think so. Both of them had to be somewhere else. They were just finishing their run."

"I see. And you came through here…"

"It's the closest path to get back to my bungalow. Moon—"

"Yes, Ms. Bannister?"

"What can you—I mean…"

He took off his sunglasses.

His eyes, she noticed, were blue, too.

Everything was blue today; the sky, the phone, Moon's eyes.

Everything blue.

What a luscious day it was supposed to have become.

She thought of Faulkner's Benji, the idiot boy, after his sister had been deflowered.

'Caddie didn't smell like leaves anymore.'

The day didn't smell like cream the way it had.

"Did he drown?"

"We don't know yet. My men are going through the pockets now to see if there's ID or money. Maybe it's somebody that lives in one of these apartments. He could have been drunk, walking out here by the coulee. Maybe he fell in, hit his head on the concrete. There aren't many cars that drive by here, but there was a pretty hard shower an hour or so before sunup. A car could have hit him, then driven off. Or of course…"

Moon did not say, "He could have been murdered."

But that's what he was thinking, of course.

As was she.

The most dependable thing about Bay St. Lucy was its stone jetty.

The half mile wood pier—for that is what it had become informally named—was a new feature, wonderful for tourists and lovers, but still redolent of Robinson gangland money, and likely, at least in the minds of oldsters, to collapse like matchsticks under the fury of the first hurricane.

The jetty, on the other hand, was an immovable thing. It extended out into the Gulf just as far as its wooden Johnny-come-lately counterpart, but it did not shake or tremble when the big swells slammed into it. It did not move. There was some question, if fact, whether it was buttressed by the giant, marble pink boulders that lined its sides with impossible angles and crags and crevices—or whether it buttressed them, with its six-foot wide core of slippery concrete and its ever present pools and puddles of spray-water that slurped when one padded across them.

Nina found herself very thankful for it.

After Moon had followed her home in the squad car and had seen her safely up the stairs, after he had watched her unlock and open her front door, after he had nodded appreciatively to Furl, who stared hatefully at him…

…and after Moon had left…

…she would have had nothing at all to do, except for the jetty.

But it seemed right and fitting that, after having discovered a corpse, she should walk on a jetty.

There was a poetic rhythm about it.

Besides, better still, a squall was approaching.

It would reach the outer end of the jetty at about the same time as she would.

She did, taking three things with her: a cardboard box of chicken livers, the ponderous dark green slicker she wore in rain storms, and a battered book of poems, the cover of which had long ceased to exist.

She put the book into a pocket of the slicker.

Then, with the latter over her arm and the box of chicken livers held tightly in her fist, she descended her stairs.

The beach was fine to walk on, of course. She did not have it to herself, for summer families had begun to arrive in Bay St. Lucy. The parents of these families stood in ankle-deep water, waving and shouting at their swimming children, while pointing at the storm and shouting words which drowned in the crashing surf some meters before reaching their targets, who, to their delight, found for the first time in their lives that their mothers and fathers had become mute.

She walked on.

The jetty was two hundred yards in front of her, the storm a mile and a half out to her right.

Neither spoke.

Neither was silent either, since the waves crashing on the jetty had been churned up and hurled toward land by thirty to forty mile an hour squall winds, and since thunder was beginning to rumble up onto the beach and announce in murmurings and rumblings that the show was about to begin.

She stopped and put on the slicker. It smelled of grease and motor oil and old, black and white movies.

It weighted her down literally but buoyed her spiritually, so that she could actually feel herself ascending to the masthead under the baleful glare of Captain Bligh.

It was also comforting to be walking along in a plastic wrapper that creaked and scratched and formed itself anew with each passing step, as though she had become a crustacean and it had agreed to be her protective shell.

She glanced again to her right.

The ocean was green now.

Come to think of it, the sky was green, a dreadful lemon yellow/green that presaged hurricanes and looked down upon the land like an oyster shell off-white deity, awesome in its calmness.

There were no birds to be seen.

It took her two minutes to reach the jetty.

For some reason she had begun to walk faster. The only reason for this that she could imagine was that she wanted to meet the storm on its own ground and would have felt remiss had it found her on shore.

She clambered up onto the jetty, her sneakers slipping comfortingly as they always did, and her eyes falling on translucent shrimp shells and cast-off fishing bobbers.

It was a fine place to be.

The spray of the big waves, the fresh breeze that was getting stronger and wetter as she bent to walk into it, the straight road of fixed rock and concrete that extended unthinkingly before her, the lines of lightning that traced marquee lights in the ink behind them, the hulk of a great ponderous tanker that inched its way along some half mile from shore and thus now found itself just being rendered invisible by clouds and rain...

...all of these things were just impressions.

They kept her senses completely glutted.

She could smell and hear and taste and shudder at and celebrate them.

There was no room in her brain for anything else.

Nothing else at all.

Seeing was not remembering.

Tasting—and, yes, she could taste salt in the air and wind—was not remembering.

There was in her mind no place for a corp—

BOOM!

Yes, good thunder! Keep at it thunder!

BOOM! BOOM!

The rain began spattering on her now; she could see its pellets dotting the water on either side of her and creating a filmy spray on the jetty in front of her.

BRRRRRROOOOOOM!

Better thunder, with a kind of consonant quality to it, a deep 'rrrrr' that added drama and discipline to what had been rather a perfunctory vowel performance that nature could easily have beaten, if it had tried.

It was trying now.

BROOOOOOOOM!   BRRRRRRRROOOOOOM DAMN YOU!"

Yes. This was perfectly satisfactory thunder, playoff thunder, going all out on defense as well as offense, executing, seeing the whole field, raising its intensity level.

Then the rain hit for real.

It poured down on her from buckets. It drenched her.

There was no sound that she could think of that in any way imitated fierce rain, rain that came from some celestial fireman's hose pointed directly down at the earth.

The closest thing she could come up with was a cross between a roar and a hiss; but since everything else was roaring and hissing—the huge breakers, the tanker's claxon horn, the surging swells out in the channel, the relentless thunder—she gave up all attempts to subdivide whatever was going on around her, and decided it was time to go crabbing.

She was not really going crabbing, for she had with her only bait and not the apparatus: string, meat-piercer, etc.

But she had no desire to catch crabs, only to watch them—and so the rest was not necessary.

She could hardly see now, the world having transformed itself into a filmy gray scrim though which all objects appeared as either moving or fixed zombies—but she knew enough about where she was to remember a small niche in the boulders, a place where she could stand on flat surface, lean against a forty-five degree angled wall of rock, peer down into a natural pool, which emptied slightly and flooded and then emptied again with coming and going surges in the swells.

Where was it?

Aha. There.

She clambered down off the jetty and stood on the surface of the great rock, her canvas shoes soaked like washrags now, water pouring off her hooded visor, the spray from crashing waves drenching her down to up even as the rain drenched her up to down.

She squatted down and opened the carton of chicken livers.

BRRRRRROOOOOOMMM!

HISSSSSSSSSWSSSSSSSSSS!

TAKE THAT, YOU DRY LAND, YOU!
WANT TO MESS WITH THE OCEAN, DO YOU?
AND BRRRRROOOOM AGAIN!
AND HISSSSSSSSSSS AGAIN!

She let the fatty chicken liver drop into the natural pool beneath her, watching as it floated for an instant and then began sinking, an amorphous whitish blob of tissue that had once regulated matters of fowl waste excretion, but that now had nothing to do in the universe except sink.

Which it did.

Slowly, in water perhaps two feet deep, extraordinarily clear.

Sink.

Sink.

Moving back and forth as the whole hole that was a pool shuddered, and the waves crashed against the massive boulders protecting it.

There.

It was on the bottom now.

Being watched by unseen eyes, hidden behind crevices and jagged outpiercings underwater.

She continued to watch.

Nothing.

But nothing was going on in her brain, either.

She was only feeling: cold, wind blown, wet, soaked, feet drenched, eyes filmed over with spray, ears inundated by the cacophony of storm surge and downpour, palms scraping on jagged granite ridges...

...there.

There!

A dark shadow moved out from the rocks below the water's surface.

It was a black hand inching its way forward, invisible fingers acting like feet to walk it as imperceptibly as moon tide toward the white patch that lured it.

A foot and a half away.

Six inches away.

And then it lurched forward, grasping the meat in what could now be recognized as claws, and ripping off shards of tissue which it began stuffing into its mouth.

There. She could see the whole crab.

Now that it was opening itself up, the yellow and blue of its legs and inner shell glimmered up from the water.

But here—on the other side of the pool's bottom, appeared a second shadow.

Then another.

Then another.

She reached into the package, grasped a cool slimy chicken liver, and tossed it down into the rapidly enclosing circle of shells and claws beneath her.

Chomp.

Rip.

There was no caution at all in the eatery below her hand now. Just tearing and grasping and engorging and tearing more and ripping, and white shards of floating chicken flesh hanging in the pool water and buoying upward until grabbed by the pincers below, which were now waving in the dark sea like machetes.

And so were more sights and sounds added to the mix.

BRRRRROOOOOOOM!

HISSSSSSSSSSSSSSS!

RRRRRRIIPPPPPPPP!

CHOMPPPPPP!

God, wasn't nature wonderful?

And so she simply sat for a time, until her package of bait was empty, and her new found friends, her small crusty pets, had given up finding anything more and had secreted themselves once again into the one bedroom, or two bedroom, or perhaps efficiency in-rock apartments they were short term leasing.

She looked up, having been thankfully oblivious even to the storm for the last ten minutes or so.

It was all changing now.

The light was different.

Rain still spattered down and pelleted the ocean, but the storm had passed and blue was beginning to replace purple.

Roar and hiss were beginning to give way to brooding moan that was the natural state of sea sound.

There. There was the sun.

It shone in morning brilliance on the eddying swells, glistening on the scudding whitecaps that were beginning to resume their normal attack on the granite rocks beside her.

And after five minutes it was all over.

A normal, summer, luscious as cream, sea gull screeching morning in Bay St. Lucy.

She made her way out of the small niche that had done her well for this orgy of feast watching, and up onto the jetty once again.

It was more drenched than ever of course, and she had to be even more careful than ever as she made her way back to shore.

Where she would do…what?

Surely there were more things that might take the place of remembering or thinking.

About corpses.

Damn.

There it was.

Why could one not sit huddled in storms, protected by granite boulders, watching animals tear apart and devour each other, forever?

Why did one have to return to unpleasant things?

Why…

"Nina!"

She looked up.

Had she been looking down?

Apparently, for she had not seen the figure that was striding out toward her, and now she did.

"Nina!"

Jackson Bennett.

What the hell was he doing here?

"Jackson!"

But here he was, or must have been, her greeting clearly having confirmed that fact.

And now here he was standing right before her, all six feet four of him, his great body at least two sizes two big for the London Fog trench coat that he wore.

"Nina, what are you doing out here?"

"Crabbing," she said.

"In the storm?"

"Best time."

"Are you all right?"

"Everybody," she said, "seems to be asking me that these days."

"Nina, I heard about this morning."

"Yeah."

"Moon called me. He asked me maybe to come out and check on you."

"Thank you, Jackson. Thank you a lot."

"Don't think anything about it. It's just...well, it must have been tough on you, finding that thing."

"It's my own fault. I shouldn't go running."

He shook his head.

"No, I guess you shouldn't. But Nina..."

"Yes?"

"There's something that you probably need to know."

"All right. What is it, Jackson?"

"Nina, they've identified the body that you discovered."

"Who is it?"

A voice within her said, 'It's no one now.'

But she ignored it.

Jackson said:

"It's Edgar Ramirez, Nina."

"What?"

"Edgar Ramirez."

"Oh my God."

"Yes. We're all pretty shocked."

"Sonia's brother."

"That's him. The engineering student."

"Jackson, what happened to him? Did he slip, or did a car..."

"Nobody knows."

"Jackson...Sonia was on the basketball team. I coached her. And her younger brother has been out to my bungalow. He's done some work for me."

"I know, Nina."

"But, but...where was Edgar working?"

"Apprenticing out on one of the deep sea rigs, apparently. I think it's called The Aquatica. It's more than ten miles out."

"What was he doing in town?"

"No one knows."

"Mrs. Ramirez..."

"Moon and several other people have been over there, and are there with her now."

'I'll have to go. I'll...I'll bring her something."

"She would appreciate that, I'm sure."

"Why do things like this happen, Jackson?"

He shook his head.

"I don't know. Look, Nina, if you want to come with me, I was able to drive almost to the foot of the jetty. I can take you back to your place."

She shook her head.

"I think I want to stay out here for a while."

"All right. I just...you're sure you're all right?"

"Yes. I'll be fine."

"All right, then. Call me in a few hours. I'd like to go over and see Mrs. Ramirez too. Maybe we can go together."

"Sure."

And with that, he was gone.

She crept back down into the niche she had found, and peered into the pool.

No crabs visible now; just clear water.

She let her eyes wander toward the beach; it was filling up with tourists, with children running headlong into the surf, screaming with wild joy.

Out farther in the water sail boats had begun to appear.

The town was celebrating summer.

She took the book of poetry out of the pocket of her slicker.

She opened it to the section labeled W. H. Auden, and found "Musée des Beaux Arts."

She read:

> About suffering they were never wrong,
> The Old Masters: how well they understood
> It's human position; how it takes place
> While someone else is eating or opening a window or just walking dully along;

And she continued to read:

> In Brueghel's Icarus, for instance: how everything turns away
> Quite leisurely from the disaster; the plowman may
> Have heard the splash, the forsaken cry,
> But for him it was not an important failure; the sun shone
> As it had to on the white legs disappearing into the green
> Water, and the expensive delicate ship that must have seen
> Something amazing, a boy falling out of the sky,
> Had somewhere to get to and sailed calmly on.

She put down the book and looked around.

There was the expensive delicate ship, perhaps two hundred yards out from her.

There was the sun, shining as it had to.

She thought of Mrs. Ramirez, who had learned, perhaps an hour ago, that her oldest son was dead.

The plowman may have heard the splash, the forsaken cry...

"Who heard the splash, Edgar?" she whispered. "Who heard your forsaken cry?"

A boy falling out of the sky.

She had somewhere to get to and she walked on.

But not calmly.

CHAPTER THREE: TEACHER, TEACHER...

By early afternoon the sky had become sticky-bright, and the town lay puddled in the aftermath of rain. Dogs, snakes, and drunks sunned themselves on benches and sidewalks, while children careened along the beach, oblivious both to the 200% humidity factor and the supplications of their parents regarding the need for everyone to take a long, quiet nap.

The small parking area fronting Olivia Ramirez's bungalow was overflowing.

Nina could barely find a crevice to wedge her Vespa in, and, as she took off her helmet and untied the big glass bowl of chicken salad from the passenger seat behind her, she was aware that even that small space had been blocked in by a pickup truck that had arrived carrying yet another family of mourners.

She began walking toward the house, picking her way carefully between still dripping fenders, windshields, door handles and bumpers.

People crossed her path, looked up at her—for otherwise everyone seemed to be looking down at the gravel in the driveway, or up at the fleecy clouds that were making their way across the sun.

"Nina"

"Chester."

"Ms. Bannister."

"Hello, Tommy."

"Oh, Nina..."

"I know, Betty."

"This is just..."

"I know. I know."

She did not, of course, but for some reason age seemed to allow her to pretend that she did.

The door to the house stood open, and Hernando Alvarez stood in it, patting the backs of all those leaving, and shaking the hands of all those arriving.

There are men in every neighborhood who assume such duties. No one has to ask them; no one has to write out their instructions. It is a duty assigned to them by dint of their white and perfectly combed-back hair, their faces browned not with a tourist tan but with hours weeks days months years' exposure to a much more hostile sun, and with a quiet dignity of movement that promised a calmness if not a cure.

People like Mr. Alvarez—who, as far as Nina knew, was still a cook at Sergio's By the Sea—made it possible for those who had to do so to sit in one place and cry, especially during those times in life when that was the only thing that could be done.

"Ms. Bannister. Thank you for coming."

"Of course, Hernando."

"They are all in back, in the living room and in the yard."

"Yes. I brought…"

"It looks very good. I think the dishes are all being lined up on the counter, in the kitchen."

"Good. Thank you. Is Olivia…"

"She is very brave."

"I know. I know she is."

The surge of people behind her had begun to build, and she let herself be carried by humanities' grief-momentum in through the entrance vestibule and on farther into the living room.

The house was redolent of smoke, incense, and candle wax. There were small alcoves in the walls where statues of Christ and Mary stood supplicating, their arms extended either to each other or to the world beyond their wall.

She nodded and murmured as she made her way through the crowd, marveling at the gallery milling around her, and about the ability of bad news to sift down into a village, through chimneys and ventilator shafts and half-open windows and half-charged cell phones.

There, in the bedroom just to the right, stood Alanna Delafosse. Behind her, just entering, was John Giusti. In the kitchen before her stood Tom Broussard and Penelope Royale. She could see on beyond, out in the small back yard, that Paul and Macy Cox were bent forward in earnest conversation with Father Gonzalez.

There, here, over there farther, dotted about the small rooms, were the basketball players she had coached only a few months ago. Alyssha, Hayley, Amanda…

How had everyone heard so quickly?

What time was it, exactly?

One thirty.

A bit over six hours since she had…

…it still was not easy to think about it, to remember it.

The way the bright red jacket had looked in the oily, sluggishly circulating sewage.

And yet she had to remember it.

Strange. She had the absurd idea that the whole thing was her fault. For if she had not gotten up to run, had not driven to Gerard Park, had not made her way back through the serpentine driveways bordering the coulee and bisecting the honeycomb of apartment cages—if she had not done these things, perhaps no corpse would have been found.

And Edgar Ramirez would still be alive.

She was in the kitchen now. An acquaintance, Pamela Donaldson:

"Nina…"

"Pam."

"We heard that you were the one who…"

"Yes."

"Oh God, it must have been awful. Are you all right?"

"I'm fine."

"You're sure?"

"Yes. I just called the police. They took care of everything after that."

"Still, I'm so sorry you had to see it."

"It's all right."

And move along, say a final something or other to Pam and go over to the counter.

Is there room?

Maybe not.

Here are deviled eggs on a platter; tuna salad; what seemed to be Caesar Salad; more deviled eggs; rolls; a platter of cold meat slices; several coffeemakers; condiments of various kinds;

The Restaurant of the Dead.

But there, there was a spot.

And in it, carefully, she placed her dish of chicken salad.

"Coach…"

Sonia Ramirez grabbed her, gently, from behind, and turned her half-around.

"Sonia…"

The two women embraced for a time, tears on Sonia's face wetting Nina's cheeks.

"Sonia, I'm so sorry."

There was no answer to this, just a tighter embrace, the girl's body shaking softly with sobs that seemed to come in rhythm with her heartbeat, and her voice spilling out birdlike and trembling.

"He was…so good. He was such a good brother."

"I know."

"He was…the best of us, you know? He was our hope!"

"I know, Sonia."

"Why does this happen?"

"It happens for a reason, Sonia," she said, knowing all the time that she was not at all sure that it happened for a reason. "We just don't understand it."

Well. That part at least was true.

"We don't understand it, honey."

"They don't even know what happened to him!"

"They will. They'll find out."

"They say he was drunk, maybe."

"I'm sure that's not true."

"It *isn't* true! Our Edgar did not drink! Not ever! He was so good..."

"I know, Sonia. I know."

"It's so terrible. It's terrible for me and for Mama..."

Sonia gestured at a spot farther back in the living room. Her mother could not be seen, covered as she was by a knot of people, all bending over her and sobbing.

"...but it's worse for Hector."

Another gesture, another spot.

This spot not filled with people, though. This spot merely a place on the pale green wall, where a young Hispanic boy with olive skin and sad cave-deep eyes was sitting in a straight chair, staring out at what seemed to be nothing at all.

"Hector is only a freshman in high school now."

"I know."

"He *needs* his big brother! There are all these drugs and bad people everywhere, and..."

She could not go on.

"Hector's a good boy, Sonia. I know that. I heard the teachers talk about Hector all last year. They had nothing but good things to say about him."

"I know, but...Edgar came into shore whenever he could, from the rig. And he spent time with Hector. 'Don't take drugs,' he would tell him. 'You can do anything you want! The world is out there, and it is waiting for you! You have a fine mind!' And now..."

"I know. I know honey."

"It is not right that Edgar should be..."

"Sonialita?"

This from a heavy set Hispanic woman, who had crossed the room and was now letting her palm rest on Sonia's shoulder.

"Sonialita...tu madre te quieres."

Sonia nodded.

"My mother is asking for me."

"I understand. You go to her. And Sonia…things happen for a reason. You have to believe that. And know that Hector will be all right. All of Bay St. Lucy is on your side. We'll be his big brother."

Sonia nodded and moved away into the crowd.

Nina made her way outside.

The grass, the shrubbery, the concrete bird bath—it was all dripping and shining and radiating heat.

"Nina…"

She turned.

John Giusti stood before her.

"Nina, we only heard, just an hour or so ago. I felt like I had to come over. Helen is on the beach. She didn't feel like she could deal with it right now. I think she'll be coming later on in the afternoon. But now…"

"I know."

"Nina, you found him just after you left us?"

"Yes, John."

"Oh my God."

"I know."

"We got to the park just a half hour before you did. Whatever happened to him might have been happening just about then."

"Yes. But no one knows. Not now, anyway."

"Here. Let's sit down."

There were two folding chairs that sat facing the bird bath.

John dried them with his handkerchief; she sat opposite him.

"I heard he was a superb student."

"The best Bay St. Lucy has produced, John, since you were winning all the science prizes ten years ago. As soon as he graduated they were onto him, the big oil companies out of Lafayette and Houma. They paid for his education at UL-Lafayette and they were right there with job offers on the day of his graduation."

"So where was he working when…"

"The Aquatica. Huge rig offshore. He was just beginning, but still making pretty good money and giving a lot of it to his family."

"Nina! John!"

She had been interrupted by the outward edges of the social amoeba that was Bay St. Lucy.

Alanna Delafosse, dressed in a onyx outfit that was black as coal, and thus only a few shades less lustrous, less mysterious, than the skin of her own bare and slender arms.

"You two dears! You were both near the park this morning!"

John nodded.

"Yes, we were."

"And it was Nina who found the body?"

It was Nina's turn to nod.

"I did."

"Oh you poor thing…you must let me…."

And so began a string of sympathies and 'you must let mes'. Paul and Macy Cox came by, Penelope Royale and her husband Tom Broussard. Edie Towler.

She learned nothing from these people, except that, yes, the body had been taken directly to the morgue and, yes, an autopsy was planned and might well have been carried out even as they spoke and no and yes and no and yes and…

Finally, Nina, beginning to feel that more sympathy was being directed at her than at Olivia, her daughter Sonia, and her younger son Hector—simply left.

Or rather, that is, she simply left but did not leave simply.

There was an ornate ritual of 'good byes' to be gone through, and there was standing in the mourning line that led to the seated Olivia Ramirez, whose upward gaze, iron grip handshake, and firmly uttered:

"Teacher. Teacher."

….might have been the hardest thing of all for Nina to bear.

And the most inspiring.

But the bottom line was, by two thirty she was gone, and wondering again.

What to do?

The jetty had done well for her in the early morning hours.

But she could not live on the water all her life.

And simply sitting at home seemed impossible. The walls would have begun to close in, and, being pretty close in as it were, even when things were at their best, could not at all have been trusted in this situation.

So she made her way to Elementals.

The town was alive as she motored through it. *This was a good thing,* she found herself thinking.

Manning Drive, Breakers Boulevard, Eglantine Way...

She passed the little streets and peered into the little shops:

Clay Creatures; Expressions by Claire; Joyce's Shells and Gifts; Maggie May's; The Social Chair; Uptown Interiors; Bay Breeze; The Blue Crab Gift Galleries; Art Alley in the Pass; Let's Make Up Gifts; Aloha Gallery; Tuesday Morning; Your Gift Cove; Jaynie's Novelties and Gifts; Charlie's Treasures...

And looking at these establishments, glorying in their bright colors and ramshackle, vine-enshrouded appearance, she succeeded in keeping almost closed completely the mental door that was labeled THINGS NOT TO THINK ABOUT BECAUSE THEY WILL MAKE YOU SICK.

But that door, badly constructed as it had been by the Creator, could never be closed entirely, and always allowed the cold draft of bad thoughts to pour through its crack.

As they were doing now.

How the hell could this have happened to Edgar Ramirez? He did not drink. He was not a crazed young teenager making his way to or from an all-night apartment bash. He had most certainly not lost his way and fallen blindly into a coulee that was as obscure and well-hidden as the Hoover Dam. Cars? Could he have been run into by a hit and run driver?

Possibly, but…

…but there were seldom if ever any cars on that slender ribbon of concrete road. The apartment dwellers came and went on a larger highway on the other side of the buildings. No, this road was almost completely devoid of traffic, which was one of the chief reasons she herself always used it to go to and from the park.

No.

It did not make sense.

And so she RAMMED her brain against that door and CRUSHED it shut so that those evil old thoughts would stay locked behind it…

…and parked in front of Elementals.

She chained the bike to its rack, walked up the stairs fronting the shop, reached into the BANNISTER CANISTER, took out the key, and unlocked the door.

Then she went inside, turned on the lights, started the coffee maker, and sold:

One Hummel Keeping Time, consigned to her by Judy Tice from Baton Rouge.

She sold this at 2:45.

(At three o'clock Moon Rivard came by to tell her that an autopsy had been completed on the body of Edgar Ramirez, but that the results were being held in strictest confidence.)

One Swarovski Duck, consigned to her by Felicity Meyer out of New Orleans.

She sold this duck at three ten.

(At three thirty, Ellen Swenson came by to look at paintings, did not buy one, but did tell her that there had been an autopsy and the official cause of Edgar Ramirez's death had been listed as drowning.)

One Hermann Traditional Mohair Bear, consigned to her by Albert Moor from Jackson.

She sold the bear at four o'clock.

(At four fifteen, two tourists, a man and a woman whose names she did not know, came by to tell her that Edgar Ramirez had died sometime between four and four thirty a.m. These people also informed Nina that the young man's blood alcohol level had been very high.)

Then she closed the shop and went home.

It would be all right, she told herself, while Vespa-ing in reverse the trail she'd taken to get here in the first place. She would fix dinner and that would occupy her mind; she would wash dishes and that would occupy her mind; she would walk along the beach and hoot at the silly tourists with their giant plastic floats and dragons, and that would occupy her mind because nothing after all was better than making fun of people dumber than oneself; and then she would read a mystery and then it would be ten o'clock and at ten o'clock it was okay to go to bed so that's what she would do.

And it would be ok.

Brrrrrrr, went the Vespa.

NOTHING NOTHING NOTHNG NOTHING NOTHING NOTHING NOTHING NOTHNG NOTHING NOTHING NOTHING NOTHING NOTHNG NOTHING NOTHING NOTHING NOTHING NOTHNG NOTHING NOTHING NOTHING NOTHING NOTHNG NOTHING NOTHING NOTHING NOTHING NOTHNG NOTHING NOTHING NOTHING NOTHING NOTHNG NOTHING NOTHING NOTHING NOTHING NOTHNG NOTHING NOTHING came through the bad thoughts door.

So she had it all planned, and knew, as she turned onto the small oyster shell drive that led down to the beach and to her bungalow, that cooking, cleaning, walking, reading and sleeping would keep the Ramirez family completely out of her mind.

Until she looked up at her porch and saw Hector Ramirez seated upon it.

He darkened the entire structure. She did not understand immediately why. It was more than those cavelike penetrating eyes, his crow-ebony hair and the equally black shirt he was wearing. No, it was his way of looking down at her, then looking out into the world, which, vacillating between various kinds of evil potentials, as it always seemed to do for a fourteen year old, had chosen the one it was going to take.

So be it, Hector seemed to be saying.

Bring it on.

She took one step up the stairwell and spoke to him.

"Hector!"

Of course, there really wasn't much else to say.

It was strange. The previous autumn he had come over to do some work for her—she could hardly remember what it was, but it had to do with a platform she was having built under the bungalow to put the freezer on, and the need for a strong back to carry lumber. He had been there waiting for her when she had arrived after errands—been there sitting on the entry porch just in front of the door, knees drawn up to his chin, just as he was now.

"Hector, how nice to see you!"

He watched her as she climbed.

This was the time for him to engage in small talk, but his brother was dead, and he wasn't in the mood for it.

Finally she was on the porch looking down at him.

"What is it, Hector?"

Even then he seemed to feel the need to look her up and down once more, just one last time, before deciding.

But he did decide:

"I need to talk to you."

She nodded, reaching into her purse for keys.

"Fine. Come in."

It was getting dark. She had to switch the living room light on.

She led Hector inside, pointed to a chair, took one herself.

Then she simply waited as he collected everything inside him, sorted it all out, translated it, evaluated it once again, and then let some of it come trickling out over the coffee table that sat between them.

"I think you are very smart."

"Thank you."

"What they say in school, when you be the principal— they say, you don't get over on her. Nobody ever get nothing over on Ms. Bannister."

"I'm not sure that's true, Hector."

"The first day you come to school, you break up that fight."

"Yes. I remember."

"How you know about that fight?"

"I don't know. I'm old. I've been in the schools a long time. Sometimes you just know things. It's hard to explain."

He looked at her. She could feel those eyes boring through her.

What was this about?

"They say Edgar get drunk. He come home from the rig, then he go out and get drunk."

"I know. That's what they're saying."

"That he fall down with his face in the water. And he drown."

"Yes."

"Bullshit."

Somehow there didn't seem to be much to say in answer to that.

"Edgar tell me all the time; don't drink. Don't take no drugs."

"Well, maybe he…"

"No. No, if he find out I drink, he beat me up. He would do it, too. He beat me up."

Again, not much to say.

The sea seemed to be growing louder as darkness fell.

Streetlights began to turn on, glowing white against the blue of coming night.

"What did Edgar do that last night, Hector?"

"The police ask me that. I tell them; I tell you."

"All right. Go ahead."

"He get home from rig in the afternoon. About four. Whenever he get back home he spend the first night with us. For Mama."

"That sounds like Edgar."

"But he is very worried. I can tell."

"Worried about what?"

"I don't know. He go into his room a lot, and, I can hear sometimes through the door, he is trying to call somebody. On his, you know, his…"

"Cell phone."

"Yeah. Finally he get through to that person about eleven."

"Who was the person?"

Hector shook his head:

"*No se*. Don't know. But he talk a long time. Then he call me into his room. He tell me, 'Hector I have to see someone. It has to do with my work. Explain to Mama. I will be back before the sun comes up."

"And you told all of this to the police."

"Yes. But there is one more thing."

"What?"

He reached into his blue jeans pocket and withdrew a small silver key.

"That looks," said Nina, "like the key to a locker."

"Yeah. His locker. Out on the rig. His computer is in his locker. 'Hector,' he tell me, 'don't give this to no police. No matter what happen. The police—I think the people out on the rig own them. Don't give this to no police. Find somebody you trust. Somebody smart."

Hector held out his hand:

"Here. Ain't nobody get over on Ms. Bannister."

She took it.

"I don't know what I'm to do with this, Hector."

He shook his head.

"I think, maybe when the time comes, you will know."

They were silent for a time.

Finally he asked:

"Would you give me a can of beer?"

She was somewhat shocked.

"A beer?"

"Yes."

"But...what would Edgar have thought?"

"He's dead."

"Hector, you're still a minor. I can't give beer to a minor."

Hector simply looked at her. Then he said, quietly:

"My mother says, 'A boy remains a boy until a man is needed.'"

A flock of gulls screeched overhead.

He continued:

"I think, teacher, a man is gonna be needed now."

She looked at him, then nodded and said:

"All right. You can have a beer."

She rose, went into the kitchen, opened the refrigerator, pulled out a can of Budweiser—one of fifty or sixty she had around the shack in the event Tom Broussard might come over some evening.

Then she poured the beer into a glass and went back into the living room.

Hector was gone.

She went out onto the porch, peered down the stairs, and out across the parking lot.

Nothing. Just the night and the streetlights and a car up on Breakers Boulevard.

Nothing more.

Except the small key that she held in her palm.

'When the time comes, you will know.'

"All right, Hector," she whispered, squeezing the key. "All right. Maybe the time has come for you to be a man."

So thinking, she went to bed.

CHAPTER FOUR: UNTIL A MAN IS NEEDED

She woke at first light and put on her sweater and running pants; then she hurried down the stairs and unlocked her Vespa.

It was a delicious morning, the air cool and redolent of salt.

Within five minutes she was at Bagatelli's, and by the time the sun had become a complete orange, hovering happily above the horizon, she was back at home with a sack of croissants.

It took her another fifteen minutes to make coffee, but breakfast was ready by the time Jackson Bennett began knocking at her door.

She crossed the living room and opened it.

"Jackson? What's going on?"

"I'm sorry to bother you this early, Nina."

"No bother. I've already been out to Bagatelli's. Coffee is ready. Can I get you some?"

He shook his head:

"No time. I'm trying to set up a meeting for ten o'clock."

"What kind of a meeting?"

He inflated his huge chest with enough air to get all of it out, then started letting all of it out.

"Last night I was working late. It must have been ten o'clock or so. But an attorney for Louisiana Petroleum called me."

"The people Edgar worked for?"

"Yes. The man said that the company had just been informed of Edgar's death. I'm not sure how they heard the news, but since rumors have been flying all over town for the last twenty-four hours, I guess it was inevitable. I'm also not sure how they came to get my name…"

"You're the town's leading attorney, Jackson."

"I don't know about that."

"Of course, you're the one they would naturally be referred to. There's nobody better. But go on."

"All right. This gentleman said that the company looked upon Edgar as one of their own, and that they wanted to make restitution to the Ramirez family."

"Restitution?"

"That's the word he used."

"But they weren't responsible for his death."

"I don't think that's what they're saying."

"Then what…"

"I'm not sure. At any rate, though, I've just come from the Ramirez home. I told them what the attorney had said, then told them also that I would be happy to act as their advisor in the matter. I suggested to everyone that we meet at city hall at ten this morning."

"And?"

"The Ramirez family agreed. But they talked for quite some time about it in Spanish. Finally, the son…"

"Hector."

"Yes, Hector. He said to me that they would do the meeting, but that they would like you to be there."

"Me?"

"That's what they said."

"Why?"

Because, a small voice within her whispered, 'nobody gets over on Ms. Bannister.'

But she did not say this.

"They didn't say, Nina. I think it's just very obvious that they all trust you. Maybe more than they trust anybody else right now. So. If you could make this meeting, I think it would make them feel a lot better. To tell the truth, there's still so much of this that we don't understand."

She thought about telling Jackson about the key, but for some reason thought better of it.

'Don't tell the police.'

Jackson wasn't the police, but as an officer of the court—she knew this because of Frank's career as an attorney—he would be bound to turn over to them any evidence he knew of.

Hector had entrusted her with this object.

Her and her alone.

For now, anyway.

"What do we know, Jackson?"

He shrugged:

"The Ramirez family all say that Edgar was at home until about one in the morning, when he left. We don't know where he was going. About four hours later, he was found with his lungs full of filthy sewage water and his blood level full of alcohol."

"He didn't drink, Jackson."

"He did last night."

"It doesn't make sense."

"No. But the state police are in town now, and anything that gives a hint about what happened, they're going to dig up. In the meantime, though…"

"The meeting. Yes, of course, I'll be there, you know that."

"Yes. I did. Thank you, Nina."

And, so saying, he turned and descended the stairs.

Although she arrived five minutes early, the major players in the drama which was to unfold were already seated in a small board room.

Leather chairs, solid mahogany table.

Edie Towler was there, looking beige and professional as always. Jackson, in his charcoal gray suit.

Olivia Ramirez, impeccably attired in black, seated at the table with a cup of coffee in front of her and Hector, in a black suit, at her side.

Then there was the attorney representing Louisiana Petroleum.

He was the perfect 'lawyer for the rich.'

Such a highly paid perfection in his dress, tie, smile, handshake, confidence, bearing…

He was above business executives. Nina had seen a lot of business executives and this man was superior.

He was higher and more impressive than senators or governors too.

And probably higher than presidents themselves, though Nina had seen none of them.

No, this man was like, was like…

A football coach.

That's it. He was like a football coach. Not the good ole boy football coaches that roamed the high school hallways of Bay St. Lucy, but real football coaches. 'Major College' football coaches, that became TV analysts after retirement. Five million dollar a year football coaches, the people that every male human being in The United States of America wanted to become.

And so she labeled him:

OIL COACH

Everyone was seated.

Peremptory introductions. Sad tones. The radiant smiles of OIL COACH darkened only slightly by the occasion. Senora Ramirez taking deep breaths and remaining astonishingly composed.

And finally OIL COACH takes the floor:

"Senora Ramirez, I, as well as everyone connected to Louisiana Petroleum, want to take this opportunity to express our grief. We had come to know your son very well. Edgar was a part of our family. He was, as you know, a brilliant young man…."

More deep breaths from Senora Ramirez, whose shoulders could be seen shaking.

Hector leaned toward her and said, softly:

"Señora Ramirez, yo y mi socio, así como todos los relacionados al petróleo de Louisiana, quieren aprovechar esta oportunidad para expresar nuestro dolor. Nosotros habíamos llegado muy bien a su hijo. Edgar era una parte de nuestra familia. Era, como usted sabe, un joven brillante..."

Ms. Ramirez smiled as much as she was able to, and nodded.

The narrative was carried on by OIL COACH #2.

"We have only just learned of the tragic events that have befallen your son. We have no idea what could have happened to him. We have, on the other hand, every confidence that the city and state authorities will locate the person or persons responsible for what happened to Edgar, and that they will see that you and your family receive justice.

He nodded to Hector, who leaned to his mother's right again and translated.

Nods all around.

Everyone understands.

This is a coach, Nina found herself mentally commenting, *of a top ten program.*

Louisiana Petroleum is probably due to play in the Rose Bowl this year.

The speech continued.

"Finding these culprits, as desirable as it might be, is not something that we at Louisiana Petroleum can accomplish. Nor can we bring Edgar back to you, his family, or to this, his community. We can do something, though. Something that might help at least to a small degree. We have done some research, Ms. Ramirez, and found that Edgar is the sole provider for your family. His paychecks have gone directly to you, and have been a major means of your support. His loss must be devastating for you financially as well as emotionally. When we lose members of our families to tragic circumstances, whether these circumstances occur in the line of work or not, we do not forget. We are a caring family."

Upon saying these words, he opened a briefcase, while Hector carried forward the translation.

When he had finished:

"Ms. Ramirez, our company would like to present your family with a check for thirty thousand dollars."

Olivia Ramirez said nothing.

"This is the base amount of money that Edgar would have earned in the twelve-month period from now until next year. It is, in short, a year's pay for him. We hope it will help to ease to some degree your pain and suffering."

Hector translated; Olivia Ramirez nodded.

More papers came from the briefcase.

"We will need you to sign these release documents. They exempt the company from wrong doing. Hopefully, this will not be a problem, since Edgar was clearly not hurt while doing his duties. They also give over to Louisiana Petroleum the permission—your permission as his mother and closest of kin—to enter his room, collect his valuables, and send them ashore to you."

Jackson Bennett intervened.

"May I see those for a second?"

"Of course."

The documents were passed around the table.

Jackson took some minutes to read them, then he nodded:

"These seem to be in order. From my experience they're fairly standard release forms."

He slid them back.

One of the coaches offered Ms. Ramirez a ball point pen.

She looked first at the daughter, who nodded.

She looked then at Nina.

Teacher,

You always know what to do.

Then she and Hector spoke for a time in Spanish.

And, finally, she herself spoke.

To the entire room.

And in perfect English.

"I am very appreciative of your offer. But one thing is very important to me."

The attorney sitting across the table nodded:

"Yes, Senora Ramirez. Just tell me."

"The things in my boy's room. For them to be touched by strangers…"

She shook her head.

The attorney:

"How should we handle this?"

Ms. Ramirez:

"In my culture it is usually done…"

Silence.

She composed herself, then continued:

"I would like for someone in my family to do this thing."

Jackson Bennett to his fellow attorney:

"Would that be possible?"

A nod.

"I'll speak to the people on The Aquatica. In general, though, I don't think it would be a problem. Groups of civilians, visitors, are flown out to the rig quite often. So, yes, if it means that much to Senora Ramirez, I'm sure it can be done."

Jackson:

"Senora Ramirez, who would you like to go?"

"My son. My son, Hector."

"All right."

"And…"

She looked at Nina.

So did Hector, and Nina could hear the young man's solemn voice from the night before.

'No one gets over on Ms. Bannister.'

But were these people trying to 'get over?'

The computer.

The computer in the locker.

For which she alone now held the key.

'Don't give it to the police. The oil men…they own the police, I think.';

Now Senora Ramirez:

"Ms. Bannister. Nina. My teacher. Our friend. You are in our family now. Would you go? Would you go out upon this place—and bring my son's things back to me?"

Nina nodded:

"Of course. Of course I will."

Olivia Ramirez nodded slowly and then said:

"Vaya con Dios."

And the matter was decided.

CHAPTER SIX: FOR THOSE IN PERIL ON THE SEA

The ocean stretched below them, massive, silver-tinged, heaving quietly in great sub-aquatic swells that seemed to have a life of their own, and that, if one were knowledgeable enough about such matters, probably did.

"For some reason," Nina was saying, "I'm more nervous about this than I thought."

She glanced at the late morning sun, now mirrored in the carpet of water that rolled blank and featureless before them to the east.

Then she looked to her right, at the figure seated beside her.

Sandy Cousins. Strawberry blonde hair, bright blue eyes.

Sandy Cousins, public relations executive for Louisiana Petroleum.

Sandy Cousins, who had met Nina and Hector at Bay St. Lucy's regional airport, and helped them get outfitted in the bright orange jumpsuits everyone on the helicopter was wearing.

The helicopter, she learned, made only two runs a day. A morning run to bring people out to the rig, and an evening run to bring back people who had completed their two-week shift.

"What are you nervous about, Nina?"

Nina looked in front of her and behind her.

No one seemed to be listening.

Perhaps that was because the various crew members being ferried out to Aquatica were lost in reading something or other, or were immersed in listening to something or other, thick black headphones sprouting like tumors from their ears.

Which was the case with Hector, seated one row in front of her.

"I don't know. I just have an image of what it must be like to be on one of those things."

"You mean an offshore rig?"

"Yeah."

The sea rolled on beneath her as she turned away from Sandy, who sat just to her right, and back to the window, which was reflecting the sun-glitter to her left.

It was as though the two of them were on a tour bus, so elegant was this sky cruiser of a helicopter—row after row of beige leather seats, all built as though meant for private clubs overlooking Central Park or Chicago's business district.

They looked to be meant for beefy men smoking cigars, except that no tobacco was allowed past debarkation point.

Or alcohol.

Or cell phones.

Too much danger of explosions.

Explosions?

Perhaps that was why she felt a little nervous.

"So what is this image you have of life on an offshore rig?"

"Narrow corridors too tight for two people to walk abreast; the men all shirtless, sweating; tiny bunks built into the side of the hull; that constant noise of 'tapokita tapokita,' pressure gauges everywhere; that 'ping' of the radar…"

"Nina, that's a submarine."

"What?"

"You're thinking about a submarine."

"Oh."

"Actually, a World War I submarine."

"I guess that's what I am thinking about."

"This is a state of the art oil rig we're going to, just finished two years ago. It cost seven billion dollars and eighteen million man hours to construct."

"No depth charges, then?"

"We don't go under the water; we float on top of the water."

"I've just seen all those movies."

"Those are war movies. We aren't at war with anybody."

"So it's safe out there?"

Sandy adjusted her glasses.

"It's perfectly safe, except that it could blow up at any minute like a hydrogen bomb."

"Thank you. I feel all better now."

"Actually, now that I think about it, the explosion would probably be bigger than a hydrogen bomb. You have to bear in mind that the rig is sitting on a field of ten billion cubic meters of natural gas, which huge tubes are sucking out of cracks in coal buried a half mile beneath the bottom of the ocean floor, which itself is more than a mile beneath the surface of the water. The field also holds about eighty million barrels of crude oil, which is being brought up with the gas, so that the two things can be separated onboard the rig."

Sandy nodded, thoughtfully, then said:

"Yeah. That would make quite an explosion."

"But it's all worth it, right?"

"Of course it's worth it, Nina! Aquatica pipes to the shore fifteen million standard cubics of natural gas a day, and that is worth about twenty-six million dollars. Just the gas, never mind the oil. In one day. From this one rig. And bear in mind, the thing that should comfort you, Nina, is that if anything does go wrong…"

"Yes?"

"You won't know a thing about it."

Sandy leaned closer, the vinyl in her inflatable jump suit hissing across the seat cover while, with every quick movement, she came to resemble more and more what all of them on the helicopter resembled: huge living Halloween pumpkins with rip cords for instant inflation.

"Don't worry about it, Nina. We're going to take very good care of both you and Hector. Everybody on Aquatica thought so much of Edgar. We're all just devastated. We were also told that you were the one who found the body."

"Yes."

"My God, what that must have been like."

Nina said nothing in reply.

"Do they know any more about how his death might have occurred?"

"Not really. Officially he drowned. There was a high level of alcohol in his bloodstream."

"That doesn't make sense."

"No. It doesn't."

And there the subject came to rest. It was an awkward feeling for Nina, who had a strong urge to confide in this bright, cheerful young woman.

It was the same urge she had felt to confide in Jackson Bennett, or in Moon Rivard.

But something prevented her.

'You don't get over on Ms. Bannister...'

How ridiculous! She wasn't a high school principal any more, and, if she was, these were not school children she was dealing with.

This was a matter of life and death.

But Hector trusted her. Only her.

Edgar had been frightened.

He had called someone.

He had left home in the early morning hours...going where?

And Nina now had a small silver key in her jump suit pocket.

A key to Edgar's locker. Where, probably, they would find his computer.

And on that computer?

Maybe nothing.

And yet. And yet...

The previous evening in her bungalow, sitting behind the glowing screen of her own computer, she had Googled "Disastrous Oil Spills," and she could remember reading the words of one environmentalist, describing the causes of one particularly bad accident:

"They were cutting corners. No one person could do it; a number of people had to be involved. But there were warning signs. The continual influx of hydrocarbons, the missed checks on well elasticity, the venting directly onto the rig—none of these things would have been disastrous, by themselves, But taken together—the main point is, when a spill happens, or when a disaster happens, it's almost always caused by greed. By someone neglecting to do the third backup check after the first two have been questionable. It's caused by a lack of redundancy. The little bit of extra care that should be taken, not being taken."

Was that kind of thing happening on Aquatica? And had Edgar discovered it?

The huge mega bus that posed for a helicopter turned westward slightly, and began to descend. She could feel her ears pop.

Then they leveled out, and the sea stretched on, endlessly, as before.

She looked at her watch—10:30.

She was silent for a time.

They both were silent for a time.

After a while, she sat back in her seat, and put on the headphones connected to the console in front of her.

There was a selection of music.

She punched the button labeled "Songs of the Sea."

The music began, punctuated, as their conversation had been, by the throbbing of the propellers.

She heard a vocal rendition of "The Tides of Old Bay Fundy."

She heard "The Lighthouse at St. Mary's."

And then another.

And then another.

And then, to their right, just on the horizon, loomed the rig.

It was a carnival of a thing, one spire jutting up into the sky, and a labyrinth of gigantic tubes, like psychedelic worms, crawling all around it.

"There it is," Sandy whispered. "There's Aquatica."

They overflew it once, then circled, came back low and hovered.

Red ants that were safety-suited workers scrambled below.

The helicopter stopped dead still in the sky and began to ease straight down, as though they were in an elevator.

There was the pad, a glaring yellow circle.

And there, on either corner of this huge square rectangle, were giant white tubes that she was later to learn supported them in the water.

The helicopter was now perhaps a hundred feet from the surface.

The last song on the band came on.

She looked down at the people waving at them, and then outward at the ocean surrounding them.

Then she half smiled and half frowned, as, almost subconsciously, she whispered the words of the song she had always, being an ocean dweller, revered:

Eternal Father, strong to save,
Whose arm hath bound the restless wave,
Who bid'st the mighty ocean deep,
Its own appointed limits keep.
Oh hear us when we cry to Thee,
For those in peril on the sea!

Going down the landing ramp of the helicopter would have been like walking into a windstorm, except the winds were coming from straight over her head and howling vertically rather than horizontally.

She could not decide what battered hardest upon her senses: the constant motion of the tarmac beneath her as the rig moved in the waves; the shouting of everybody who was run-walking around her; the noise of the propeller blades fifteen feet above her head; or the dazzling array of colors, huge red tunnel here, orange pipe here, yellow oil derrick there, and underlying everything and overarching everything, the blue of the sea and the identical blue of the sky.

"Over there! Over there! That way, Nina!"

She was bending almost double as she walked, terrified of being decapitated by the rotor blades, although she knew quite well that they were spinning at least twenty feet above her head.

"There! Through there! Watch out for the cranes! The crane operator has probably the most dangerous job on the craft. A supply boat is unloading now, and the ocean chop is pretty strong. The crane offloads huge containers of machine parts that may weigh as much as a ton. Once a few weeks ago one of the containers almost swung into a departing helicopter. It was pretty scary! Come on though—everything looks clear now!"

Sandy hooked an arm beneath her elbow and led the way through a churning crowd of orange people arriving on the rig and orange people leaving it.

"Over here! Come this way!"

Figures everywhere, all of them wearing yellow construction helmets, all of them shouting through cupped hands.

They made their way along, out of range finally of the fierce copter downdrafts, able to smell the wind off the churning waves that surrounded them, able finally to stand upright and breathe deeply.

"My God," she found herself whispering, for no other reason than to express the other worldliness of it all.

Too loud, too bright, too unstable and rocking, too far removed from her little stable coffee and beignets world.

"My God."

What would Furl have made of all this?

"Welcome to Aquatica!"

This from several people, all smiling and waving to them.

And now they were off the landing pad altogether, the derrick soaring like the oil well that it, of course, was. Two hundred feet into the sky, just thirty yards in front of them.

She found herself, still arm linked with Sandy, who would have been only slightly taller than herself, had she not been elevated some two inches by what seemed like black combat boots, shined to a mirror polish.

Between the orange jump suit, the huge dark green sunglasses, the bright red scarf around her neck, and the yellow helmet, there was little of an actual woman to see. And now Sandy had donned plastic work gloves the same color as the jump suit.

Nina might have been listening to an erector set.

"Come this way! Let's get you inside!"

The prefabricated being in front of her turned abruptly, waving as she did so, and strode off over a tangled mass of multicolored cables, finally disappearing for an instant into the two-foot wide opening that separated the outer rail of the Aquatica from a gleaming blue-metal building to their left.

They made their way along, gamely, going single file now.

"Down here!"

They could see the pumping, downward motion of an arm, ten feet in front of them.

This, Nina would later recall thinking, *is the most orange place I've ever seen. It's like a huge University of Texas Homecoming Oil Rig.*

She bent her head again, and now was on a narrow stairwell heading down into what was darkness for three steps, and then became lighter.

"Through here. We've set up a meeting room for you and Hector!"

"Fine."

Sandy left and the two of them followed.

They climbed the stairs, turned right down one corridor, went up another short flight of stairs and were on deck.

The churning of huge compressors rocked the air around them. Beyond the rail and trailing down to the left were huge brown octopus arms, each one a tube at least five feet in diameter.

Nina remembered the figures she had been quoted: ten billion cubic meters of natural gas; eighty million barrels of oil.

Per day.

The immensity of the thing.

"What about that cable—the silver one? It looks different."

Sandy nodded:

"It is different. It doesn't carry oil or gas. It connects to an electric generator on the mainland. We get our electricity through it."

They squeezed through another opening. Pipes and valves surrounded them and orange-clad figures scurried everywhere, taking readings, checking gauges. While beyond the rails, and fifty feet down, the giant tentacles spread out from the ship and disappeared in the green blue immensity of gulf waters.

"You see, Aquatica prides itself on being a very green pumping mechanism. Most stations burn some of the oil they pump out of the fields down below in order to create their own electricity. That's all right but it spews hydrocarbons into the atmosphere. That's where we get global warming. We're trying to fight against that. Oh, here, turn right and go up that ramp."

They did so.

"Now—that door in front of you, lift that handle and push."

Nina was the first in line and so she did so.

A stateroom lay before her, perhaps thirty feet square, darkened by green curtains and viewed impassively by mural paintings of ocean scenes.

In the middle of the room stood a central oak table, upon which a coffee service had been set.

"We know you might not be too hungry, given the job you've been asked to do. But the pastry chef made croissants and scones. We also have coffee and tea. If you want to sit down and just have something to keep you going…"

And, as they seated themselves, had coffee poured for them, and watched the pure butter melt in pastries that would have done Bagatelli's proud, she struggled to make sense of the reality that surrounded her, as opposed to the presuppositions she had brought out to Aquatica.

Horribly cramped quarters, sweating shirtless men, depth charges….

World War I submarine movies.

How stupid you are, Nina!

And there was also a stereotype in her mind of the ruthless oil barons who must have created these rigs in order to plunder the environment and ruin the world's supply of fish and wildlife.

That was not what she was seeing.

She was seeing an environment where everyone they passed seemed to work in teams of two, checking and double checking to be sure that nothing had been missed.

Where giant signs saying 'Be Safe!' seemed to be everywhere.

"Ms. Bannister? Hector Ramirez?"

They stood, and Nina noticed that a line of people had formed between them and the door.

"Yes, I'm Nina. This is Hector."

"And so very nice to meet you two indeed; I'm Tom Holder. I'm the Tool Master on the rig."

"Nice to meet you."

He was dressed exactly as all the other workers; orange jump suit, yellow helmet, sunglasses.—but he was much larger than everyone else. He was also completely bald, and, with glittering eyes, he looked menacing indeed.

Somehow the cockney accent added to this air of threat, and was not completely belied even by his broad smile.

"We 'preciate you're coming out, we really do! Everyone here on the rig thought Edgar was a first rate bloke."

"I can see that," said Nina.

And the line continued.

Various sizes of people, various accents…for, she learned, if Aquatica recruited mainly in Southwest Louisiana, that did not mean all of its workers were Cajuns.

"Man, we were bros. We hung tight, you know?"

"*El mejor Amigo. Mejor.*"

"I had, I think you say, inwited him. Yes, yes, inwited. To visit me in Germany. In Hannover. I think he would have liked it there."

And on.

And on.

The line of people who had conspired to kill Edgar Ramirez and who were attempting to get rich at the expense of the earth's welfare continued to snake its way along.

This could not be true, Nina found herself thinking. These are gracious and highly professional people.

And yet….

…and yet…

Edgar was dead. And in no possible stretch of the imagination could he have gotten drunk and stumbled into the coulee.

No, he had been frightened.

Of something he had seen out here.

It just did not make sense.

He had come into Bay St. Lucy from his two-week shift out here.

Frightened.

Of what?

Finally, it had become, somehow, twelve o'clock.

"There's one last stop, if the two of you don't mind. Before we go to Edgar's room."

"We don't mind," said Nina.

"We need to go on over into the control room. Phil Bennington is rig director. He asked me to bring you by."

"Sure."

"So, if you'll follow me…"

They did so, leaving the room by a far entrance, and struck as they looked down by five huge torpedo-like growths that seemed to sprout from Aquatica's hull and extend down toward the surface of the ocean.

"Life boats," said Sandy.

"Those are life boats?" Nina found herself asking. "They look like dark red okra pods, but two hundred times bigger."

Sandy smiled.

"They're specially designed. They've got to be able to withstand a fall of twenty feet into the ocean."

"They're not lowered?"

"No, they're exploded out from the ship. If an emergency happens, there might not be time for a lowering. They're also fireproofed and insulated, so they can navigate in and through a burning oil slick for half a mile."

"You don't use them a lot, I hope."

Sandy shook her head.

"We have them. That's the most important thing. Here, though. Turn right, go up these stairs, then left. That's the control room."

They did so, then entered something out of a James Bond movie.

Control panels were everywhere, as were huge TV monitors showing every room on the oil rig.

"Phil? Here are Ms. Bannister and Hector, Edgar's brother."

A red-haired man with dancing blue eyes crossed the room, beamed at them, and shook their hands.

"Thank you both for coming out. Welcome to Aquatica. I'm Phil Bennington, rig master."

"Nice to meet you."

"I can't tell you how much I'm going to miss Edgar. He was one of the best I ever worked with."

"It will mean a lot to his mother that you said that."

"Tell her he was the best, and that his rig boss said that."

"I will."

"Look. On these monitors you can see every area in the rig. All workers have micro chips in these clips around our necks. Two hundred and fifty-three people. They're all out there now, all accounted for. Well, I'll promise you: Edgar knew every one of them. Sometimes we would scan the monitors, just to be sure everyone was in the right place. If Edgar didn't recognize someone, he would ask. It was important to him."

And so, on it went.

Finally, they were through.

And five minutes later, they were following Sandy Cousins down the corridor that led to Edgar Ramirez' room.

Individual rooms for each worker.

Carpeted halls leading from room to room.

Little sound at all except for the ventilation motors overhead and the soft sounds of music coming from closed doors to their left and right.

Sandy had reached the door and was unlocking it.

She swung it open inwardly.

The room that looked back at them could have been any dorm room, but a little nicer and with no beer cans;

"All of the rooms are like this," Sandy was saying. "We have two hundred and fifteen people on board at any time. Everybody gets an individual room with a TV and stereo system."

"Now: We've left these baskets here so you'll have something to put Edgar's things in. Also, on the table, there's a vase of flowers for...well, we put it together ourselves. If you could, we would like you to take it to Edgar's mother, brother, and sister. That is, if you don't mind doing it."

"We don't mind," said Nina.

The three of them had begun to enter the room when a fourth figure approached, walking briskly up the hallway.

"Ms. Bannister?"

Nina turned.

The man walking toward her looked the epitome of a southern gentleman. His hair was wavy and so well coiffed that he might have been a character actor. With his ruddy face and twinkling eyes; he could have been the perfect Mississippi/Louisiana plantation house owner except for the absurd bright orange pumpkin costume he wore.

"Ms. Bannister?"

"Yes, I'm Nina Bannister."

"Brewster Dale here. Ah have the honor to be in charge of security for Aquatica."

She could have been listening, she told herself, *to Foghorn Leghorn.*

"And this is the young Mr. Ramirez?"

Hector nodded.

"A great loss for all of us, Sir. My condolences. You must be suffering greatly. All I can say to you is—well, I can quote the bard as I always do. He said: 'Given the choice between the experience of pain and nothing, I would choose pain'."

"The bard?" asked Nina. "Did Shakespeare say that?"

Brewster Dale shook his head.

"My only true bard is Mr. Faulkner, Ma'am."

Sandy smiled:

"Brewster is our scholar out here on Aquatica. He knows everything there is to know about William Faulkner."

And Dale would have blushed, had his complexion not been so red as to render doing so impossible. Or at least undetectable.

"I flatter myself as being somewhat knowledgeable on the subject. At any rate though, I'm sorry to have to bother both of you at what I realize must be an extremely difficult time. But we do have some rather tight security precautions on Aquatica."

"What kind of precautions? Surely Edgar wasn't stealing anything."

"No, no, I'm absolutely certain that he wasn't. A young man of sterling character, absolutely sterling."

A shake of the head:

"But the problem is as follows:. we are using some very advanced techniques out here. I'm not sure whether you have ever heard of 'industrial espionage?'"

"Only in books."

"Well, the concept exists outside of books, too. There are a great many competing companies that would like to have a look inside what we're doing out here. Companies in the oil industry. It has happened in the past that employees—especially engineers with advanced degrees—have downloaded advanced programs to personal computers, and sold the contents of those computers for a good deal of money. Not everyone has read Mr. Faulkner's line: 'I say money has no value; it's just the way you spend it.' from *Intruder in the Dust*. So it is my job to make sure they have no way to spend it, and I accordingly build in various mechanisms to protect us from this kind of thing, but even at that, we do not allow personal computers to leave Aquatica without some of our people checking them out first."

"I see."

"Once again, we should never wish to imply that young Edgar would do anything like I just described. But if he has a personal computer, I do need to check the files."

"I understand."

They entered the room.

There was a single, neatly made bed, and, bolted high against the wall, a television set.

Against one of the walls stood the six foot tall metal locker.

"When Edgar came home," Nina said, "he left the key to his locker in his room. Hector gave it to me. I've got it here."

"That's good," said Dale. "Otherwise we would have to break the lock and force the locker open. If you want to go ahead and open it…"

Nina stepped forward, taking the small, glistening key from her pocket.

Metal rasped against metal; there was a small 'clang,' and the door of the locker swung upon.

The locker was completely empty, except for two things: a small poster of a nude woman on an equally nude beach, and, lying on a shelf perhaps three feet off the floor, a black laptop computer.

"Well," said Nina. "Edgar was a man."

There were smiles throughout the room.

"Most lockers out here," said Sandy, "have posters like that inside them. Except for the women's lockers. We have pictures of naked men."

More smiles.

Brewster Dale lifted the computer gently from the shelf, turned, took it to the writing desk that sat beneath a window, unwound a power cord, and plugged the prong into an outlet socket.

The screen lit up, flashing with a dozen or so icons.

"Can you get into Edgar's files?" Nina asked.

"Yes."

"How?"

"The young man was required to register his password. I have it."

His fingers rattled on the keys. Finally, he said:

"I want to change places here, so the light from the window comes in over my shoulder. There don't seem to be too many files here. Maybe, if the rest of you want to pack the clothes and personal belongings, I can be done with my work in only a few minutes."

He moved, then looked wistfully out of the window and quoted his favorite author again:

"'Some days in late August at home are like this, the air thin and eager like this, with something in it sad and nostalgic and familiar...' I do love the novel *Light in August*."

Nothing could follow that but some moments of silence. Then the three of them set about packing.

It was, after a time, a kind of eerie scene. There was the purr of the computer, a barely audible scrabble of muffled voices from outside on the platform itself, and the hiss of various fabrics as they slid them out and folded them, then placed them neatly in the containers provided.

Nina was simultaneously a bit frightened, and a bit relieved.

What if Dale found something?

If anything truly incriminating to Louisiana Petroleum *were* on the computer, then surely the company would not allow the information off the rig.

They could simply wipe the files clean.

They could also accuse Edgar of—what had been the term?—industrial espionage.

And in so doing, they would have all the reason they needed to avoid paying the Ramirez family the thirty thousand dollars that had been promised them.

On the other hand, perhaps nothing was on the computer.

Then at least the matter would be over as far as she was concerned.

And over as far as her responsibility to the Ramirez family was concerned.

Hector had suspected something, had told her of his suspicions, and had asked for her help.

She was helping him.

If nothing was there...

...of course something might be there, for all she knew, and might be being erased even now.

This was all so far beyond her...

Dale, face intent, glowed in a combination of late morning sunlight and computer luminosity.

The screen was turned away, so that all she could see was the back of the computer.

And, looking up only occasionally, she kept on about her work.

All three of them did.

Hector's face showed no emotion at all as he went about packing his dead brother's belongings.

A white shirt here to be folded; a light blue shirt from a hanger on the other side of the closet; there, lying neatly folded in one of the drawers, a small stack of cloth handkerchiefs with the letters "ER" monogrammed in one of the corners.

Haunting work.

The fabric remains of young Edgar Ramirez, who, when he hung them here and folded them here and stacked them here and arranged them here...had no idea that within a matter of hours he would be dead.

The three of them and Dale finished, apparently, at the same time.

He closed the computer, looked up, and smiled:

"Nothing there out of the ordinary that I can see. Some video games. Nothing more. Are you finished with the packing?"

"Yes," Nina said, nodding.

"Well. Do we need to call some people to help carry the boxes?"

Sandy answered:

"I think the four of us can get it all. So it's all right for Nina and Hector to take the computer?"

Dale nodded:

"No problem at all as far as I can see. And I am sorry for having to do the check. It's just that with technology this advanced..."

"We understand," said Nina, quietly.

"And, madame—I must ask, although I believe I know the answer quite well..."

"Yes?"

"You are from Mississippi, are you not?"

"Yes, I am."

He beamed:

"'To understand the world, you must first understand a place like Mississippi.' I believe Mr. Faulkner wrote that in *The Mansion*. But at any rate, it has been a privilege."

"A privilege for us, too, Mr. Dale."

Sandy:

"Well. Are we ready?"

To which Hector replied:

"I must ask one thing."

They all looked at him.

"What is it, Hector?" asked Sandy.

"It is the place of my brother. I would like to say a prayer for him. I and...his teacher. Ms. Bannister."

"Would you like us to leave the two of you alone?"

He nodded:

"It would be better. If it could be done."

"Certainly. We'll just go down the hall. Take all the time you want."

And they left.

Hector closed the door.

"You want to pray, Hector?" asked Nina.

But Hector merely shook his head.

"I have already prayed," he said.

"Then what..."

"Look."

He opened the locker door.

There was only the nude poster inside.

"You want to take the poster, Hector?"

He shook his head, while he carefully began to untape the poster.

"No. I want what is behind it."

He pulled the poster carefully away from the wall behind it.

There, taped against the gray metal, was a flash disk.

"I want this."

He peeled the clear tape off it, and handed it to Nina.

She put it in the pocket of her jump suit.

"You don't get over on Ms. Bannister," he said, quietly.

She shook her head:

"You don't get over on Edgar, either," she answered. "Or his brother."

They left the room together.

CHAPTER SEVEN: A LATE NIGHT PHONE CALL

Darkness came late to Bay St. Lucy in the summer months, there being no reason for it and no money to be earned by it.

The money lay in the glaring white and then golden-shadowed late afternoon hours, when vacationers gleefully romped on the beaches and sailed in the surf, eating ice cream cones and covering themselves with sand.

That was vacationers.

It was not Nina Bannister.

These particular golden hours, for her, consisted of a forty-minute helicopter ride back from Aquatica, a meeting at the airport with Jackson Bennett and a van he had rented for the occasion, a half-hour spent unloading Edgar Ramirez's clothes and other possessions from the helicopter into the vehicle, and a ride across town to the Ramirez residence.

Hector was generally silent during this time.

So was the flash disc that felt like an overly thick fifty-cent piece in her pocket.

She wondered about what was on it.

She wondered also whether she should give it to Jackson, who was the wisest man she knew. But no. The arguments concerning the flash disk were exactly like those concerning the key to Edgar's locker. Jackson, as an officer of the court, would have to turn any evidence—and this disk certainly would qualify as evidence—over to the police.

And that would constitute a problem, since the data on the disk had almost certainly been stolen from Louisiana Petroleum.

It was confidential.

And now she had it.

So she attempted to push these thoughts out of her mind, while she followed another theory.

Something was wrong, and it nagged at her.

It made her nag at Jackson during the drive across town.

"Jackson, I assume no further progress has been made in this case."

He shook his head and gripped the van's steering wheel tighter.

"They don't even think it is a 'case.' As far as anybody knows now, the kid just got drunk, fell into the coulee and drowned."

"All right. You've talked to the police about this, haven't you?"

"They've told me everything they've been able to learn."

"All right; then let me ask you a question."

"Fire away."

"What did they find on the body?"

"What do you mean?"

"Personal effects. Things like that."

"His wallet. Several keys. He had a wristwatch on."

"Money in the wallet?"

"Yes, a little over fifty dollars. Nobody had touched it, which means robbery couldn't have been the motive."

"Credit cards in the wallet?"

"American Express. Visa."

"And that's all they found?"

"I think so."

She nodded.

"Okay. Okay."

She said nothing else.

But it didn't make sense. And it nagged at her.

The nagging continued through the next hour, while they took Edgar's things into the Ramirez home. There were a great many hugs during this procedure: Olivia Ramirez, Sonia, a few neighbors...

...what do you do with the clothes of your dead eldest son?

But Nina had a chance to do the one thing it seemed she had to do.

She had to look at Edgar's room.

During all the coming and going, she asked Hector to show her the room, so that she could take into it a plastic crate filled with shirts and trousers.

It was much as she imagined it to be, and not much different from the room on Aquatica.

Spare, well kept.

With a bit of change sitting on the dresser, and a few pictures, a pair of nail clippers.

"Hector, tell me again: when did Edgar start making calls?"

"About nine o'clock, I think."

"He didn't complete any of the calls?"

"I don't know. Maybe one or two. But he kept calling. He would kind of curse under his breath, and just whisper, 'Be there.' And then some bad words."

"Right. And he left..."

"After midnight."

"Having never gotten the person he was trying to call."

"No."

"Okay. Let me just look in here."

The bathroom. Same story. A few clean towels, some toiletries.

Nothing else.

And nothing else on the body.

No. It didn't make sense.

And she would have to make sense of it.

It was quite dark when she returned home.

She let herself in the front door, bent to pet Furl who was rubbing against her ankles, put her things away in the closet, went into the kitchen and poured herself a glass of milk.

Then she returned to the living room, sat down in the chair facing her computer, slipped the disk into the side port, and turned the machine on.

It took some seconds to warm up.

Almost subconsciously she looked around, out the deck window, out the front window.

Nobody.

Come on, Nina, don't be such a coward.

No one knows you have this thing.

At least, no one that you know of.

The icons on the glowing screen; that one. Scroll down. Click on 'computer.'

Removable Disk (E);

Click on it.

Wait.

Whirrr.

Then a screen full of data.

Incomprehensible charts, graphs, figures after figures after figures, a few of them highlighted in red, the rest inscrutable black against the white background of the screen. Occasional columns with equally inscrutable headings and apparent acronyms: LGTPR, HDS, CTPR, AMALOGUE, STPYS…

…and on, and on.

Finally she stood up.

What could she have expected?

If Edgar had found something, it was here. But it was in code. And no retired high school English teacher was about to unscramble it.

She turned off the computer, removed the disc, thought about putting it in the desk drawer, thought better of it, and slipped it back into her pants pocket.

Then she simply paced, while Furl watched her do so.

They found his wallet; they found his keys; they found his credit card; she saw his room…

It didn't make sense.

And she had to make sense of it.

So she ferreted in her closet for raingear. And old tarpaulin of a slicker; thick yellow rubber boots that came up halfway to her knees.

She put these things on, went out the door, and down the stairs.

She unlocked her Vespa, started it, and chugged up the driveway toward Breakers Boulevard.

Two minutes driving.

Five minutes driving.

Tourists heading back to various motels and B&B's, all of them wearing bathing suits or short-sleeved shirts.

While she looked like the ancient mariner.

There it was, up ahead, Girard Park.

She skirted it, then drove slowly past the apartment complex, turned once...

...and was now, once again, driving along the drainage canal.

There it was, fifty feet in front of her, now twenty.

And now she was there, where she had sighted the body.

She stopped the Vespa, took a flashlight from her raincoat pocket, flipped it on, and shined the beam down onto the murky stream of drainage waste that eddied below.

Nothing. Just small circles in the water that were the thick lips of feeding carp.

"Ok, Nina," she told herself. "You've got to do this."

And she did. There was no other explanation.

And so, inching backwards, on all fours, she made her way down the concrete sides of the canal.

Down, down...

Finally, she could feel as the surface of her vinyl boot entered the—water?

No, not water, but she had to pretend.

She straightened, then turned, and peered in the direction of the stream.

She could see it for approximately fifteen feet; then it entered a kind of tunnel, semicircular, impenetrable to her sight.

She made her way toward it.

Slosh. Slosh.

The smell had drifted up into her nostrils some time ago, but it was worsening now.

The thick gray fish moved away from her as she walked, but still nudged her ankles.

It was as though she was making her way through a herd of water cattle.

She had to bend to go into the tunnel, above which was a thick cement walkway.

The light of the flashlight bored its own tunnel into the blackness that stretched before her.

She scanned the stream, nothing.

And the sides of the rounded tunnel, nothing.

On and on.

Slosh. Slosh.

Far behind her, she could hear music coming from one of the apartments.

It had to be here.

There was no other explanation.

It might be useless.

And yet. And yet...

Think back, Nina. Think.

She had found the body at around six o'clock. But before that, around four o'clock, there had been a rain shower.

The coulee would have been up for a time, the stream of refuse running faster. It would possibly have...

There.

There!

Caught within a tangle of bare tree limbs that had been washed down into the coulee and carried this far before sticking on something.

There, glowing incandescent blue in the yellow glow of the flashlight.

It was there, after all!

She reached down and wrapped her hand around it.

Smooth and glistening, it nestled into her palm.

It was a blob of inert plastic.

Having been here four days now, it might be useless.

But she had found it out of the water, which had carried it this far, and then had receded.

Also, this thing had been Edgar's.

Edgar the engineer.

Who would have made it a point to own only the best of equipment.

Only the best computer.

And only the best cell phone.

The cell phone that he had been using all evening, trying to reach some unknown party.

The cell phone that he had—MUST have—carried with him when he left home, it being nowhere to be found in his room.

The cell phone that had not been found on his body.

And that, it must then follow as the night the day, had been jarred from one of his pockets during his fall…

…and carried away by the current.

So that the police did not find it.

But she had.

And she held it in her palm.

"Work," she whispered.

"Work, damn you."

She flipped it open.

The small window above the key pad lit up.

"Yes."

There, just below the window, was a green button.

She pushed it.

And there, before her, lay a series of telephone numbers.

The last ones that Edgar Ramirez had attempted to call.

"Yes."

She put the phone in her pocket, turned, and walked out of the tunnel.

For some reason, she drove back to Gerard Park.

She wasn't absolutely certain why. Perhaps it was a feeling that she did not want to go back to her bungalow right now; or it was simply the perfumed and balmy early summer air of Bay St. Lucy; or it was the streetlamps beginning to glow blue throughout the copse-lined walkways where only a few days ago she had come to do her morning run…

…or perhaps, it was something undefinable that draws people into parks and that makes parks necessary, especially town parks, especially parks with small gazebos where families gathered to have small picnics and drink cans of beer and listen to music on portable radios.

But whatever the reason, that was what she did.

The park was not particularly crowded. It was not a place that Bay St. Lucy advertised to its tourists. It was a more private experience, a refuge from the vacationers rather than a lure for them.

So Nina had no difficulty in finding one of the white gazebos that seemed meant for her. She drove the Vespa up to it, parked, rammed her foot down on the kickstand, and got off.

Then there was the rain gear.

She shucked it off, storing it in a compartment behind the driver's seat that had apparently been constructed by Vespa's engineers for the sole purpose of hiding toxic vinyl.

Then, shaking her head like a dog that has just been thrown into a lake—and crawled out—she walked up into the gazebo, waved at an acquaintance that happened to be walking by on the running trail fifty feet distant, and sat on one of the white wooden chairs that had been placed around a metal table in the precise center of the edifice.

She looked up, through a circular opening that had been made in the top of the structure, probably, she imagined, to let through smoke from a charcoal grill that someone might want to be cooking with.

One bright star.

"Star light, star bright," she whispered. "First star I see tonight."

There, farther on toward the center of the park, a teenage boy and his girl friend were throwing Frisbees, wildly, having no idea where the miniature plastic flying saucers would end up, not caring at all, both of laughing girlishly even if only one of them happened to be female.

"I wish I may, I wish I might,

Have the wish I wish tonight."

And so thinking, she pressed the green button for recall.

She pressed the phone to her ear.

Buzz.

Buzz.

Bu...

Click.

"Narang here."

Even as the words embedded themselves in static, it dawned on her immediately that, having no idea whom she was calling, she also had no idea what to say.

Hi. I don't know you but I'm Nina and you don't know me either. My whole name doesn't really matter or who I am or where I'm from or are right now but you may be the one who killed Edgar, either that or the one who might have been able to keep him from getting killed. We don't quite know which right now and we're not even really sure he *was* killed but his lungs were all filled with sewage and his blood was all filled with alcohol and that really isn't like him so could you help us?

The static once again:

"Narang here! Who's calling?"

"I'm sorry..."

"Yes? Yes, who's calling, please?"

Did she want to give her name?

No.

So what could she say?

"Do you have the wrong number? Who is this? Who is calling?"

"I'm calling from Bay St. Lucy."

A pause.

"From where?"

"Bay St. Lucy. It's in Mississippi."

"Yes. I know of it. But I don't…"

"I'm sorry to bother you. I need to know, though: with whom am I speaking?"

Yet another pause.

She could feel the tension as something in the phone that was being held to her ear was whispering:

He's going to hang up now.

But he did not.

"This is Professor Daruka Narang."

A British accent, with perhaps a touch of New Delhi or Bombay thrown in.

"And…and where are you located, Professor?"

"Please tell me who this is? Are you soliciting? Because I do not do business…"

"I'm not soliciting."

"All right, but I still don't wish to…"

"I'm a friend of Edgar Ramirez."

The name seemed to dispel the static.

So that the following pause, though longer, emanated a kind of warmth.

Impossible as that might have been.

The voice at the other end, when it came back, was somehow softer.

"Edgar?"

"Yes. Do you know him?"

"Of course. Of course. He is one of our students."

Was, thought Nina.

But she did not say that. Not yet. Although she knew that she would eventually have to.

"Are you calling me on behalf of Edgar?"

"Yes. In a way."

"I'm very sorry but I do not understand you."

"Are you Edgar's teacher?"

"Yes, yes…in the department of geological sciences."

"Located at…"

"At the University of Louisiana, here in Lafayette."

All right.

So that explained it.

Edgar knew he had discovered immensely complex, but also immensely important, data.

He might not be able to make sense of it himself.

So he would ask for the help of his old professor.

Who was now on the other end of the phone, asking:

"I really must ask that you identify yourself."

Okay, here goes:

"My name is Nina Bannister."

"And you are a friend of Edgar's?"

"I'm a friend of Edgar's family."

"His family?"

"Yes. I'm not sure you knew, but Edgar lived here in Bay St. Lucy."

"Lived?"

"Professor Narang, I must tell you that Edgar Ramirez is dead."

Strange. She had never before in her life told someone that someone else was dead.

It made her feel, also, as if she were dead.

The phone was also dead—even if only for an instant or so—the park was dead the dogs that should have been running around in the park were dead, the Frisbee flying over a small stream was dead, and so was the stream and so were the stars and so was all the town…

…for just that instant.

Then:

"Oh my God."

There is nothing one can say to 'Oh my God.'

So she simply waited.

"How?"

"I…we're not sure."

"But…was it an accident, or…"

"His body was found in a drainage canal."

"A what?"

"A kind of a runway for storm water."

"I cannot believe that I am hearing this."

"I know."

"But how…how could this have happened?"

"No one in Bay St. Lucy is certain, Professor Narang."

"But…but Edgar was working on an oil drilling platform, wasn't he?"

"Yes, Professor."

"Then how…"

"He had come home. Maybe to visit his family, we don't know."

Pause.

She continued:

"But Professor Narang, the bottom line is this. Edgar may have found out that something was wrong on The Aquatica. That's the rig he was working on."

"Wrong?"

"I know, it sounds crazy. His brother says he was worried, even scared. He spent three hours the night before he was killed…"

"Killed?"

"I'm sorry, I shouldn't have said that."

"You think someone killed him? Killed Edgar?"

"I don't know."

"But…"

"But he spent three hours of his final night attempting to call you. I know that because I recovered his cell phone. That's how I got your number."

Pause.

She continued:

"Professor, Edgar's brother Hector and I went to the Aquatica this morning to get his things. We found in his room a disc drive that he had hidden. On this drive is a huge amount of data."

"What kind of data, Ms. Bannister?"

'I don't know."

"You haven't looked at it?"

"Yes. Only a short time ago, but it's incomprehensible to me."

"And you haven't shown it to anybody?"

"No. I'm absolutely certain that he wanted you to see it. You and no one else."

"Ms. Bannister, please tell me clearly what you are trying to say."

"All right. I think Edgar, brilliant engineering student that he was, had found out something very wrong was happening aboard Aquatica. I think he recorded his findings on his computer, then transferred them to this disc that I now have. I think someone may have followed him from the Aquatica to Bay St. Lucy, killed him, and made it look like he had gotten drunk, fallen into the drainage canal, and drowned."

"My God."

There was that phrase again.

Surely someone would come up with a reply to it.

"All right. Then precisely what is it that you want me to do?"

"I want you to look at what's on the disc."

Static.

More static.

It was quite dark now, and several yellow stars had crowded their way into the cupola above her.

"All right. I do not see how I can refuse."

"Can I somehow send you this data electronically?"

"Ms. Bannister, this data. I assume that no one on the Aquatica knows you possess it?"

"That's true."

"Then I feel we should avoid sending private and confidential information flying through digital space. But if you have a disk and you wish to show it to me.."

There was, she knew a flight from Bay St. Lucy tomorrow at two p.m.

It was the regular commuter flight to New Orleans.

From New Orleans there would certainly be flights to Lafayette.

As for money, she had a bit in the account, left over from her months as being a principal again.

"I'll come to you."

"All right. When can you be here?"

"Tomorrow evening. I'll take the commuter flight from New Orleans, and I'll probably arrive about six or so. I'll have to check the times. I'll also have to get a motel room. But when I do, I'll…"

"No. No, the motel is not good. There is a young woman here in the department., a graduate student. She is…was… a friend of Edgar's. I feel certain that she will wish to help in this matter. She has a small place near campus, I think. I can have her meet you at the airport here in Lafayette. I feel certain she would not mind for you to stay with her."

"All right. I'll be there."

And thus it was determined.

She was first going to take Edgar's cell phone back to the Ramirez home and ask Hector to take care of it.

Then she was going to Lafayette.

CHAPTER EIGHT: ALLONS A LAFAYETTE!

The flight from Bay St. Lucy arrived in New Orleans at two. There was a connection to Lafayette leaving at four fifteen. Shortly before six, the Delta jet touched down at the Lafayette Regional Airport.

She took a small travelling bag from the overhead compartment, made her way up the aisle and out into air that was heavier, more ponderous and liquid-sweet than Bay St. Lucy—yes, she remembered now, what the swamplands here were like, remembered them from drives she and Frank had taken through the Cajun prairie.

"Nina!"

A striking young woman was striding across the tarmac, waving her arms.

"Are you Nina Bannister?"

She was a tall woman, five seven or five eight, and her flaming red hair washed about her shoulders as she walked.

"I'm Nina!"

"Annette Richoux! A student of Professor Narang. Like Edgar."

The woman was wearing dungarees and a short sleeve white shirt that showed the muscles in her lithe arms.

Nina began making her way tentatively down the ramp.

"Can I help you with your traveling bag?"

"No, I've got it."

"Any trouble with your connections?"

"No. Everything went fine."

"You're going to stay at my place while you're in town. Hope that's all right with you?"

"Of course. I hate to put you out."

"No, it's no bother. It's just...is it true what the professor told me, about Edgar?"

"Yes. It is."

"I can't believe it."

They looked at each other for a time.

Then they cried for a time.

Then, shaking their heads, they walked together toward the parking lot, with Nina saying:

"I don't know if what I'm doing is right. About this disk."

"Don't worry about it."

"Maybe the information on here is not..."

"We're not even going to talk about it, ma chere. It's Friday night, gettin' to be seven o'clock. And I might as well let you know right now—I'm a Cajun girl. Born and brought up not too far from here."

"If you want to go straight home, I'll understand."

"Home nothing. We're going dancing."

And they did.

Within minutes, the two of them were winding their way through the streets of Lafayette, Annette Richoux laughing as she drove.

"Naw, nobody can make head nor tail of me. I was born up in Eustace. My folks were ranchers. They're gone now, God bless 'em. I grew up as a tall drink-a-water nerd, always reading. Nothing to do with boys. Never did have anything to do with boys. I discovered men sometime in my early twenties and I haven't looked back. I'm brilliant, by the way, but I don't let anybody notice, at least not socially. No way to tell you how I got interested in geology, and then the oil part of it. I guess it has to do with the fact that I was always around drillers, growing up where I did."

Nina, settled back and told herself that this entire thing was absurd.

She was here because of a murder..

What was she doing going dancing?

"It's been a little while since I danced."

"How long?"

"Forty-three years."

"That's nothing. It'll come right back to you."

They swerved onto a street called Johnston Avenue, which, Nina could not help noticing, had the traffic density and speed of an interstate highway and the engineering features of a ditch.

They talked casually and perilously as sixty miles per hour in-city traffic shot beside them and around them like so many harmless multicolored lights, and they negotiated the nonsensical and directionless turns of downtown Lafayette.

Finally, they pulled beneath a massive live oak tree that overhung the front porch of an establishment whose battered sign pronounced: "The Blue Gator."

"Annette! My favorite young genius student from the great university!"

"Hello, Pierre!"

A man as massive as the tree itself rolled out of the clapboard door and down a wooden walkway that was certainly destined to collapse at any time, allowing him to submerge on his own.

"Nina, this is Pierre Boudin! He owns The Blue Gator!"

"Hello, Pierre."

"And hello back to you, Miss Nina! You'all come right on in! Guests of honor at the Blue Alligator!"

His face was a combination of ripe tomato and under-inflated basketball, and his eyes—mere slits now—had not existed for years as actual openings. But the vines that tangled and sprouted from the white shirt barely covering his chest certainly were organic in nature, and thicker, healthier, more deeply-rooted, than human hair could ever have been.

"Abidas?"

"Yeah, Amber for both of us. Red Stick Ramblers playing tonight?"

He nodded:

"You know it!"

"The Red Stick Ramblers, Nina," said Annette, "are the best Cajun band there is."

They followed the tree man up the walkway…which sank appreciably but did not overflow…and, with Pierre standing behind and holding the door open for them, entered the Blue Gator.

It was, observed Nina, a great deal like Pierre himself. Not so huge, nor bulky, but certainly tangled and completely untrustworthy. Immediately to their right was the bar, lined with bottles of Abida Beer. To their left was the dance floor. It was perhaps fifteen feet square, and completely bare now, save for one solitary jazz musician, a tall black soprano saxophonist, who poured forth mournful and delicate tunes that absolutely no one was listening to.

Beyond, though…

…she could see, peering through the garish yellow light, was a crumbling garden, vines overhanging bare rafters, tables scattered here and there, some with tablecloths, some bare and reflecting in their green metal tops the half moon that peered mockingly though the places in the roof that were not roof.

"Nina," said Annette, "maybe you can go back in the garden and find us some place to sit. I got this T shirt on, and these jeans. That's nothing to go dancing in. I'm gonna change into something sexy; I'll come and find you."

So saying, she turned and disappeared.

Nina, left to her own devices, made her way back into a jungle of furniture and vine-tangles that seemed to keep opening out from itself, passing a bench here and there, and overhearing patches of conversation.

"Non, c'est…c'est bien trop…"

"Oui, je crois bien que…"

French. English. Cajun. Creole…all of it seeping out of the woodwork from people defying characterization: yes, that was a university group; there were three people who seemed to have come from a nursing home; and there was a family, along with an infant in arms and a two year old.

Finally, she found a rickety table and sat down, overhearing a conversation beside her as two men discussed fishing.

They were both talking at once, shaking their heads, agreeing, disagreeing, citing geographical features of southwest Louisiana, moving into and out of the feeding habits of the red bass, and culminating in a reminiscence of Earl Long.

Pierre brought two bottles of beer. She began drinking one.

Somehow the softness and gaiety of Lafayette began to wash over her.

How many days ago was it that she had come upon Edgar's body?

Four? Five?

It was all a haze.

And then, the wake at Olivia Ramirez's home; the strange encounter with Hector; the meeting with the oil executives; the bizarre helicopter ride to the equally bizarre carnival ride that was Aquatica; the inky waters of the coulee…

…and now this.

A different world.

Everyone was smiling here.

How long had it been since she had smiled?

And while thinking these things, she let another idea play in her head.

There would be any number of men here for her to dance with.

She could not dance; but she would learn.

There would probably be one man later in the evening.

He would be a perfect gentleman.

And she could, if she wished, go to bed with him.

This evening, for that matter. This very evening. She was of an age, as was he, when, at an appropriate time on the dance floor or in the back seat of the car returning home, she could simply say matter of factly:

"Let's stay together tonight. I miss being with someone."

And he, though perhaps a bit shocked, would have too much gallantry and pride, if not desire (since Nina still could not believe she was actually a woman who could instill sexual desire in men)...to refuse.

And tonight, for the first time in so many years, so many years...she could have sex.

Frank would not be standing by the bed, shaking his head.

She could have sex.

But she would not.

She had just begun to speculate concerning the reasons why not: this delightful sense of freedom in smaller things, the love of reading until whenever, (and of reading whatever without having to summarize it or explain it); the lessening of sexual desire (or was it there and simply being ignored?); and the simple and exquisite sense of self-reliance that, while probably illusory (because she did need love, did she not? And what about the 'no woman is an island thing?)...was growing yearly more enjoyable...

...to speculate on all of these reasons why she would not have sex tonight or any other night in her future, when she was joined at the table by Annette, who undoubtedly *would* have sex tonight...

She wore a black dress bare on one shoulder, red hair glistening in whatever meager yellow light was dispensed by a precariously hanging single bulb, small cigar swinging at the end of an immensely long arm...

"The beer came," Nina said.

"Good. Now...look across the room, over there, leaning against the bar. See that oily-haired and muscly guy?"

"I do."

"That's my boyfriend. Wait. I'll go get him."

Annette crossed the room, accosted the man she had been speaking about, embraced him quickly, laughed, embraced him again, kissed him lightly…

…and after two minutes or so, was back with him.

"This is Guidry," she said.

"Hi."

"Hi."

And so, for a time, Annette and Guidry talked about fishing while Nina simply listened.

Pierre Boudin, happy as a pig-clam, worked his hall. He brought them two more bottles of beer—okay, so they weren't quite ready for more beer, but they would be—sat with them, agreed with them, laughed with them, folds of flesh rolling and tangled torso-growth sprouting in the warm, fetid air.

…until, the beer-clock above the bar inching its way to seven o'clock, they rose and made their way toward the dance floor.

It looked different now. The single melancholy saxophone player had disappeared, swallowed by the swamp upon which this entire precarious enterprise floated. In his place, still not attracting a great deal of attention, were scattered musicians, none of whom seemed to know each other, all of whom seemed unaware of their surroundings. A fiddle appeared, was scratched, then tuned, then set aimlessly aside. A bass joined it, huge, burnished, immovable, more like a piece of bedroom furniture than any possible musical instrument; and there, as much smaller as it should have been than the bass was larger…was the heart of the band, the box accordion.

Annette watched the Red Stick Ramblers set up like she would have watched a mother give birth.

Her eyes glittered, black and shining, star-scattered rhinestones on the strap of her dress.

"How long," whispered Nina, "have you known Guidry?"

Annette stared back at her for an instant.

"What?"

"How long have you known Guidry?"

"Oh. What time is it now?"

"It's seven o'clock."

"'Then—five minutes, I guess."

Nina could find nothing to say for a moment, and finally stammered out:

"I thought you two were a couple."

Annette nodded, impatiently:

"We are. Now. Remember how I told you I discovered men in my mid twenties…"

"…and never looked back."

"That's' right, ma chere, that's right."

"And you're not looking back now."

"Not a bit of it.

Nina knew nothing to say.

Finally, she tried to stammer something out, but nothing came.

"What? What is it, Nina?"

"Annette—it's just—it all seems so inappropriate. I mean—one of your classmates is dead."

"That's right, Babe. He is. He is dead."

"I mean—how can you just go dancing?"

Then, from somewhere in the collection of half rooms that were nothing like an actual building, a clock started chiming.

Bong. Bong…

The Red Stick Ramblers belted out:

"GEAUX GEAUX GEAUX de GEAUX GEAUX GEAUX!

MEAUX MEAUX MEAUX de MEAUX MEAUX MEAUX!

And Annette shouted back at Nina:

"How can you not?"

The music pounded and throbbed and wailed and squawked and dipped and soared and cried and always tailed off in its plaintive syllables of "oh oh oh, de oh oh oh," spilling out into the sweating air with five vowels and an 'x'.

The dance floor, Nina estimated, was fifteen feet square.

There were now eleven thousand people on it.

Where had they come from?

True, there had been customers, lag-abouts and stragglers, disreputable types scattered about this trail of rooms furnished like an alley...but nothing like this!

Annette had disappeared, sucked into the dance quicksand that was heaving and boiling so close to the musicians themselves that dancers, their heads cocked back and eyes boring straight up into heaven, had to neck-jerk slightly to avoid fiddle-bows jabbed into earrings.

"May I?"

A man was standing just before her with an arm outstretched.

He looked...

Oh, hell, what did it matter how he looked.

"Do you wish to dance, Miss?"

"Sure."

She took his hand, felt herself being led forward, albeit, coincidentally and irrelevantly, backwards...and bathed in the dance as she would have in the ocean swell of a beach.

There was no room on the dance floor, and there was everywhere room.

It was, perhaps, his skill in guiding them; or it was the massed radar of the beings around them, who, like a cloud of bats, emitted and received in return navigational force waves operational only in fields of rhythm.

He held her closer to him, palm pressed firmly against her back. At that moment, she did not so much reconsider going to bed with him, as to postulate for the first time going to bed with all of them. They could every one...all of the bodies large and small, bespectacled and red haired, glamorous and wizened, mammal and near-reptilian...all sleep exhausted, some time far later in the night or early morning, in a bed of reeds and mango peelings, snoring out, like a huge multi-limbed Cajun bear, the muted syllables:

All bad things, all evil deeds, disappeared.

OH OH OH, de OH OH OH!

"You a good dancer, Miss!"

"Thank you!" she shouted to the six faces closest to her. All of them smiled back.

Saturday morning.

Seven thirty a.m.

It was a little, dilapidated house and Nina loved it. What was this place where the strange Annette Richoux lived, and to which a taxi had dutifully returned her around midnight? A bungalow? No. A cottage? That would be putting an optimistic spin on the thing. It was literally no more than an outbuilding, a something that would have passed for slave quarters if slaves had existed at the time of its construction. It contained only one large room, partitioned by half walls and dotted here and there by what passed for a tiny kitchen, a questionable bathroom, a bed nook—and, at her first glance, it was semi-coated by badly peeling grey paint, seemingly bought as surplus from the German army.

Tucked away in the forest...well, all right, it wasn't exactly a forest, but everything here in the swamplands, only some miles from the huge Atchafalaya Basin...everything in this coastal Cajun marshland seemed only a live oak, only a cypress spear away from what could have easily been called a swamp...tucked away in this near forest, with a crumbling red-brick wall separating it from the lane, and a delightfully dilapidated off-green swinging gate allowing entrance to the yard-patch...

...tucked away just far enough from the sight of those few students who might be passing en route to the mile distant campus...

...it looked exactly like what her own bungalow would have been, had it been surrounded by a swamp and not fronted by an ocean.

"So, you sleep okay, Nina?"

She was sitting beside the bed, having accepted a cup of tea.

"Best night's sleep I ever had," she replied. "I was dead tired."

"Well, darlin,' you looked good out on that dance floor."

"I was just jumping around."

"That's all dancing is."

"I don't know...the rest of you made it look better."

"Well, we were born here. Or close by, anyway."

"What time did you get in, Annette?"

"I don't know. Doesn't matter."

"Where is Guidry?"

"Where is who?"

"Okay. I get it."

"Here. Want a beignet? I got 'em at Poupard's Bakery when I was driving back, about five. That's the best time. They're fresh."

She did want a beignet. Then another.

Sugar was getting everywhere.

It did not seem to matter.

"I had a good time last night, Annette. I really did."

"You deserved it. You've been through some stuff."

"I guess so."

Silence for a time. Then:

"Nina, I can't tell you how much everyone in the department thought of Edgar."

'"He had that effect on people."

"I hated it, that he got hired by LP."

"Why?"

Annette shrugged:

"Writing about oil companies...big oil companies...is what I do. I don't like them."

"Why not?"

"Because they're frauds. They claim to understand what they're doing. But they can't. The whole damned thing is too big. The depth of the wells, the complexity of the operation—there are too many people involved. Too much chance of a mistake. A lot of mistakes. And then all hell breaks loose. It breaks loose, and they can't put it right again. And everything dies. Hell, we don't even know how long the dying goes on."

"And this is what you write about?"

"Hope to make my career about it. Even though it's sure to hold me down."

"How?"

"When we go onto the campus, you look around you."

"At?"

"The buildings. Especially the geology building."

"What will I be looking for?"

"The money that built them."

"Which comes from?"

"Big oil, baby. Big oil."

"So they don't like you because you don't like them."

"It would never be admitted. But that's the way it is."

"They hired Edgar anyway."

"They have money. They need engineers now. Half the young people in our department are already under contract, even before the ink is dry on their diplomas. Hundred and twenty thousand."

"What?"

"One hundred and twenty thousand dollars a year. Starting salary. They spend two years on the rig, then they start up in the company."

"Edgar had his family to support."

"Yes, he did. So there wasn't much of a choice about the matter."

"No. Guess there wasn't."

Pause.

"You want another beignet?"

"I've had plenty."

"Well. The dancing is over then. You know what we need to do, Nina."

"Yes."

"So. Let's go meet Professor Narang. And look at this mysterious flash disc of yours."

Within ten minutes, they were walking into DeGolyer Hall, which, Nina ultimately realized, housed all offices belonging to the geological sciences. Then there was a stop at the departmental office, another at Annette's office—small and crammed with books lying around like refuse—and finally they were opening the door of a larger viewing room, with computers hooked to overhead projectors.

"My esteemed Ms. Bannister!"

Professor Daruka Narang beamed at her.

He was standing behind a podium, looking up at the two of them as they entered.

It was a classroom meant for perhaps two hundred students, almost empty now except for the three of them.

"Dr. Narang?"

"Yes! Yes!"

He was a small man, immaculately dressed. He had a perfectly trimmed goatee, which shone black against his olive skin.

He gestured broadly:

"Come. Both of you, come down. I have some tea here. Could I offer you a cup of tea?"

And in fact he was standing beside a small table with a makeshift tea service on it.

They descended the steps.

"Thank you so much for letting me come, sir."

"No. It is our pleasure. Has Annette been gracious to you?"

"She has indeed."

"I took," said Annette, "Nina dancing."

"Wonderful! Wonderful! Please—take a cup of tea. There is sugar here, if you wish."

"Thank you."

It was so strange, thought Nina. *Tea. Dancing.*

And the memories of Edgar.

But she drank, and chatted, and talked about the flight into Lafayette…

...and went through all the common courtesies with this man, as though the three of them were celebrating the queen's birthday at some salon in London.

Finally though, after she had said some words about her own identity, and what Bay St. Lucy was like, and what Edgar's family was like...

After the three of them had completed the pleasantries expected of them, the work at hand was ready to begin.

She produced the disc, which she had been carrying in her purse.

Annette inserted it into one of the computers.

Another computer began buzzing, and finally the screen behind the podium broke into bright illumination.

Professor Narang, horned-rimmed glasses on now, fingers crawling over the keyboard like the legs of a tarantula, became immersed in the data filling the air and covering the walls around them.

And there was a mass of data.

The same data Nina had seen on her own computer, which now seemed woefully inadequate.

But the figures on the screen changed as the speed of Narang's typing increased.

Now there were graphs—line graphs, bar graphs.

Now there were lists of names, rosters, departmental flow charts.

Then numbers again, and letters in some kind of code.

And this went on.

Two minutes.

Five minutes.

Finally, Narang began whispering at the keyboard, and, from time to time, the ceiling of the room as he threw his head back, attempting, it seemed, to get his breath.

Finally, he looked at Nina and asked:

"Do you see this?"

Nina shook her head.

"I see, but I don't understand what I'm looking at."

"All right. Follow the pointer. This is not easy. But it is all here."

"What is?"

"You must simply look…"

The moving cursor:

Narang:

"These figures are from Tuesday, May 2, a bit over a month ago. The well has reached a depth of 13,293 feet below the sea floor. The final string of production casing from the wellhead at the sea floor to total depth has been put in the hole, and cemented in place."

Nina understood none of this, but it had a kind of haunting quality about it, and she could not take her eyes off the figures sprinkled over the screen before her.

"The well plan calls for fifty-one barrels of cement. Look…look here: this graph shows that they have used only twenty-three barrels. This will be in no way sufficient to ensure a seal between this 7-inch production casing—do you see it on the chart?—and the 9 and 7/8-inch protection casing they had put in before."

The professor was immersed in his subject now, and his eyes could be seen glittering behind the lenses of his glasses.

"Now please watch, Ms. Bannister. Mud has been lost to the reservoir while drilling the bottom portion of the well. This is the phenomenon which we generally refer to as 'lost circulation.' It usually indicates good reservoir quality, an interval of lower pressure or both, and can result in an enlarged wellbore or "washout." This is important—*exceptionally important*—because it might have been difficult to create a good cement seal between the casing and the formation. It also would have been impossible to ensure the effectiveness of the cement seal without running a cement-bond log."

Silence for a time, save for the humming of the computers and the projectors.

"All right. We shall proceed. It is now four days later. The cement that they did pour contained—and you can see that in the spectrum analysis over on the second chart there—a nitrogen additive to make it lighter so that it would flow more easily and better fill the area between the casing and the lost circulation-washout zone. That might make some sense, but surely they must have recognized that it also lowered the cement's ability to make a good seal, and cause gas from the reservoir to dilute the viscosity of the cement."

A door opened.

Someone looked in, and asked if the three people in the room needed anything.

They did not.

The door closed.

More:

"The next day. They have waited about 20 hours for the cement to dry. Oh my heavens—they are displacing the drilling fluid in the wellbore and riser with sea water. Sea water is much lighter than drilling mud so there is going to be less downward force in the wellbore to balance the flow of gas from the reservoir."

And so it went.

Narang spoke primarily to Annette, who nodded, obviously understanding what to Nina was simply gibberish.

But clearly something was wrong on Aquatica.

Finally, lights went up in the room.

"What's going on out there?" asked Nina.

"Oh a great deal. And none of it very promising. But I can promise you, dear Ms. Bannister, that you have done a very good thing, and a very brave thing, by bringing me this disc."

"It was just a thought of mine. Edgar's phone. If I could find it, I would know who he was trying to call."

"And a brilliant thought it was."

"Can you do anything with this information?"

"Oh yes, oh yes. I can first decipher it, calculate the extent of damage that has already been done, make certain projections—and then begin contacting the right people."

"Great. But…I feel like there is probably something I should do."

"There is, dear lady. There certainly is. And you are going to do it with Annette, right now."

"What?"

"Go and eat lunch."

There is only one reason why one should not live in the charming and magical city of Lafayette, Louisiana, this being the traffic. Even at normal times of year, getting from one point to another is difficult, the original city planners having neglected to take into consideration the concept of the left turn.

But there are very few normal times of the year, normal being an abnormal phenomenon for Cajun thinking.

Rather, there is always a parade of some kind going on.

Mardi Gras season, for example, always begins with Epiphany and worsens, so that by February fifteenth, one week before the day itself, traffic is almost intolerable. The city is paralyzed, its major streets cordoned by gray metal barricades that resembled modular prison cells.

But it is not only Mardi Gras. There are late spring parades, early summer parades, fall parades. Car travel becomes impossible, each turning being met with flashes of blue squad car lights, as stern policemen, either on horseback or motorcycles, stare at drivers and make small circular motions with their hands, ostensibly suggesting another route to the grocery store or the bakery or the filling station or whatever…but signifying in actuality that the vehicle must simply stop and remain immobile until the parade is over.

This is why Professor Narang suggested to Annette that she and Nina walk to The Olde Tyme Grocery.

The Olde Tyme Grocery is one of hundreds of reasons why one *should* live in the charming and magical city of Lafayette.

Food.

The Olde Tyme Grocery was just an expanded shack, perhaps a half mile from campus.

But it had a kind of splendor about it, just the same.

One walked into a scene of chaos, tunneled through a constant crowd, bellowed as loud as possible either SHRIMP! or OYSTER! or CATFISH!

...and then flattened oneself into one of the far shack corners like a hat rack until an echo-bellow approximating the order-bellow rolled through and over the crowd signifying that the sandwich itself was ready.

There remained a bit of hand-to-hand combat involved in reaching the counter, paying the bill, getting the treasured grease soaked sack, and escaping into the balmy swamp air again—(tables existed at The Olde Tyme Grocery but were only available during those hours when the establishment was closed)—and going somewhere to eat the food.

'Somewhere' in this case was the alligator pond in the center of campus.

Annette and Nina chose one of the metal benches separated by a sidewalk from the three-foot high metal fence separated by no more than a few reeds and a fallen tree from the four-foot alligator, which, gray as the mud it was lying on, stared implacably and enigmatically at them as they unwrapped their shrimp po-boys.

Nina wondered what to talk about first.

She could talk about the huge battered shrimp that seemed to dwarf not only the buns that semi enclosed it but also all of the living wildlife—birds, fish, squirrels, turtles—that moved about the placid lake before them.

Or she could talk about the wisdom of eating anything at all this close to a four-foot alligator, which, though admittedly not a ten-foot alligator, was still a good deal more significant than the four-inch pet alligator Nina's parents had once bought for her in a pet store.

She chose that for a time.

"Don't the alligators worry you?"

Annette chewed for a while, closed her eyes, savored the sauce even as it was dribbling down her cheek, wiped herself clean with a brown napkin, and finally recognized that another being was with her on the bench.

"What?"

"The alligators."

"What about them?"

"Aren't they a little close?"

"Close for what?"

"You trust them?"

Annette shook her head before taking another bite.

"I don't tell them any secrets, if that's what you mean. How's your po-boy?"

"Good. Great, really. These shrimp are huge. I just mean...well, there are students passing by here. And little children. And pets."

"They don't bother the gators."

"No, that wasn't..."

She continued to look at Annette, who, mystified, looked back at her.

Finally, it was time to change the subject.

"So what do we do, Annette?"

"Eat."

"I know. But after that?"

"After that, Nina, you take it easy. Go home. Sit by the ocean. You've earned a rest."

"But Aquatica..."

"What's going on out there is what's going on everywhere in the deep-water industry. They're cutting corners."

"So what will happen now?"

Annette nodded:

"Narang will happen now. Edgar, and you, have done a helluva thing by getting him this disk."

"He's that good?"

"He's amazing, Nina. Do you know anything about him?"

"No, practically nothing."

"Born in New Delhi but raised in London. Educated at Cambridge. Then Harvard."

"Why is he here?"

"Because big oil is here. Right in Lafayette."

"He hates big oil?"

A pause. Then:

"He doesn't hate big oil as such, Nina. He hates big oil and greed when they join up."

"Doesn't that always happen? Isn't that what you just said?"

"Not exactly. There are fine people in the oil business, and Narang knows every one of them. From New York, to Washington, to New Orleans....he's not a firebrand kind of guy, not a demonstrator who would get himself kicked off a rig. Right now I can promise you, he's making calls."

She stood up, walked in a tight circle around the bench, and continued:

"If I were to take that disc anywhere—LP, the police, the EPA, anywhere—I'd just get laughed at."

"Despite what's on it?"

"The things that are on it are not that obvious. It takes a world class physics person to see what their long term effects are going to be. That's Narang. Nina, he will get Aquatica fixed, if anyone can."

"And for the time being?"

"I don't think there's an immediate danger. A month down the road, maybe two months. But it won't happen. Narang won't let it."

"I just feel like I should…"

"What you 'should,' ma chere, is fly back home. Go out to eat. Let us handle it from here."

"Will you keep me updated?"

"Of course we will. Don't expect to see any big splashy news stories, though. Everything will be kept very quiet. And besides, the things that are going to happen—increased viscosity tests, heightened awareness of various density parameters—these things don't make the big headlines anyway. But don't you worry. They'll be getting done."

"So you think I…"

"Should go back to Bay St. Lucy, feeling good about the whole thing. When does your flight leave?"

"Two fifteen."

"Great. I'll take you to the airport."

"I feel like I should at least say good-bye, express my appreciation to Professor Narang."

Annette smiled and shook her head:

"If either one of us walked into his office right now, he probably wouldn't even know we were there. That disc you brought him is like a bone for a dog. He'll be thinking about nothing else for the next few days and weeks."

"Well, then…"

"Well, then, thank you, Nina. I thank you, and maybe the whole gulf coast needs to thank you. Now let's catch your flight to New Orleans."

The flights back were as uneventful as those coming had been.

On both legs, though—Lafayette to New Orleans, New Orleans to Bay St. Lucy—she was surrounded by a pleasant, comforting, golden glow.

The glow might have emanated from a small amount of alcohol, since she allowed herself a glass of cold, dry, Chardonnay on each flight.

Or it might have come from a bit of smugness, of self satisfaction.

This was not English literature. This was engineering. Physics. Chemistry.

Areas about which she knew nothing at all. And from the time she had set foot on Aquatica with Hector, she had felt silly, guilty, and out of place. She was intruding in a billion dollar industry, when she should have been staying in her little beach-front shack, petting Furl and taking her morning walks along the beach.

And yet, and yet…

She had done something good.

Something was wrong, something so complex that she might never understand it.

And now it was going to be fixed.

She told herself, as she watched the sun go down and finally got a glimpse of the airport lights at Bay St. Lucy, that she would never hear anything more about Aquatica, and that everything would be all right.

And about both of these things, she was to be proved completely wrong.

INTERLUDE

He had long since forgotten what bar he was in.

There were so many in the Quarter. All he knew was that he had studiously avoided the known tourist spots—Pat O'Brien's, The Napoleon House, The Olde Absinthe—simply on the off change that he might be seen.

But he would not be seen.

He had been too careful.

The plan had taken months to perfect, but he had overlooked no detail.

And tomorrow—today, actually, since it was almost 3 a.m.—today, in little more than seven hours he would be on a tramp steamer heading to Hamburg.

A day or so in that festive German port city, with its sailors' quarters and legalized prostitution, then on to London.

London with money.

He knew a woman there. She had no idea that he was coming, and she would probably be shacked up with someone. But she would be glad to see him.

She always was.

And as for his days on the Aquatica, the work he had done there…

…that was all in the past.

So that when the fruition of that work actually took place, he would be half a world away.

Such were his thoughts upon paying his bar tab, tottering his way drunkenly along whatever semi-deserted street—for streets in the Quarter are never completely deserted—finding the key to the apartment door, slipping it into the lock, and turning it.

Click.

Sleep would be good.

He had never been able to sleep well on the rig.

But he had escaped the rig.

And all the gibberish, the 'once in, never out;' malarkey…

That was to be proven wrong, once and for all.

He was, upon thinking about it, not at all convinced that such a character as The Tool Master really even existed.

He pushed open the door and stumbled inside.

Ah, the bed, waiting there for him.

"We don't," came a voice behind him, "encourage desertion."

He thought about turning around.

And that was the last thought he ever had.

CHAPTER NINE: BEING COMPLETELY WRONG

The following morning Nina received an invitation.

It was the kind of thing she might ordinarily have turned down, preferring instead to get back into her routine of beach walking, Furlcurling, shackcleaning, and gift shop managing.

But these had not been ordinary days for her.

These had been days of deep melancholy mixed with utter confusion.

She had been dealing either with things she did not understand at all, or things she found completely depressing.

And so when Tom Broussard arrived on her porch at a little after ten a.m. (she had just brewed a new pot of coffee and was sitting on her deck watching a bright green plastic dragon try to strangle an eight year old boy in the surf, much to the boy's—and his parents'—delight), when Tom, Bay St. Lucy's favorite pornographic novelist, announced that he and his wife Penelope were planning a small overnight camping trip to one of the offshore islands and Nina should come along…

…she accepted without reservation.

Nor was she wrong to do so.

The trip proved to be everything she had hoped it to be.

She arrived on her Vespa at the dock around six p.m., helped Penelope and Tom load the two tents they would be taking, as well as a small supply of rations (fish were to provide the major portion of what was to be eaten, and these fish would be caught later), lugged some of the coolers of beer onboard (the hosts were taking a thousand cans of Schlitz and a six pack of light beer, half of which were for Nina)—and then settled into her cozy stern niche as The Sea Urchin, Penelope's squalid and efficient little fishing boat, bravely attacked the incoming tide and threw itself and its crew against a series of waves tinged gold by the setting sun.

An hour and a half later, they had caught five whitefish. These Penelope dutifully cleaned while Tom built a driftwood campfire. And now they were sitting on the beach of DuBois Island, a place virtually unknown by tourists for the simple reason that it contained nothing of interest save dunes, scrub brush, and isolation.

So for a while they simply talked of this and that—why various members of the Democratic Party should be shot for what they were doing to the country, why various members of the Republican Party should be shot for what they were doing to the country, the last brutal murder Tom had planned and executed by typewriter, the number of pieces the corpse had wound up in and where they were by Chapter Six...

...and other such conversational morsels.

...which they chewed over along with the fish, while two of their party guzzled beer after beer and the other of their party drank *a* beer.

One, which lasted an hour and a half.

And then a second, which lasted until bedtime.

The stars, Nina could remember thinking, as she drifted off to sleep with the unmistakable aroma of sea air and tent fabric filling her nose, were superb.

And that, then, was the way her night had gone.

Absolute perfection.

No coulees, no corpses, no computer disks, no oil rigs, no incomprehensible data...

...just the exquisite kind of an evening that those people who live on the sea coast can experience whenever they want, and that everyone else in the world cannot.

The following morning was just as good.

They awoke at first light of course, Nina feeling a slight twinge of dizziness from her two cans of light beer, Tom and Penelope feeling no effects at all from their two hundred cans of actual beer. The air was deliciously cool. They combed the beach, noting the sand crabs, quivering bits of unidentifiable marine life, and white/pink ribbed shells that lay in dark, hard-packed sand; and they rekindled the fire, poking it a bit, prodding at the hissing coals, and blowing on various sides of a driftwood teepee until it had begun to crackle again and could prove a satisfactory base for the beat-up old coffee pot they had brought along.

They ate a 'b' breakfast.

Bear Claws, beignets and bagels from Bagatelli's.

A day old, perhaps, but who cared?

And so Nina was, for a time, cured.

The events of the previous week had been no more than a dream.

She felt this way, at least, during the boat ride back to Bay St. Lucy.

She felt this way for the entire afternoon, as she puttered around Elementals, shifting pots and paintings and ferns and tea services for absolutely no reason, and selling something now and then…

..and she felt this way for most of the early evening, during which she apologized to Furl for leaving him unattended, and fried in her favorite little skillet two of the filets that had been given to her by Tom and Penelope.

She even felt this way as, at approximately nine p.m., she began to read her Dorothy Sayers.

It was, in fact, all the way until ten minutes after nine— Lord Peter was just exiting the Bellona Club—when the cell phone buzzed, that she stopped feeling this way.

"Hello?"

The buzz on the other end sounded far away.

She wondered how she could differentiate near and far buzzes.

Weren't all buzzes the same?

There was no time to speculate about this, because a voice had now embedded itself in the buzz, or, she mused, embuzzed itself.

"Am I speaking now with Ms. Bannister?"

"Yes?"

"Ms. Nina Bannister, of Bay St. Lucy?"

"This is she."

"This is Professor Daruka Narang calling."

Oh shit, she thought.

So much for remote islands, campfires, and sleeping under the stars.

"Yes, Professor Narang?"

"I am calling you because…well, because a somewhat difficult situation has arisen."

Of course a 'difficult situation' had arisen.

What had any of them expected, if not that?

"All right. Tell me."

"I completed this morning a thorough examination of the materials you supplied me with."

"Okay."

"The situation at Aquatica is quite serious, perhaps more serious than I might have conjectured upon a first glance at the available data."

"How serious is it, Professor?"

"We may be talking about something quite imminent, and something quite large."

"An explosion?"

"Yes, and one which would involve many fatalities on the rig itself. Also, given the amount of oil and gas involved, the environmental aspects would be absolutely devastating. Unprecedented, I would say."

"My God."

"Yes, it is indeed quite serious. Which is why we have come to the matter of my calling you."

"What can I do?"

"You have done much already, my dear Ms. Bannister. But there may remain a more difficult challenge still."

"Tell me."

"I shall. You must understand that my normal path of action in a situation such as this would be somewhat subtle. I would make specific contacts and offer specific recommendations. Certain scientists and engineers, certain specialists familiar with the problems particular to the offshore drilling process..."

"Yes."

"But now more drastic measures seem to be called for."

"And so?"

"So I have written an article outlining, rather graphically, the urgency of the problem. And this article I have submitted, by means of a few special contacts I have collected over my career, to *The New York Times*."

The words *New York Times* seemed to send a small electric shock through Nina's cell phone.

"*The New York Times*?"

The current seemed to disappear when she said the name of the newspaper. Perhaps because of the question mark she had inserted.

"Yes. It is a publication of quite extensive circulation."

"I've heard of *The New York Times*, Professor. But, I have to ask: if the situation is that bad, shouldn't you just call Louisiana Petroleum immediately?"

"Perhaps. It is an option that I have naturally considered. But I must point out, that Louisiana Petroleum has allowed this situation to come about."

"Yes, yes, I see."

"But the bottom line is, I have just finished talking on the phone with several of the newspaper's editors."

Darkness had fallen on Bay St. Lucy now. She could see through the kitchen, on beyond the plate glass sliding door that led out to her deck. The waves were scudding in, silver breaker foam glowing in moonlight.

"Because of the urgency of the situation—and perhaps because of my modest reputation—they are agreeing to print the article."

"When?"

"Well, that is the question, my dear Ms. Bannister. This is a story of immense ramifications."

She could feel what was coming.

She did not like it.

But what had been to like since her discovery of Edgar's body?

Nothing.

"This being the case, the editors have naturally asked me the source of my information. I explained that all data had been collected from the mainframe computers currently operational on Aquatica, and was, unmistakably, accurate. However..."

"However, they still wanted to know where you got the data."

"Precisely."

"And you told them?"

"That I had it from an unnamed source."

"I see. That didn't satisfy them, though."

"Not entirely."

"But Professor, I see stories all the time that come from 'unnamed sources.' I thought reporters were not required to reveal their sources."

"They are generally not so required. But this is a very difficult area. You have also read, I am certain, of reporters who are required to do so by the courts. And these reporters frequently..."

"Go to jail."

"Precisely. You must understand, Ms. Bannister, that my recommendation in this article is to shut down Aquatica immediately. To evacuate it, and to set about a series of extensive checks and repairs that would cost months of time and billions in revenue."

"So they want to know where you got the disk."

"Yes. They do."

"And the truth is, I stole it."

"Well..."

"I and a fourteen-year-old boy."

Silence.

The waves continued their long, silent, scraggly roar.

"Did you give them my name?" she asked, almost as an afterthought.

"No, dear lady. No. I must have your permission to do that."

"And what do you think will happen if I let you give them my name?"

"Oh. Oh, dear. Well, I believe the expression is 'all bloody hell will break loose for your life.'"

She smiled at the phone, and then at Furl, who was watching the conversation from the straight chair on the far side of the room.

Neither smiled back.

"Yes. I guess it will."

"Again. I can quite easily proceed with channels that are..."

"Slower."

"Yes. And I can almost certainly avoid bringing you into the situation. But..."

"By that time, Aquatica may have blown up, and killed everybody out there. Not to mention destroying half of the gulf coast."

"Oh no, not half."

"No?"

"No! All!"

She breathed deeply.

"All, my dear Ms. Bannister. This is an installation much larger than any we have dealt with previously, and sitting on much greater energy reserves. If all elements converge at precisely the right—or in this case, wrong—instant, then we are talking about an enormous explosion, which would release millions of gallons of oil per minute, and which could not possibly be stopped for weeks. The effects of such a calamity would be..."

She interrupted him.

"Yes. I understand. Listen, do you have to give them Edgar's name?"

"I don't know. But I fear, yes. He was the young engineer who originally downloaded the data. Without him..."

"I know. All right. Listen, you have to give me a little time."

"Certainly. Certainly. If you wish to call me…"

"I've got your number."

"Excellent. Now, as to how much time you will need…"

"Just a minute."

She set down the cell phone, walked across the room, petted Furl, who said 'rrggghh', wagged his tail, and then, in a reciprocal gesture of affection, bit the back of her hand.

"Damn cat," she whispered, wondering if the bite would draw blood.

It did. Just a tiny red spot. But blood, still.

Then she walked out onto the deck and looked at the ocean.

She remembered the way it had looked last night, just before she had gone to sleep on the beach.

And how fresh it had smelled.

Then she walked back into her living room and picked up the phone.

"Okay," she said. "Use my name. Use both of our names."

Static.

Then:

"This is very brave of you, Ms. Bannister."

"Yes, well. I'm that kind of a gal."

"Pardon?"

"Nothing. Just…go ahead and tell them. Tell them the whole story."

"I shall. I shall, immediately. You understand, the newspaper may well wish to contact you."

"I imagine," she whispered, "that a lot of people may soon wish to contact me."

"I'm sorry. I did not precisely understand you."

"That's all right. Write the story well, Professor. A lot of people are depending on you."

"Oh, I shall. I shall indeed."

"Good night, then."

"Good night, Ms. Bannister. And all my best wishes."

She clicked the phone shut.

She sat quite still for some time, wondering how she could have done such a thing.

She was admitting to being a thief.

Admitting it to everyone in the world.

And how could she have done this without consulting the Ramirez family?

What would happen now?

She had just finished mentally asking herself that question, when the phone rang again.

She flipped it open.

"Hello?"

"Hello? Nina Bannister?"

"Yes?"

"This is Liz Cohen of *The New York Times*."

She looked at the back of her hand; a drop of blood was growing out of the small hole Furl had made in it.

It was, she surmised, to be the least of her worries.

The following afternoon she found herself in Jackson Bennett's Mercedes-Benz, heading out of Bay St. Lucy, driving toward a cabin somewhere in the forests of Mississippi, to meet with the writer she had spoken with the previous evening.

Elizabeth Cohen.

Feature journalist.

Who had asked her almost immediately:

"Are you the source?"

"Yes."

"Is the information in fact valid?"

"Yes."

And finally:

"Do you have a lawyer?"

She did.

And so Liz Cohen had called Jackson Bennett and arranged this meeting.

It had furthermore been decided:

The journalist was to fly out of New York at midnight, land in New Orleans at 3 AM, rent a car, and drive to the meeting place suggested by the attorney of Nina Bannister.

Because there was no question of holding this meeting at Nina's house.

Or at Jackson's office.

Or anywhere else in Bay St. Lucy, for that matter.

No, this had the potential to be one of the biggest stories of the…what? Year? Decade?"

This meeting had to be secret.

And so, accordingly, Jackson had suggested a cabin.

It was a nice drive. The radio emitted a bit of elevator music, which mixed with the murmur of the engine to have the same lulling effect that windshield wipers do during a long trip in rain.

The chain restaurants and filling stations came more sparsely as they left town. Finally, there were just pines and blue sky, the sun behind them getting multi-colored as its rays deflected through whatever layers of waste and garbage in the atmosphere made it look golden and magical.

"I had bought this cabin we're headed to," Jackson was saying, "several years ago as a kind of time-share venture with a couple of other guys. For the first year or two, I spent a good deal of time in it. Four or five of us would do a boys' night out occasionally, playing poker and drinking beer until late Friday night, and canoeing off the hangover at whatever time Saturday we decided to get up."

After a time, they turned off the main road and started meandering over the deep-rutted gravel lane that led through thick firs and balsams, getting just a glance here and there of a placid lake.

"Jackson, I want to thank you for helping me in this."

"Nothing to thank, Nina."

"I've probably messed this whole thing up. Going out there and getting that disk, without telling you—and now, *The New York Times*…"

He shook his head:

"Nina, whatever it is, I'll hear about it when Ms. Cohen does. It would be very easy for me to say, you should have done this, or you should have done that. But the truth is, we wouldn't have a Bay St. Lucy now—at least Bay St. Lucy as we know it—if you hadn't been smart enough to do the right thing when everybody else was doing the wrong thing. Helen Reddington would be in jail if you had used bad judgment. You didn't. You saw something nobody else could see. Hell, you almost won us a state basketball championship."

She could not help smiling at this.

"Whatever is going on here, you've earned the right to be given the benefit of the doubt. And I'll help you in any way I can. Now…let's just meet with Ms. Cohen, and see if somehow we can stay out of an all-out battle between the biggest oil company in the world and the biggest newspaper in the world."

"They stopped at a grocery store. Jackson went in, stayed for a time, then returned with a sack full of groceries, two bottles of red wine.

"There's a little kitchen in the cabin. This interview might take some time. We might as well be eating while it's going on."

"What did you get?"

"Stuff to make stroganoff."

"That's as good a last meal as any."

They kept going, deeper into woods, but still skirting the lake.

After about twenty minutes, they turned off the main road and started meandering over a rutted gravel lane that led through thick firs and cedars, getting just a glance here and there of the water.

The cabin looked as though it had always been there. There was a pier leading out to the green-glass still lake, the surface of which was dotted only by a few double-bump bullfrog heads and up-jutting logs that had once been willow trees. A swing and flier-chairs still sat placidly in the screened-in porch.

They stopped and got out of the car.

The lake had begun to make its evening sounds. There were the tree frogs and humming mosquitoes of summer evenings, and crows still circling and cawing. Some kind of animal, maybe a deer, could be heard crunching quietly over the fallen leaves and decomposing twigs.

"I always carry a key to this cabin on my keychain. Never know when the place might be useful. Sometimes I ask key witnesses to stay out here, relax before their appearance in court."

They walked across the porch, which overlooked the lake.

Jackson unlocked the door and pushed it open.

Nina had the bag of groceries in her arms. She took it inside.

It was a sparse cabin, but neatly made up. She could see dust particles floating in a shaft of light coming through the west window.

The cabin still had the musty smell of a place infrequently occupied, but, as she opened the window over the sink and felt the cool, pine-cone scented air float in, she felt the same sense of ease that the beach had given her two nights ago.

She looked through the window.

On the other side of the lake, two hundred yards or so away, a deer walked into a clearing. She could see him stop, raise his antlered head that was somehow not-brown not-gray but the exact color of the whole surrounding forest—then lower his head and meander away.

Twenty minutes later, Liz Cohen's rental car pulled into the driveway, and the woman herself got out of it.

"Hey! Nina? Jackson?"

They both shouted back various greetings.

She beamed.

"Liz Cohen. Nice place you got here."

"Thank you," answered Jackson. "Come on up!"

"Will do!"

She bounded up the steps.

Nina was uncertain whether the woman was so striking because she had NEW YORK written all over her, or because she was a little over six feet tall or because of her dense black curly hair, or because of the way she had of slightly leaning forward, not only into a room but into the world.

They all shook hands and then Liz Cohen said:

"So where is the booze?"

"Kitchen," answered Jackson.

"What have you got?"

"Two bottles of red wine," said Nina.

"That might not be enough. Given the story you're going to be corroborating—hell, given your own story—that might not be enough."

Jackson smiled:

"There's a bottle of scotch underneath the sink. I always try to keep a full one there. Never hurts."

"That's what I like to hear. Can we go inside?"

"Sure," he answered.

They did.

"Bedroom back here?"

"That's right, Ms. Cohen. Just take your things back there and put them on the bed."

"Liz," she said, disappearing through the door. "Liz is fine."

Within a minute she was back.

"Okay to smoke in here I hope."

"Sure," Jackson added, "but it will be more comfortable out on the porch. Why don't you two ladies go out there, sit on those rockers, and look out over the lake while I make the drinks."

"Great idea. Come on, Nina."

They found chairs and sat down. Liz lit a cigarette, took a deep drag on it, held the smoke inside her for a cancerous amount of time, and then expelled it toward a stuffed owl that was sitting improbably on the far side of the porch.

"It must be fascinating to work with *The New York Times*," Nina said. "How long have you been there?"

Liz looked at her through a haze of smoke and asked:

"Do you really care about that?"

Nina thought for a time and said:

"No, not really."

"Good. No, I think I'm gonna like you, Nina. Now what the hell is going on?"

"Aquatica is going to blow up."

"Well. I gotta say, that's a story. There's at least a Pulitzer in it. If you're not full of shit, of course."

Jackson arrived with the drinks.

"Nina is not full of shit," he said, sitting down. "If she says it's true, then it's true."

Liz nodded and produced a smart phone from her purse.

"Thanks for the Scotch. Tastes great."

"We try," answered Jackson.

"So, I might as well tell you: we're ready to run with Narang's story. He called us yesterday then sent the story electronically. Somehow the feature got routed to me. Didn't take much checking. He's one of the pre-eminent authorities on this kind of thing."

"I know," said Nina.

"I've got to ask you some things. I'll be typing as you talk, so don't worry if I look distracted. I'm not."

"I understand," said Nina.

"All right. The big thing, of course, is, where did all this data come from?"

"From Aquatica."

"They just volunteered it?"

"No, I went out and stole it."

"You what?"

"I stole it."

"From Aquatica?"

"Yes."

"Oh this just gets better and better."

"Nina."

"I'm sorry, Jackson; this is the story and I've got to tell it."

"Don't worry, counselor," said Liz. "She'll be out in twenty years, with good behavior."

"I don't," said Nina, almost despite herself, "feel like behaving good."

"No. I guess not. So go ahead. Tell the story."

"Almost exactly a week ago, I found a body in one of the drainage canals in Bay St. Lucy."

"*You* found it?"

"Yes."

"Come on, the two of you are making this whole thing up. This is a gag that one of my old boyfriends is pulling."

"No," said Nina. "It's the truth."

"The young man's name," said Jackson, "was Edgar Ramirez. The cause of death is still listed as drowning. There was great deal of alcohol in his bloodstream, and it seems he may have fallen."

"Fallen," said Liz, "into a drainage canal?"

"That's the current theory."

"Bullshit. But go on."

Nina did.

"Edgar's brother contacted me."

"Why?"

"I don't know."

"Everybody," Jackson said, "has gotten into the habit of contacting Nina when there is a murder to be solved."

"I can see. Go on, Nina."

"Edgar had just come home from a two week shift on Aquatica. He was an engineer out there. He was apparently very upset."

"About what?"

"We don't know. But he spent most of his first evening at home trying to call someone."

"Who?"

"That's coming."

"Okay, so we put the Pulitzer on hold. But keep going."

"He left home about midnight. That was the last time anybody saw him."

"Until you found his body."

"That's right."

"Fine. So how do we make the little jump from there to you committing industrial espionage on a billion dollar oil platform?"

"That," said Jackson, rocking forward and finishing his glass of Scotch, "is what I would like to know."

"When I came home that night, I found Edgar's brother, Hector, sitting on my porch. He said Edgar had confided in him that there was something very wrong; he had documented it, and it was on his computer."

"Which was where?"

"In his room on Aquatica. Louisiana Petroleum offered to clean out the room and send Edgar's belongings back to his mother, but…"

"…but you knew they would confiscate the computer. And whatever was on it."

"That seemed probable."

"Certain, more like it. So you went out there?"

"Hector and I did."

"And packed up his things?"

"Yes."

"But the computer? Surely they didn't just let you have it, and anything that might have been on it?"

"No, they checked it thoroughly, while we sat there and watched. They found nothing."

"Nothing? Then I don't see…"

"They left and Hector asked if we could be left alone in his dead brother's room to pray. They said okay. But as soon as they were gone, he opened Edgar's empty locker—we had checked there first thing and emptied it out. Behind a pin-up poster of a naked woman was a flash disk. Edgar had downloaded the vital files onto it, then hidden it."

"Behind a naked woman?"

"A picture of a naked woman."

"Yeah, we're back to Pulitzer again. The only question is, I'm just not sure who's going to play you."

"Play me?"

"In the movie. I'm thinking Meryl Streep."

"She's too tall."

"She can play short. So how did Narang come onto the scene?"

"Edgar had been trying to call somebody all night. But nobody knew who."

"Yeah, I got that."

"But I kept wondering…if he had been doing all that calling, where was his cell phone?"

"Where indeed?"

"They hadn't found it on his body, and it wasn't in his room."

"So you figured?"

"It was still in the drainage canal. So I went back there, poked around, found it, and called the last number that showed up on the call window."

"Jesus."

"No, Narang."

"You're a smartass, too. God, I like you."

Liz thumbed madly on the keypad of her smartphone for more than a minute; then she said:

"Okay, the whole story's sent. We're leading with Narang's piece, then printing a byline that essentially goes over what you just told me. The digital version of the paper goes on line at five a.m. tomorrow morning. As for whether this is a Pulitzer or not, I don't know. But I can tell you…"

There was a buzzing sound.

"That's my phone," said Jackson Bennett.

He looked at the window on the phone.

"My office. Something must be going on, or they wouldn't be calling me out here. Wait a minute and let me take this."

He flipped the phone open, and for a time Nina could hear only half of a conversation.

"Yeah. Yeah."

Pause.

"What?"

Second pause.

"Just say that one more time. All of it."

Third pause.

Finally:

"Okay. See you as soon as I can."

Phone flipped shut.

Jackson:

"That was my office, like I thought. They just heard from the Coroner's office."

"The Coroner's office?"

"Yes, Nina. The Coroner's office. They've run further tests."

"And?"

"Edgar Ramirez was murdered."

"Oh, my God."

"He was drugged and then forced to drink almost a bottle of whiskey. Whoever did it hoped the whiskey would cover the drugs. And it did on preliminary tests. But they kept on looking, and...well, it's like you must have thought all along. Somebody killed the boy."

Liz Cohen stubbed out her cigarette and said:

"Okay, then let me get this straight. Ms. Bannister, retired school teacher and ex-principal, along with *The New York Times*, are going to be accusing one of the biggest oil companies in the world of murdering a twenty-one-year old Hispanic boy in cold blood in order to hide the fact that their greed and incompetence are about to blow up one hundred and twenty workers and destroy the entire ecological system of the United States Gulf Coast? Is that what is happening here?"

Nina thought for a time, then said:

"They'll be mad, won't they? When the story comes out?"

Liz said nothing, but her thumbs continued to work on the keypad.

It was soon obvious that she was not texting, but making an actual phone call.

Finally, she spoke into the glowing plastic appliance in her palm:

"Tom? Liz. You got the stuff I sent you? Good. Well get ready, it gets better. The kid they found in the ditch? He was murdered. No. No, you heard right. Drugged and then drowned. No. No, I don't know what drugs exactly, but I'm sure as hell going to find out. I'm driving into Bay St. Lucy right now and heading to the Coroner's office. I'll send you an update in less than an hour. Okay."

So saying, she hung up.

Then she looked at Jackson and asked:

"Are you a good lawyer?"

He merely shrugged.

Liz continued:

"Well, you better be. Because you're gonna have one pissed off oil company looking for Nina Bannister in the morning."

"They are," Jackson said, "going to be looking for *The New York Times*, too."

She stood up, and smiled.

"Yeah. Well, we're big kids. I'm going to get my things out of the bedroom and head back to town. I may have to batter down the doors of the Coroner's office, but I will find out what kind of drugs were used on that kid. And I'll get a direct report from your coroner. Sorry I can't stay for the stroganoff."

"That's all right," said Jackson. "I probably need to get back to town too. All hell is going to be breaking loose."

"You better know it."

She disappeared for a time into the bedroom, then reappeared with her briefcase.

"Nina Bannister," she said, extending a hand, "you are one brave woman. And everybody on the Gulf Coast may owe you more than they realize. As well as those folks on Aquatica."

Nina took the hand and returned as firm a handshake as she was capable of.

"I do what little I can."

Liz smiled, looked first at Jackson and then at Nina, and said:

"What was it that Margaret Mead said? 'Never doubt that a small group of thoughtful, committed citizens can change the world; indeed, it's the only thing that ever has.'"

Nina nodded and added:

"Right. Margaret Mead's dead, isn't she?"

"Well," said Liz, opening the door to the porch, "there is that to consider. You two have a nice evening. I may not see you again. Hope you enjoy the story."

And with that she was gone.

Nina and Jackson watched her get into the rental car, and watched as its tail lights disappeared into the forest.

For a while, there was only the sound of cicadas and crickets.

The woods and lake had become purple and murky as night fell.

"What," Nina asked quietly, "is going to happen now?"

Jackson shook his head:

"I wish I knew. I'm not that smart."

"Well, you're the smartest we got around here. So I'll try it again: what's going to happen next?"

"Okay. Louisiana Petroleum is a multi-billion dollar oil company that employs more than two hundred attorneys. All of these lawyers, and all of the company's top executives, and all of their workers, and all of their workers' families, are going to go completely ape in about ten hours. Maybe sooner if this thing leaks before *The Times* actually hits the street."

"Yeah; so that's bad."

"Well, they're probably going to take note of the fact that they're being accused of murder and environmental destruction on a mass scale, all because of a small computer disk that you stole from them."

"I was hoping they would miss that."

"No, I don't think they will."

"What can they do to me?"

"They can sue you for about a trillion dollars in damages."

"That would almost empty my checking account."

"Well, they might be satisfied just to take Furl and call it even."

"No way."

"I didn't think you'd want to do it the easy way. Nina, what is it about you, anyway?"

"What do you mean, Jackson?"

"For the last, oh, eighteen months or so, your life…"

"I know what you mean."

"Why can't you just be a retired senior citizen, sitting on her deck and watching the ocean?"

"That was my plan. It really was."

"I know. But, there was the Robinson case, and then the Reddington murder and then the bizarre deal with April van Osdale…"

"I know. I know. I keep thinking, 'well, this horrible thing is over. Now at least now I can settle back and enjoy my golden years."

"But it doesn't seem to happen, does it?"

"No, it doesn't. It almost seems like I'm caught up in this series of wild murder mysteries, and the writer keeps churning them out, each one more unbelievable than the last."

"Yeah. Well, I hope they're selling."

"They can't be. People who read mysteries like a little English village and a quiet, simple murder. I could even stand to be involved in that. Maybe I could even solve the murder. But what do I get? The biggest oil well in the whole world, which is ready to blow up and destroy the entire Gulf Coast of The United States. How would Miss Marple deal with that?"

Jackson shook his head and rose to his feet.

"I don't know, Nina. But what I imagine is this: Louisiana Petroleum will issue a statement first thing tomorrow morning. They have offices in a number of major cities, but I think their CEO is based in Lafayette— although the majority of their lawyers probably are based in DC. Anyway, they will, of course, deny everything. They will skewer *The New York Times* for daring to run such a damaging and untrue story. All this time, phone calls will be going on behind the scenes. There will be threats of huge lawsuits."

"And they will probably want to have a few words with me."

"Just a few. Which is why...."

He took a deep breath.

She interrupted:

"What, Jackson? Which is why what?"

He exhaled, and then said, quietly:

"Nina, I don't think you should go back into Bay St Lucy tonight. I have to. *The Bay St. Lucy Gazette* is going to get hold of this story as soon as anybody does. They're going to want to talk to you. I'll intercede. In fact, I may go straight to their offices now, and give them a heads up on what's happening. They'll contact Louisiana Petroleum, or Louisiana Petroleum will contact them, I don't know. But at any rate, by early tomorrow morning, LP will know that I'm representing you."

"You will represent me?"

"Don't I always represent you? I'm like Perry Mason: every Sunday evening, same time, same place..."

"I know, Jackson. This time it seems we're a little out of our league, doesn't it?"

He smiled and shook his head:

"Not a bit of it. You beat Hattiesburg and the McNulty girls; you shouldn't have a problem with some huge, floating filling station. The thing is, though, it just might be better for you to stay here tonight. A lot of people are going to start wanting to talk with Nina Bannister, starting in just a few hours. Nobody knows you're here. Nobody even knows about this cabin. So just try to get a good night's sleep. There's coffee and a coffee maker. When I went into the grocery story I picked up some cereal and milk. I mean, it isn't Bagatelli's but..."

"There's Furl."

"I'll go by tonight and change his litter, give him some fresh food."

"I don't have a book to read."

"You don't need a book. You *are* a book."

"Yes. I guess that's true."

"I'll also go by and talk to the Ramirez family. Try to tell them what's coming."

"Tell them I'm so sorry to have gotten them into this."

He shook his head:

"You didn't get them into it, Nina. Edgar got them into it, maybe because he thought it was a good idea not to destroy a major portion of the ocean. And Hector got them into it, maybe because he knew his big brother had been killed, and he thought somebody ought to do something about it."

"The proverb he used," she whispered. 'A boy remains a boy until a man is needed.'"

Jackson walked toward the doorway, turned, and said:

"Well. A man may be needed now."

"Several of them. And maybe a couple of women, too."

He smiled:

"As far as the women are concerned, one may be enough. It has been in the past. Anyway, I promise you, Nina. No one will bother you out here tonight. Get a good night's sleep. I'll send a car out to get you, maybe about nine tomorrow morning. I won't be able to come myself because I'm sure to be in one meeting after another; also, I don't want anybody to follow me. But there's a young man I trust. He'll bring the car out, and we'll sneak you back into Bay St. Lucy. After that, we'll just go by instinct."

"All right, Jackson. Whatever you think."

"That's it then. Okay, goodnight, Nina."

He walked through the door, down the stairs, and out the pathway toward his car.

She could hear it driving away.

And she was alone.

What to do?

Something told her that she should be uneasy. The evidence had come in, and Edgar had indeed been murdered. Chilling thought. Whoever had killed him was going to know about her.

Somehow, though, as she walked to the window and peered out into the forest, she felt comforted. The pines and cedars seemed to wrap her in a blanket of security, and the night sounds had a restful quality. She looked around her, in the kitchen. There was the plastic-wrapped packet of ground beef that Jackson had bought at the grocery story. A can of mushroom soup. A small sack of noodles.

And two bottles of red wine.

She didn't need two bottles, but…

…where was a corkscrew?

There, before her, in the drawer.

All right, then…

…stroganoff for dinner.

So she boiled the water, dumped in the noodles, and cooked her meal.

Half an hour later she was finishing her second glass of red wine.

She had moved outside to the small pier that extended out into the lake, and was sitting on a plastic folding chair. The Mississippi sky sparkled above her, stars glittering like tiny jewels on an ink-black gown. They were reflected in the calm lake, which moved not at all except when a heron chanced to land on it, or a fish jumped out of it, plopping on re-entry.

What would tomorrow bring?

Lawyers, lawyers, lawyers, all yelling at her, all accusing her of something.

She could have left well enough alone, couldn't she?

And then she was conversing again, as she did so often at times like these.

"But it's true, I could have. When Hector came to the house and I found him there, sitting on the front porch—I could have just told him to go on home."

"Yes, you could have."

"Then none of this would have happened."

"Well, not to you, anyway."

"Of course not. And when you think of it, why am I involved in this anyway? Aquatica indeed! I'm an old retired English teacher. What do I know about oil rigs?"

"More than you used to."

"Maybe. But not much more. And *The New York Times*. Me in *The New York Times*! The only thing I know about *The New York Times* is their crossword puzzle. And even that's too hard."

"Except for Monday."

"Yes, except for Monday. So what do I do now? What if they sue me?"

"They can't sue you."

"Why can't they?"

"You don't have anything."

"Oh. Well, there is that to consider."

"Of course, there is."

"Still, I feel like I've made a horrible mess out of things."

"Look at the lake."

"What?"

"Look at the lake."

"Why?"

"Because, one way or another, it feeds into the ocean."

She did look at the lake. Bullfrogs ringing it had begun croaking in chorus, not far from where she was sitting. More fish were jumping now, one out there, to the right, another closer to the center. And there, on the far side perhaps two hundred yards from her, a deer stepped out of the undergrowth and began to drink. She could see his button eyes gleaming, even in the distance.

"And the ocean, Nina, feeds into it."

She nodded.

"The oil would be here, too, wouldn't it?"

"Yes, it would, Nina. It might take time. But the oil would be here, too."

"Okay."

Silence for a time.

"Okay. So I'll just do the best I can."

"Of course, you will. You always do."

"Whatever's out there waiting. Bring it on."

"They will and you'll handle it. You always do."

"You have a lot of confidence in me."

"I always have."

"I know that."

"And I always will. Now go to bed, Nina Bannister. Get some sleep. You're going to need it."

"All right. Good night, Frank."

And so thinking, she rose and went in to bed.

CHAPTER TEN: WOMAN OF THE YEAR!

She awoke with first light and glanced at the small alarm clock someone had left on the bed stand. Five forty five.

She got up, dressed, and walked outside. The air was deliciously cool. The world was still gray on its way to blue and green, and mist hung over the lake.

She found a walking trail and began to encircle the lake.

By seven-thirty she had completed her walk, made coffee, and completed half of the bagel Jackson had bought the day before.

She was wondering how she might spend the next two hours when a car pulled up to the cabin.

"Ms. Bannister?"

A fresh-faced young man emerged from the innocuous black sedan, which seemed to have been built for no other purpose but to avoid detection.

She thought she remembered him from Bay St. Lucy High School.

"Ms. Bannister?"

"Yes?"

"I'm Terry Anthony. I was a senior last year."

"Oh yes, Terry, I remember you. You were on the A Honor Roll for the last two six-week periods."

He beamed.

"Yes, ma'am."

"What are your plans, Terry?"

"I got accepted to The University of Mississippi."

"Excellent."

"I'm planning to go to law school. But for right now, this summer, I'm interning with Mr. Bennett. Just doing errands, and seeing a little bit about what a lawyer does."

"You couldn't do better."

"No, ma'am. Anyway, that's kind of why I'm here. To pick you up and bring you back into town."

"I thought Jackson said it would be about nine."

"Yes, Ma'am. But apparently a lot is going on. He thinks you need to come on in now."

"I see. All right, then. I'll get a few things together, and we can go."

She went inside, packed her travel bag quickly with the change of clothes she had brought out and her toiletries, then returned to the car.

Terry was standing beside it, holding open the back door.

"Are you going to be my chauffeur, Terry?"

"Yes, Ma'am. Just get in and make yourself comfortable."

"Thank you."

She slid in, putting her things on the vacant seat beside her.

He started the car, then leaned back and said:

"Ms. Bannister?"

"Yes?"

"Mr. Bennett said I should give you something."

"All right."

"He said not to let it upset you."

This upset her, but she still found the presence of mind to reply:

"I'll try not to. What is it?"

"This newspaper. It hit the streets about an hour ago."

He handed her a copy of what she immediately knew to be *The New York Times*, even before she saw the paper's masthead or read the headline, which screamed:

DISASTER IMMINENT! MAJOR OIL INSTALLATION ON BRINK OF EXPLOSION!

By...Daruka Narang.

"Okay," she whispered to herself, unfolding the paper in her lap while Terry eased the car out of the driveway. "Okay, let's see what you wrote, Professor."

She read as follows:

"According to unimpeachable data recently obtained from the main computer bank of Louisiana Petroleum's flagship offshore drilling rig Aquatica, the installation stands on the brink of a major catastrophe, perhaps unparalleled in the history of environmental disasters. Due primarily to greed and mismanagement, at least eight crucial subsystems are in danger of near-simultaneous failures, the combination of which stand to unleash a devastating explosion of almost nuclear destructive potential, which will in turn unleash more than a billion gallons of pure crude oil into the Gulf of Mexico."

"Wow," she found herself muttering as the car wound its way toward the major highway back to Bay St. Lucy. "The man can write."

The article continued:

"Eight Steps to Doomsday":

1. Dodgy cement. The cement at the bottom of the main borehole has failed to create a permanent seal, so that gas and oil have already begun to leak through it into a pipe leading to the surface The cement formulation chosen—a less expensive and more easily applied brand—has clearly proven itself incapable of performing its crucial task.

2. Valve failure. The bottom of the pipe to the surface contains two valves designed to stop the flow of gas to the surface. Both have failed completely, although no one on Aquatica at this moment seems aware of the failure, or of the imminent danger arising from it.

3. Pressure tests misinterpreted. Six pressure tests have been carried out in the last three weeks, all of which should have served as warnings. All of these tests have, inexplicably, been either ignored or misinterpreted.

4. Leaks not spotted soon enough. Unexpected increases in the pressure in the well should have been spotted at least ten days ago by the crew at the surface. These increases have been occurring with ever heightening frequency during the last days, and have not been interpreted as leaks.

5. Third valve failure. A mixture of mud and gas has already begun seeping onto the floor of the ocean. This seepage should have been prevented by the blowout preventer which sits on the ocean floor at the top of the borehole. The blowout preventer—again, a less expensive model than should have been installed given the size of the gas field being dealt with—has completely malfunctioned.

6. Some moments before an actual explosion takes place, the crew of Aquatica will have the option of diverting mud and gas away from the rig, venting them safely through pipes over the side. Instead, as the system is now designed, the flow will be diverted to a device on board the rig designed to separate small amounts of gas from a flow of mud. This device is called a mud gas separator. The problem is that the mud gas separator currently in place is no more than one-third the size necessary, given the volume of gas and oil involved. It will fail, and be overwhelmed immediately by escaping gasses.

7. Questionable gas alarm. The rig has an onboard gas detection system that should sound the alarm and trigger the closure of ventilation fans to prevent the gas reaching potential causes of ignition, such as the rig's engines. This system HAS NEVER BEEN TESTED.

8. No battery for BOP. The anticipated explosion will almost certainly destroy the control lines the crew will be using to attempt to close safety valves in the blowout

preventer. However, the blowout preventer has its own safety mechanism in which two separate systems should shut the valves automatically when it loses contact with the surface. Presently one of these systems seems to have a flat battery and the other a defective switch. Consequently, the blowout preventer WILL NOT CLOSE."

"Consequently, in light of these appalling observations, I cannot but call upon the Louisiana Petroleum Corporation to shut down its Aquatica operations immediately, and evacuate all personnel on board. The installation should remain isolated for at least forty eight hours, during which time no drilling should be done, and residues of gasses now trapped in precarious locations should be allowed to disperse. Following this cool down period, and only after a complete check of all available data has been undertaken by objective scientific observers, a select and highly trained team of maintenance engineers must be dispatched to Aquatica to begin the process either of repairing the institution, or, as painful as it may be economically to the corporation and its shareholders, of dismantling it entirely.

Note: It gives me, as a scientist who has spent a career studying the benefits and pitfalls of offshore oil drilling, no pleasure to report these findings. I can, on the other hand, be heartened by the fact that they come as predictions before the fact rather than regrets following it. At the present time, no lives have been lost, no oil has been spilled, and no damage has been done either to the Gulf of Mexico nor the residents of its coastal cities."

"Time, though, is not on our side."

Professor Daruka Narang

PhD., Chemical Engineering

The University of Louisiana at Lafayette

This was the lead story in *The New York Times*.

A second story, though, ran some inches below it:

"WOULD BE WHISTLE BLOWER MURDERED"

"*The Times* has learned that a young engineer assigned to Louisiana Petroleum's offshore vessel Aquatica was brutally murdered three nights ago, possibly as retribution for his attempts to report safety violations occurring aboard the installation. Edgar Ramirez, a recent graduate of The University of Louisiana at Lafayette, had returned to his family from a two-week stint on the vessel, and was apparently attempting to contact authorities to make clear his findings. He was attacked scant hours before he was able to do so, then drugged and thrown into a drainage canal, where he drowned."

"The body of young Ramirez, *The Times* has also learned, was then discovered by a resident of Bay St. Lucy, retired teacher and high school principal, Nina Bannister. It was Ms. Bannister who, along with fourteen-year-old Hector Ramirez, the victim's younger brother, took it upon herself to go to Aquatica, locate the hidden 'flash disk' on which Ramirez had recorded his findings, and transfer it personally to Professor Daruka Narang, who wrote the above article."

"Final note: when this reporter remarked to Ms. Bannister at the conclusion of their personal interview: "Nina Bannister, you are one brave woman. And everybody on the Gulf Coast may owe you more than they realize. As well as those folks on Aquatica…."

…Ms. Bannister answered simply: 'I do what I can.'

'What you can,' Ms. Bannister, is quite a bit.

Quite a bit indeed."

SPECIAL TO *THE NEW YORK TIMES*

ELIZABETH COHEN

Okay, thought Nina. *So I'm famous.*

She let that thought circulate through her mind during the half-hour ride back to Bay St. Lucy and had to be called out of a mental haze by her driver, Terry, who was trying to communicate with her.

"Ms. Bannister?"

"I'm sorry…"

"Ms. Bannister? I think maybe you were napping. I'm sorry to bother you."

"No, not napping. Just thinking about what it's like to be splashed over the front page of *The New York Times*."

"Yeah! I guess that's got to be pretty exciting."

"Well, it's pretty something."

"It's just that Mr. Bennett had some kind of instructions for when we get into town. And we're only a mile or so out right now."

"What instructions?"

"He asked me to have you wear these."

"Sunglasses?"

"Yes, ma'am."

"Oh, my God. Why do I have to wear sunglasses?"

"I guess he doesn't want anybody recognizing you."

"Is it that bad?"

"I don't know, ma'am. Things have been pretty chaotic this morning. Mr. Bennett can't seem to get off the phone. People are coming into town from all over."

"Louisiana Petroleum people?"

"Yes, Ms. Bannister, and lots of others, too. There's a kind of panic going on. And also Mr. Bennett thought…"

"Yes, go ahead, Terry, out with it."

"He thought it might be best if you kind of scrunched down in the seat."

"Scrunched? Is that a word?"

"It's the word he used. I guess he means for you to…"

"I know what he means. But I'm only five feet four. I'm scrunched when I'm sitting up straight. Besides, the car has tinted glass windows."

"Yes, ma'am. I'm only telling you what he told me."

"All right, all right," she answered, putting on the glasses and sliding down so that her head was below the level of the back windows. "Now I know what Greta Garbo must have felt like."

"Who?"

"Don't worry about it, Terry. Just drive. Get us there in one piece and maybe I'll give you my autograph."

"Yes, ma'am."

She could feel the car slowing now, and she could imagine the familiar turns that took them into downtown Bay St. Lucy.

Overhead she could now hear the throbbing pulse of rotor blades.

"Helicopter?" she asked.

"Yes. They've been flying in since about six o'clock this morning."

"From where?"

"Just about everywhere. All right. We're here, but I'm supposed to take you around back and park in the alley."

"Wonderful. I'm breaking into my own husband's old law office."

The car parked.

She got out, looking warily up and down the alley, and running toward the rickety back stairs which she had not climbed for at least twenty years.

They held her, though they wobbled a bit and forced her to grab tight to the paint-peeling bannister.

She remembered Frank having painted this bannister all those years ago, beaming as he attached a cylindrical tube designed to hold messages that were, for reasons of security, meant to be delivered out of sight of the general public:

"The Bannister bannister canister!"

And she had answered:

"Oh, Frank, honestly!"

How many times had she said 'honestly' to her husband?

And just what did that mean, anyway?

She opened the door.

There was a restroom just to her right, and a dark corridor.

She followed the hallway, turning first right, then left.

Then another door.

And Jackson's office.

Jackson Bennett himself turned as she entered the room.

"Well," he rumbled. "The film star!"

She walked across the old office, took off her sunglasses, and put them on the arm of the couch.

"What is happening, Jackson?"

He shook his head:

"What isn't happening? The whole world is in chaos. Look. I've been watching TV for the last ten minutes. The networks are breaking into all the regular shows. It's the biggest story of the decade."

"What is that you're watching now?"

"CNN. Louisiana Petroleum is having a live news conference, out of Lafayette. There. There's their president, and, I don't know, a bunch of muckety-mucks. Here. Sit on the couch."

She did so, feeling as though she were living in a dream.

Jackson had, some years earlier, installed a flat screen television on the wall that Frank had always kept covered with maps.

It seemed a sacrilege, but one must, Nina had concluded at the time, keep up with progress.

Now the area that had been central Europe was plastered over by the face of a man who, dressed in a black suit and red tie, looked to be the model of all corporate presidents.

"I think," said Jackson, "this guy's name is…"

"It doesn't matter what his name is," Nina interrupted. "He's the president of a corporation. He plays golf and has silver hair. That's all you need to know."

Jackson chuckled.

"I guess that's right. Well. We'll listen to what he has to say."

They did.

"First, I want to assure everyone here present at the press conference today, and all those people who might be watching across the country—that every allegation made in this morning's *New York Times'* story is completely without foundation. We have no idea how this particular professor got hold of his information, but it's insane. There is no drilling installation in this country, or in the world, for that matter, that is safer than Aquatica. Every gram of cement, every valve, every pipe, must meet, and have met, the highest specifications. There is no 'seepage' of gas, no malfunctioning gas alarms, no malfunctioning blowout preventers—and we are completely at a loss to explain how these absurd allegations could ever have been made. Now—rather than my going on and saying the same things over and over again, I'd like to open the floor for questions. Yes, Allyson?"

Reporters had surrounded the podium like a pack of dogs. They fired questions one by one, and he answered with the same flat equanimity.

"Are steps being taken to evacuate the facility at this time?"

A shake of the head:

"No, of course not. There is no reason to evacuate Aquatica."

"Have you been in contact with the crew?"

"John…"

How did this man seem to know the first names of all of these national reporters?

That must come with the territory, Nina decided, if one is a CEO.

"John, not only are we in contact with the crew of Aquatica now, but we are in contact with them daily, and even hourly—as we are every day of the week—without exception! We have people in Lafayette who are seeing the same images that the people in the control room at Aquatica are seeing. And I must tell you, everyone out there is just as shocked as we are here in the company's main offices."

"Is there any panic on the vessel?"

"Of course there's no panic on the vessel! Nothing is wrong on the vessel! The only panic on Aquatica stems from the fear that families and loved ones on shore are going to believe some cock and bull story—I'm sorry, but that's the only way I can describe it—about misinterpreted safety checks and dodgy cement."

"Have you been in contact with the EPA?"

"Patricia, we are ALWAYS in contact with EPA. A team of EPA inspectors returned from Aquatica just last week. I met with them personally here in Lafayette. Their only concern—and this was in fact somewhat troubling, because we take these kinds of things very seriously—was that the lobster they were served for dinner was two days old."

"Sir, do you think this is funny?"

"Do I think a nationwide demand that we shut down and dismantle our flagship oil rig—at a cost of billions of dollars—because of an absolutely ludicrous story, supplied apparently to *The New York Times* by a retired school teacher who stole a young engineer's flash disk from what should have been a secure computer—is funny? No. No, I don't think it's funny, and the professionals who work on and are extremely proud of Aquatica don't think it's funny; and their families, who now may be terrified for absolutely no reason, don't think it's funny; and the residents of every town on The Gulf Coast, who are now imagining their beaches covered with oil and their livelihoods threatened—don't think it's funny either. Insane perhaps. Ludicrous. But no, not funny."

"Do you have any comment about the death of Edgar Ramirez?"

"We regret it deeply, because the young man was one of us, a part of us. We have expressed our most sincere condolences to his mother, and to the rest of his family."

"You deny then that anyone from Louisiana Petroleum had anything to do with his death?"

"Of course, we deny it! It's as insane and ludicrous as everything else in this hodgepodge of a story! Also, we are demanding that *The New York Times* retract this garbage immediately."

"And if they do not?"

"That will be a matter for our legal department to deal with. I'm not prepared to comment on it at this time."

"Have you been in contact with Professor Narang, or with Nina Bannister, who according to *The Times* is the original source of the story?"

"Again, I'm not going to comment on that. But I do want to do something else at this moment."

He turned and addressed someone standing behind him:

"Are we ready? Have we got the signal? All right then…"

He spoke once again to the reporters:

"If you'll look at the big screen to my right, you'll see that we have a direct hookup with the main control room on the Aquatica."

The screen on the TV flashed once. Then the scene changed and Nina saw the same control room she had visited some days earlier.

Staring into the camera were three familiar figures, all outfitted in the bright orange jump suits and yellow helmets.

The CEO continued to speak:

"The people you see before you," he said, "are three of Aquatica's top officers: Dr. Sandra Cousins, materials engineer and public relations specialist, Mr. Tom Holder, first drilling assistant, or Tool Master, and Dr. Phil Bennington, rig master. I'm going to let you direct your questions to them. Bill, you've had your hand up. Go ahead and address your inquiry to any one of them. They can see you now, and they can hear you."

The reporter stepped forward and shouted at the screen:

"This question is for Dr. Cousins!"

Sandy Cousins, looking pert and sunshiny as Nina had remembered her being, spoke up to answer:

"Yes! I hear you!"

"Do you feel as though you are in any danger out there?"

She shook her head emphatically:

"No, not in the least! I'm one of the people in charge of importing materials we use to line the well. This story—and by the way we just were able to read it a little more than an hour ago—this story is complete fiction. Please, please, please, do not believe a word of this! Also, as chief public relations officer I'm in contact daily with people who are frightened of the dangers of deep-water drilling. All that I can tell you is, we share their concerns. And we're dedicating our professional lives to making sure that nothing harmful happens, and that we continue to follow safe drilling procedures."

A second reporter:

"I'm Randy Thomas of *The Memphis Star*. This question is for Mr. Holder."

"Aye, Mate!"

"Mr. Holder, you fill the position known as Tool Master?"

"I do. And I have filled it for three years now. Been in offshore drilling for seventeen years, I have, my entire professional life. Started as a roustabout on a rig off Liverpool and worked my way up."

"*The Times* story says that at the bottom of the main drill pipe there are two valves designed to stop the flow of gas to the surface."

"Aye, that's the only thing the damned story got bleedin' right. Sorry about my language."

"That's all right, sir. But these valves…"

"These valves are exactly built to specifications. Not only that, but they're checked daily. We checked them an hour ago. There's nothing wrong with them! Also, if I might add, we didn't do six pressure tests in the last two weeks; we did fourteen, since we do one pressure test every day. There is no increasing pressure down there, and there hasn't been since Aquatica began operations three years ago."

"I see. As for the blowout preventer…"

"There is one. It was installed two months ago. And the reason we installed it is because it is a state of the art mechanism. It was developed by The Luebke Corporation based in Bremen, Germany. It's the best in the world. There was nothing wrong with the old preventer, but we're constantly scouring all markets to find the best supplies available. When a better part is developed, we know about it, we buy it, and we install it."

"So, in your opinion, Professor Narang's allegations are…"

"His allegations are something that Sandy wouldn't want me to say."

All three of the figures on the screen smiled.

Another reporter:

"Dr. Bennington, I'm Susan Baker of *The Corpus Christie Caller*."

"Yes, Ms. Baker."

"As Rig Master, you oversee all operations on Aquatica, is that right?"

"Yes, it is."

"Your final comments concerning this story?"

He shook his head.

"I'm just…I'm just speechless. Nothing about it is true. We have had nothing but the most minor problems on Aquatica for months now. I've been in this business twenty-three years. This installation is absolutely without parallel in terms of safety and efficiency. We have back ups to every back up. We have only the top people working here.

"And you feel safe?"

"Absolutely. If I didn't, I wouldn't stay out here a minute. Nor would I allow my crew to do so."

"Thank you, Phil."

"My pleasure."

And the screen went blank.

It lit up a second later to reveal the executives on the podium.

More questions:

"Are the people at Louisiana Petroleum aware that messages from environmental groups all over the country—and the world—are pouring in, demanding that Aquatica be shut down and dismantled?"

A nod.

"Of course we're aware of those demands. That's why this story is so irresponsible, so insanely thoughtless. If it were true, then all of these demands would be thoroughly justified. And we would shut down immediately. BUT IT IS NOT TRUE! THERE IS NOT A THREAD OF TRUTH IN ONE DETAIL OF IT!"

"So what are you doing in response to the demands?"

He huddled with two of the men on the podium with him, then addressed the reporters again:

"All I can say is, we're going to get to the bottom of these allegations as quickly as possible, and we're going to have them completely retracted. Then we're going to find the people responsible for making such claims, and we're going to be sure that they are held accountable for the damage they've brought about. Damage both to our good name and to the oil industry as a whole. Now, that's all I'm going to be able to say at the moment."

The men left the stage.

Jackson turned off the TV and looked at Nina.

"Okay. So what do you make of that?"

She shook her head:

"All I know is, Professor Narang is supposed to be one of the most intelligent men in the world regarding such matters."

"Fine. But surely all these folks out on Aquatica wouldn't be denying these allegations if they thought there was any danger."

"I wish I could talk to Narang."

"Nobody can find him. After he wrote the story, he apparently went into seclusion."

"Probably," she said, "because he knew the firestorm that he was going to start. What about Liz Cohen?"

Jackson merely grunted:

"Can't reach her either. The newspaper is not commenting, and they won't take my calls."

"So how much trouble am I in, Jackson?"

He smiled.

A thin smile, but still a smile.

"It depends on who you talk to. I've had about fifty calls from LP people this morning. They want me to produce you, and they want you to produce the disk, which they claim you stole from them."

"Only because I did steal it from them."

"Yes, there is that. Where is the damned disk?"

"Narang has it."

"I guess that would make sense. Anyway, LP wants their own engineers to look at it. They're also offering to make it available to anybody else who wants to analyze it. According to them, none of the stuff Narang claims is on it, could possibly be there. Anyway, they want a chance to clear their name."

"And if they don't get the disk?"

He shrugged.

"They're threatening to bring charges against you."

"What charges?"

"Theft. Industrial espionage."

"And if they do?"

"We'll have to produce you in court."

"Well. I can't deny that I stole the flash disk."

"Of course you can."

"How?"

"By telling the truth. It wasn't their flash disk. It was Edgar's. You brought it home to his family just like you brought his shirts."

She thought for a time and then said:

"I had almost forgotten the way lawyers think."

"Yeah, we're all very proud of that. Of course, what they're going to say is, it isn't so much the physical disk you stole as the information that was on it. So it becomes an intellectual property case."

"And then?"

"Then we've already reached a district court in New Orleans and we all get to go to Pat O'Brien's."

"Hats and horns. Jackson, I'm tired. I'm tired just thinking about all this. I want to go home."

He looked at her.

"You want to go home?"

Then he shook his head and said, quietly:

"I had forgotten. You don't quite realize what's happening, do you?"

"What do you mean?"

He rose, and beckoned for her to do the same.

"We need to take a little ride."

"Where?"

"Just..oh, just around in town. There are some things you need to see. Things I can't quite explain."

"What are you talking about, Jackson?"

"Just come on. I'll show you."

"Do I need the sunglasses? Do I have to scrunch?"

"Negative on both. We'll be going in my own car, not the one the boy picked you up in. Windows are completely tinted. No one can see you."

"Is it that important that they don't?"

"You'll see. Terry?"

The young man stuck his head in the door.

"Yes, Mr. Bennett?"

"Bring my car around back, will you?"

"Yes, sir."

He disappeared.

"Still the back stairs?" asked Nina.

"I'd take you out off the roof if I could."

"So it's that bad."

"Don't worry about it. Just come along, and enjoy the view."

The first thing she noted about 'the view,' as they made their way down the stairs, was that a great many people were getting it from a higher vantage point than she enjoyed.

Helicopters were everywhere.

Red helicopters.

Green helicopters.

Blue helicopters.

"My God," she whispered, as she opened the car door and entered the front seat, "are we being invaded?"

Jackson turned the key and started the engine.

"Yes, we are, Nina."

"But why? Aquatica is ten miles offshore and LP is headquartered in Lafayette. What does everybody want with little old Bay St. Lucy?"

"You'll see."

They pulled out of the alley.

The town had transformed itself, and was continuing to do so.

Busses crowded the narrow streets.

Bands of people were parading past the souvenir shops.

"Who are all these people?"

"These people? You haven't seen anything. Here, I'll turn onto Breakers and we'll take a look at the beach."

He did in fact turn onto Breakers Boulevard, but the beach could not be seen.

It was obscured by crowds of bandanna-wearing, bearded, sign-waving people.

"I will ask again, Jackson: who the hell are all these people?"

"These people," he growled, slowing the car as it merged into a line of vans and RV's, "are the environmental fringe. They've been pouring into town for the last two hours. As far as I can tell, all the 'beds and breakfasts,' all the hotels, everything—is now booked up for the foreseeable future."

"But why? Why are they in Bay St. Lucy?"

"Because we are now the center of the 'Protect the Environment' movement. And we are that center because we have one thing."

"What?"

They were passing a large and raucous crowd of people who had built a campfire on the beach and were passing around what were quite obviously marijuana joints. These people, while not sucking hard on their tokes, were waving signs.

Half of the signs said:

"Down with Big Oil!"

...and had a picture of an exploding oil well on them.

The other half of the signs said:

"NINA!"

..and had a picture of Nina on them.

"Oh my God!" she whispered.

...while Jackson continued, saying:

"We are the center of the 'Protect Your Environment" movement, Nina, because we have *you*."

"Oh my God."

"You haven't seen the morning edition of the *Bay St. Lucy Gazette*. It's covered with stories about you. They reprinted stuff about the Robinson case, and the Reddington murder. There are about five different photographs of you, even one of you being carried off the court after the Hattiesburg game."

"But...but look at that poster, the big one that's been nailed to the pier. Is that..."

"Yes."

"That's Furl! They've got Furl's picture on that poster!"

"That's because one of the stories this morning talked about you and Furl, and your shack. It even ran a picture of Furl."

"But how did they get it?"

"Beats me."

"And that printing...what does that sign say, those letters just under Furl?"

"It says, 'Furl hates Big Url."

"What?"

"Furl hates..."

"I know, I see it now. But that's awful! That's the worst pun I've ever heard!"

"What did you expect, Nina? Whoever came up with it was probably stoned out of his mind."

"This cannot be happening. I'm dreaming all of this. Look! Look over there. Why are they waving those huge pictures of Willie Nelson?"

Jackson sped up slightly in order to get the car through what was either a low-hanging patch of fog across the road, or a cloud of marijuana smoke that had drifted up from the beach.

"It was just announced half an hour ago. Willie Nelson is coming here next week to do a special 'save the earth' concert. He's also writing a ballad that will be called 'Nina the Queena the Good Greena Earth,' that will be sung to the tune of 'Home with the Armadillo.'"

"I'm going to be sick."

"Not, hopefully, in my car."

"But...Jackson, it's like I said: can't I go home?"

He shook his head.

"Are you joking? Your home has become a shrine. People are standing around it in rows fifty feet deep, as though it was a Greenpeace cross between Canterbury Cathedral and Mecca."

"But what about Furl?"

"All I know is that he hates Big Url."

"Stop that, Jackson."

"Sorry. I thought a little humor..."

"No."

"Okay, okay. Furl is at my place. The girls are loving on him. He's having the time of his life. And I've already heard from two Los Angeles producers who want to make a TV series about him."

"Please stop joking, Jackson. This isn't really very funny."

"I'm not joking. It would be a kind of cross between Rin Tin Tin and Lassie. Every week Furl would ferret out some big environmental polluter and rip him to shreds."

"Okay, and don't tell me. They'd want Meryl Streep to play me."

"She's too tall."

"She could play sh…oh, the hell with it, I don't want to go through that all again. But Jackson, where can I go? I'm tired. I'm really confused. And I'm scared. I feel like World War I is breaking out and I'm little Nina Sarajevo, sitting there right between all these giants: the oil industry on one side and the recreational drug industry on the other. Where am I going to sleep for heavens sakes?"

"I've got that covered. I and your friends. You're not alone, Nina. This is Bay St. Lucy, you know."

"It looks like Woodstock."

"How would you know anything about Woodstock?"

"I read."

"Like I say, don't worry about it. I'm taking you home right now. It's just that 'home' is going to be in a different place for a while."

"How long, do you think?"

"Not long. Maybe a few years, I don't know."

"I just want to walk along the beach and read mysteries. Is that asking too much?"

Jackson nodded:

"Nina, it seems to me you're right in the middle of a mystery right now. And if you don't solve it—well, there may not be a beach to walk along.

Within five minutes, they were turning into the lush-groved driveway of Auberge des Arts, formerly known as the Robinson mansion.

"You're bringing me here?"

"Absolutely."

"But Alanna…"

"It was Alanna Delafosse's idea. She's a very perceptive woman, Nina. As soon as the story broke this morning, she was on the phone to me. She asked how you were, figuring, I guess, that if anybody knew your whereabouts, it would be me."

"Which was true."

"A lot of what Alanna thinks is true. So anyway, by that time the town had already begun to fill up. Craziness was already happening, both here and in Lafayette. As well, by the way, in everywhere else from LA to DC to the Amazon Rain Forest. We both decided you couldn't go back to your place. But we also realized that the mansion was perfect. It was built to keep the Robinsons safe from Chicago and New Orleans gangsters. Surely it can keep out Willie Nelson fans."

"And Alanna is okay with this?"

"She was really the one who suggested it. After she did, I called Moon Rivard's office and asked him if he could spare some additional security people."

"I see a couple of them now, in one of those police cars parked beside the gazebo."

"Yeah. We don't want to make it too obvious. But this place is an absolute fortress. If whale lovers break in, you can hide in one of the getaway tunnels."

They pulled to the main entrance, where Jackson stopped the car and got out.

Nina did likewise, watching as she did so, the front door of the mansion swing open and Alanna Delafosse swing outward, ripping across the wide porch floor with hurricane like winds and enveloping Nina in a storm surge of python embraces, kisses and tears.

"My darling! My darling, Nina! How are you, my dear girl? How are you?"

"Well, I can't breathe."

"I know. I know. It must be overwhelming. Whatever can I do to help?"

"Put me down."

"I know. I'm overly affectionate."

"No, you're just really strong."

"There. Is that better?"

"Well, my feet are on the ground anyway. Now if we can just free up my ribcage..."

"Of course, dear. Come inside. Come in quickly, before you're seen. Jackson, did you have any trouble getting her here?"

He slammed the back door of the car after grabbing Nina's overnight bag, and he made his way up and onto the porch.

"I think we're all right."

"You weren't followed?"

"No."

"Would you know it, if you had been?"

"Well, I've seen a lot of movies. There's usually a chase scene, and we didn't have one."

"That's a good sign."

"I hope."

"Here, both of you, right through here."

They entered the main hall, where Nina could still imagine images of Eve Ivory standing proudly on an interior balcony, looking down at the assembled township gathered like peasants awaiting the pronouncement of their doom.

The great hall clock ticked, its pendulum rocking somberly left and right, as though wagging a long finger toward them in a continual admonishment that they were allowing time to pass.

Tempus fugit.

Tick tock tick tock.

"Jackson," asked Alanna, who was dressed in a long garment that might have been a robe or the map of a children's playground, "are you still receiving calls?"

He nodded as they walked through the hall.

"Everyone's calling everyone."

"And everyone, of course, wants to see Nina."

"Seems that way."

"Oh, my poor darling…"

Alanna stopped halfway across the hall and turned abruptly, taking a step toward Nina, who shouted:

"Don't grab me again!"

"My poor child…"

"I know karate."

Alanna smiled.

"Of course you don't know karate."

"No, but I've read books about it. Anyway, you need to find a way to comfort me without squeezing me."

"Of course. But come now, both of you. We'll go into the study. There are no outside windows there, so no one can peek in and spy on us.

"My God," said Nina, following dutifully along, "I feel like I'm public enemy Number One."

"You are public enemy Number One," said Jackson, "to big oil. Especially to Louisiana Petroleum. To what seems to be everybody else in town, you're a symbol. You're one small person—no reference to your size, sorry.."

"It's all right, I'm used to it."

"...but let's say one average person who has taken it upon herself to fight a huge corporation. Going out there on your own, getting that disk somehow, smuggling it to Narang…"

"I didn't 'smuggle' it. I got on a plane and carried it to him."

"Yeah, I know, but 'smuggle' sounds a lot better."

"Jackson, where the hell is Professor Narang?"

He shook his head.

"No one seems to know, and everyone in the country is trying to find him."

"He's got to stand by the claims he made in his article. Otherwise, I look like, well…"

"An idiot."

She paused, then said:

"That wasn't exactly the way I was going to put it."

"I know."

"I was thinking more in terms of 'a person not so highly informed as she had once thought herself to be, given a particular set of circumstances'."

"Yeah. An idiot."

"Well then, if you insist."

"Here," interrupted Alanna. "I've made the study my business center for the morning. Jackson, you may put Nina's travelling bag over there on the couch. Nina, once Jackson has left, you can help me take the calls and make the engagements."

She found herself in front of a huge mahogany desk and pulled by furniture-gravity down into the bowels of the biggest green leather chair she had ever seen. It enveloped her with its cushions much as had Alanna enveloped her with her arms, but it was more stern, and it offered less possibility of escape.

She was to be here, in this chair, for the rest of her life.

"What arrangements?"

Her voice, after leaving her lips, was confused and depressed for a time, being caught in a gravitational vortex spinning like a charybdis whirlpool between the sun that was the desk and the earth that was the chair. Finally though, if found a black hole through which it could flee, and it wafted across the room to the other people listening for it.

"What arrangements?"

Alanna looked at her in bewilderment.

"Child, do you not understand what has been happening?"

She shook her head.

"Everyone seems to be asking me that this morning. And the answer is always, 'no.'"

"Nina, because of you, Bay St Lucy has become the epicenter for worldwide environmental awareness. You are now to Big Oil as Anne Frank was to Hitler."

"I'm Anne Frank?"

"Yes. Of course, you're hiding in a somewhat larger space, but..."

"This is surreal."

"Yes, isn't it wonderful?"

"'Surreal' and 'wonderful' aren't necessarily the same things, Alanna."

Alanna Delafosse reacted to this statement with shock and dismay, and it was with a funereal voice that she asked:

"They aren't?"

Nina shook her head.

"Don't worry about it. Anyway, so I've become the Anne Frank of Bay St. Lucy. What does that have to do with these engagements that you're talking about?"

"Why, it has everything to do with them! We already have a sparkling summer series planned!"

"A what series?"

"A summer series, darling. Artists have been calling me since six o'clock this morning. So many New York contacts were made last summer, you remember, due to the unfortunate Reddington matter..."

"The murder, you mean."

"Well, I *said* it was unfortunate. I try to avoid being overly dramatic."

This was the most precisely and thoroughly incorrect statement Nina had ever heard, and she would have spit out the food she was chewing, except that she was not chewing any. So she simply said:

"All right, go on. So we know a lot of artists from New York."

"Well, they've all been calling."

She thought for a time, then said:

"Okay, I saw the sign about Willie Nelson coming."

Alanna shook her head in disgust.

"Darling I do not deal with people who have names like that."

"Like 'Willie?'"

"No, like 'Nelson.' It sounds so...so plebian."

"I'm sure the man has always struggled against that. So who do you deal with?"

"Sergie Eisentein."

"You're right. That's a long way from Willie Nelson."

"And artists from around the country. Chamber musicians. We've just scheduled an oboe concerto for August the eleventh."

"That's going to be fun."

"Oh, it shall be, it shall be! Nina, it's such a remarkable thing: we tried so hard to make our town a cultural mecca last summer, and it failed. But—well, you saved Bay St. Lucy when it was threatened by Eve Ivory and Big Tourism. Now you're going to make it a center for environmental awareness. And that awareness is going to draw the entire art world to us! You should be so proud— our own Anne Frank!"

"Couldn't I be somebody else? Like Davy Crockett?

"Davy Crockett," Jackson growled, "got killed too."

"Well," Nina fumed, "that's just a bad thing about doing people favors, isn't it?"

No answer.

Finally she said, to Jackson:

"So what is next for me, really? Besides getting to go to Auschwitz, I mean?"

He shook his head:

"I still don't know, exactly. But you need to stay here under wraps this afternoon. I think we can trust Alanna to help us out there."

Alanna beamed:

"We shall take these calls for a time, my dear. Then we shall have a light lunch. Perhaps cucumber sandwiches. Then you need to take a nap. For heaven's sakes, you've earned one…"

"That all sounds good, Alanna. It really does."

And then, later on in the afternoon…how about working in the garden?"

"The auberge has a garden?"

"Of course we do. My great pride. In fact, we have several: a flower garden, an herb garden, and a vegetable garden. Tomatoes, squash, bell peppers—and all in need of watering, weeding…."

"Alana, that would be wonderful."

"I even have gardening clothes for you to wear. Overalls, a sweatshirt…"

"Great. Just let me hide under some plants for a time."

"It shall be done. And then, I've ordered white wine and oysters for dinner, and I shall reserve a film for us to watch in the movie room."

"What film?"

"I thought perhaps 'Norma Rae'"

"Alanna!"

"Or something else. Whatever."

"That all sounds fine, Alanna," said Jackson. "But Nina…"

She perked up.

"Yes?"

"At some point, we've got to make you available."

"Available to whom, Jackson?"

He shook his head:

"That's the question, of course. And I'm going to spend this afternoon trying to find an answer. My best guess is this, though. There will need to be a meeting some time tomorrow. They're maybe going to want that meeting to be in Lafayette, or New Orleans. Maybe Jackson."

"Who will be there?"

"Attorneys for LP."

"That sounds like fun. Are they going to charge me with anything?"

"They would, but, like you said earlier, you don't have anything they want. Except…"

"Except what?"

"Nina, they're going to want you to apologize."

Alanna interrupted:

"Why should she apologize? She's done a courageous thing; the whole nation is applauding her."

"Yes," Jackson continued, "and that's what LP hates. The more they love Nina, the more they hate big oil. They are continuing to insist that none of these claims are true. Now they're going to want you to substantiate that fact."

"How can I substantiate it, Jackson? I don't know what all that data means!"

"I know."

"If they have a problem, it should be with Narang. And I'm sorry, I just don't think he's going to back down."

Jackson shook his head again, and rose.

"Like I said, I just work here."

"Oh, and by the way: I'm not going to be able to pay your bill."

"You've never paid any of my bills. As far as I remember, you still owe me fifty-thousand dollars or so for the Reddington Case."

"I can give you five at the end of the month."

"Or maybe you could just come over and do the windows."

"In addition to the five?"

"Let's not worry about it now. You get some sleep. Then do a little gardening. Then get some sleep again. I'll send the kid for you tomorrow morning. But I will say this: if I find out anything this afternoon, I'll be sure and give Alanna here a call. Whatever happens tomorrow morning…"

"It would be nice if I had the night to worry about it."

"Well, now that you put it that way…"

"No, Jackson, please do call. I want to know what's coming."

"All right then. So have a nice rest of the day, Nina."

And, so saying, he left.

The rest of the day was indeed nice. She was taken to a small but exquisite bedroom where she buried herself under thick but exquisite comforters and listened to the soft chiming of a wrong (at least as far as time goes, given the questionable truth of the assertion that any clock can be wrong about its own specialty, that being chronology) but exquisite Dresden alarm clock, and dreamed an exquisitely incomprehensible dream which she did not, alas, remember any of upon waking.

Which she did around four o'clock.

Then Alanna outfitted her in rags, took her out to the garden, and abandoned her there.

Bliss.

The afternoon sun dropping lower and lower in the summer sky, the clouds becoming golden-tinged, the dirt porous, cool, and sticky in her fingers, the green tomatoes ranging from bb size to huge, pale green, and globular—she forgot everything but a drizzling hose and a six inch trowel.

By dinner time, she was covered in dirt and sweat, and her legs were beginning to cramp from bending low and crawling on the ground.

The dinner was wonderful, of course, as she knew it would be. Alanna had turned the Auberge des Arts into a kind of fine restaurant/bed and breakfast, with the sole difference that, instead of random tourists, the clientele tended to be writers, musicians, painters, and storytellers, who stayed for some days and lived sumptuously, in return for the community service of doing school readings or private workshops.

These people paid nothing for their meals, the fare being bought with money left in coffers from the sale of the vast Robinson estate.

And so: fresh oysters, asparagus, pate de foie gras, and lobster.

Plus cold, dry Chardonnay.

Nina had showered and changed, and was able to watch the sky darken through vast picture windows in the dining room as she chatted with Alanna about this or that completely irrelevant subject, munched the food that was set in front of her, and tried to keep from her mind the fact that vast forces were preparing either to vault her to the top of the universe or chew her up and discard her like so much garbage.

It was only over cheesecake and coffee that Alanna added:

"By the way, dear, I did not tell you: we shall be having one other guest over tonight."

"Really?"

"Yes. I'm sure a great many of your friends would have liked to dine with us, if for no other reason than to offer you their support. But Jackson and I felt that, given the particular circumstances, confidentiality was the best policy."

"I agree."

"There will be one exception, though. Ah. Here it comes now!"

The same prim, white-jacketed young girl who had served the dinner now served a laptop computer, which she placed carefully in the center of the table.

"Our guest is a computer?"

"Our guest will be arriving through means of the computer."

The screen lit up. Alanna's fingers played on the keyboard for a time.

And there, indeed, was the guest.

Nina exulted when she saw the familiar image:

"Margot!"

For there before her, courtesy of Skype, was Margot Gavin.

It was a remarkable thing: the chiseled face, the gray outlandish hair, and equally outlandish baggy sweater— the two of them might as well have been sitting back in the vine-entangled garden of Elementals, having a first-of-the-morning cup of coffee.

"Margot Gavin! I can't believe it!"

"Nina! Oh my God, it's so good to see you!"

"And you too, Margot! It seems like forever since we've talked!"

"Well, it has been!"

"Do you like being married?"

"Oh it was a bit of an adjustment for a while until Goldmann suggested we imitate the two leads in a Congreve play that he happened to be reading. 'Good

Mirabell, says wonderful Millamant...don't let us be familiar or fond...let us be as strange as if we had been married a great while, and as well-bred, as if we were not married at all.' And that is the lifestyle we've been attempting to achieve."

"And Candles?"

"The plantation is most certainly haunted. We hear strange noises every night."

"Have you seen ghosts?"

"Oh my heavens, no. There are always artists here from Chicago. The ghosts are too frightened to come out, and so they remain hidden within the woodwork. But enough of that. You, I hear, have succeeded in keeping busy."

"I've been puttering around."

"A little walking on the beach, a little fishing?"

"Yes, and I read this or that, whenever I can."

"And you attempt to single-womanly destroy the world's largest oil corporation."

"I attempt to—oh yes, I'm doing that, too. Almost forgot, isn't that amazing?"

"Well, you have so many other things on your plate."

"Yes, it's hard to find time for all of them."

They smiled at each other. Finally, Margot said quietly, the smile having faded:

"So how are you, Nina? How are you holding up?"

"I'm good. I really am."

"We were shocked to read *The Times* this morning."

"Everybody was, I guess."

"I won't even ask you how all of this has come to pass. I'm sure you're sick of telling the story."

"I'm not sure I even remember the story. It all seems like a dream. And it has, for days now."

"Then I'm sure you want nothing more than to keep the entire thing as far from your mind as possible. I only wanted to tell you one thing, and then I'm going to let you go. But this one thing is very important."

"All right, Margot. Tell me."

"Well, Goldmann and I have been keeping up with events that have been going on across the country all day. Across not only the country but the world."

"Well, *The New York Times* gets around."

"Yes, it does. At any rate, there are sit-ins, demonstrations, and rallies in every state of the union. People are gathering in front of office buildings and chanting "Down with Big Oil!" and "Save our Planet!" You're causing destruction of property, Nina. Because of you, people are being carted off to jail. There is chaos everywhere, and everyone is smoking marijuana. And so, Nina, I simply had to tell you, tell you personally while I'm looking at you…"

"…yes, Margot?"

"…that I've never been so proud of you in my life!"

"Oh, Margot! That means so much, coming from you!"

"I've got to go now…"

"But I wanted to talk, I wanted to…"

"I'm going to cry! Good night, Nina!"

And the screen went black.

The following morning at nine o'clock, Nina was delivered to the Bay St. Lucy town hall.

No meeting in New Orleans. Or Jackson. Or Lafayette.

All parties had decided this was the best course of action.

And just as there was no flight to any of the major cities listed above, there was absolutely no publicity about the meeting that was to take place.

There would only be, Nina had learned from Jackson's phone call two hours earlier, a few select people in the room, and they would have arrived under cover of strict confidentiality.

Sandy Cousins. Phil Bennington. Tom Holder. All from Aquatica.

All people whom she had met days earlier, and who were now being flown into town by helicopter.

One lawyer—and only one—representing Louisiana Petroleum.

Two other administrators, Jackson had not been able to ascertain precisely who.

And no—absolutely no—reporters.

And so, here she was.

A room she had seen a thousand times before, with its sterile white ceiling lights, its large, circular meeting table, its pull-down wall screen designed to display power point presentations.

She took a deep breath, nodded to Jackson who stood just behind her in the hallway and opened the door.

Several people from LP were already seated at the table. There were two 'suits' almost certainly either executives or lawyers. There was one large swarthy man who seemed of middle eastern descent and who wore a dark sport coat and tie—and there were four people she remembered from the drill rig: Sandy Cousins, Tom Holder—or the Tool Master—Phil Bennington, rig master, and Brewster Dale, Faulkner scholar and head of security.

A man who was almost certain to be livid with her.

They were all, when she thought about it, almost certain to be livid with her.

All of the figures rose as she entered the room.

And Sandy Cousins circled the table.

She stood two feet from Nina.

The two women looked at each other, face to face, expressionless, for what must have been five seconds.

Then they fell into each other's arms, sobbing.

Nina was aware of the other figures—at least some of them—encircling them.

And then she was aware of the utterly remarkable nature of the entire order of things.

This was exactly the way it had been on the Aquatica.

She had expected villains. Stock ocean polluters, concerned only about making money.

She had found, instead, gracious and giving people.

One of whom she was now embracing.

Finally she was able to speak, her voice wavering, her eyes watering with tears:

"I'm...I'm so sorry if I've done wrong!"

Sandy smiled at her through an equally dense film of tears:

"It's all right, Nina."

And now Brewster Dale was laying a palm on her shoulder:

"If Mr. Faulkner were here, Ms. Bannister, he would repeat the words he wrote in *Intruder in the Dust*: 'Never be afraid to raise your voice for honesty and truth and compassion against injustice and lying and greed. If people all over the world...would do this, it would change the earth.'"

"But...you've all been so nice to me. Somehow I feel ashamed for taking the disk!"

Again, the honey-soothing Mississippi drawl:

"And again, Mr. Faulkner would tell you: 'Unless you're ashamed of yourself now and then, you're not honest.' I believe that comes from *The Reivers*."

"I just...I'm scared for you! All three of you! And everybody else out there!"

Sandy shook her head:

"Don't be. We're fine! Aquatica is safe, Nina!"

"But it isn't safe! It can't be!"

Phil Bennington put a palm on her shoulder:

"Ms. Bannister, it's like I said yesterday on television. I've been in this business all my life. If any of those things *The New York Times* said were true, don't you think I would know?"

"But I—I just..."

She could not speak for a time.

Finally, Sandy said:

"The only danger we're in, Nina, is from boats that have come out to Aquatica, filled with protesters. A few came very close to the rig yesterday afternoon, shouting through bullhorns. And saying some pretty dreadful things."

Tom Holder interjected:

"A couple of coast guard vessels have come out though. The blokes are giving us protection now."

Nina took two deep breaths and said, finally:

"I'm so sorry that this is all happening. I don't want to be anybody's hero."

Sandy took her hand and said:

"We know that, Nina."

"But Edgar's brother was terrified. He knew that Edgar had been murdered. And he was convinced that Edgar had discovered something terrible that had been happening on Aquatica."

"Then why," asked Sandy "didn't you share all this with us when you came out?"

"I guess—I guess I just didn't trust you. And still—still it doesn't make sense to me. It's all crazy. I found out that Edgar had been trying to call Narang, his old professor. So I got hold of the man. He agreed to look at the disk."

There was movement from the other side of the table.

The tall, burly, dark-skinned man rose.

"Where," he asked, his voice tinged with a slight lilting accent, "did you meet Professor Narang?"

"In Lafayette. I flew there two days ago with the disk. A graduate student in the department—her name was Annette Richoux—met me at the airport. We went dancing…"

"Dancing?" asked the man.

"Yes, I know it sounds crazy. But I think she just wanted to get my mind—both of our minds, because she had been a good friend of Edgar's too—off the things that had happened. Anyway I spent the night at her little house beside campus. The next day we went and met Professor Narang."

"Where did you meet him?"

"In the geology building. There's a projection room. He was already there. We put the disk in the room's computer, and he started analyzing it."

"Was anyone else there with you?"

"No, just Annette and the professor. The more he saw of the data, the more frightened he seemed to get. He told me that a complete analysis would take a long time, so I flew back home to Bay St. Lucy. That night he called me though. He said it was worse than he had initially thought. Something drastic needed to be done, or the whole installation might blow up."

"And so he wrote the story that appeared in *The New York Times*."

"Yes."

"Saying that the entire Gulf Coast was in danger."

"That, and that the explosion would be big enough to kill all of you. Instantly."

She paused to get her breath.

Her heart, she realized, was pounding.

"But they wouldn't run the story," she continued, "without substantiation. They had to know where the disk came from. So a reporter flew down to Bay St. Lucy and I told her everything."

"That was, I take it, Ms. Cohen."

"Yes, Elizabeth Cohen."

"And so," he said, with a half smile, "the world came to know of Ms. Nina Bannister."

"Yes. But again—I didn't mean for it to be this way."

He nodded.

"I understand. I think we all understand."

"It's just—I'm still terrified. I don't want you to go back out there!"

Brewster Dale merely smiled:

"You cannot swim for new horizons," we read in *Absalom Absalom*, "until you have courage to lose sight of the shore."

"Nina," Sandy said, "like I told you. We're in no danger. The gulf is in no danger. The only real danger now is all of these people who seem to hate the oil industry. Which is crazy, because all we're trying to do is keep their cars running and keep them warm at night."

"But Sandy—how can you know you're safe? Professor Narang is absolutely certain of what he wrote. And he's one of the leading authorities in the world on these matters!"

For an instant, there was complete silence in the room.

Then the tall man with the slight accent said, quietly:

"Ms. Bannister, there is no danger. Of that, I can assure you, having read all of the data available."

"But how can you know?"

Silence again.

Then:

"Because, Ms. Bannister. I am Professor Daruka Narang."

He then looked at everyone else in the room, pointed to Nina , and said:

"And I assure all of you: I have never before seen this woman in my life."

CHAPTER ELEVEN: NOTHING THAT DOES NOT ANSWER

An enormous amount of time went by.

It might have been seconds. It might have been years.

But there are moments that cannot be escaped from, that cannot be used to jump forward. They are such quicksand that the foot one braces with sinks into them, and existence stops, it being unable to progress in time.

So that time, at least for all practical purposes, ceases to exist.

Somewhere in the vacuum of her mind appeared Jane Austen's words—words that had been her guide and inspiration during the Robinson case, the Reddington affair, the bizarre twist involving April van Osdale. The words stood out quite clearly, as though they had been printed on the screen in the meeting room:

"A mind lively and at ease can do with seeing nothing, and can see nothing that does not answer."

Nothing that does not answer.

"Nina?"

What was that?

Someone was asking her a question.

Who was it?

Jackson.

She should answer Jackson, of course.

But they were all looking at her. Why would they be looking at her like that?

But she should answer Jackson.

"Yes?"

That was the appropriate thing to say, wasn't it?

"Nina. What's going on here?"

"I...I don't know."

The tall, burly, dark-skinned man continued:

"And I must tell you, Ms. Bannister.."

"Yes? Yes, what must you tell me?"

"Ms. Bannister, I know our department quite well. I am, in fact, its chairman, and have been for some years. There is no graduate student in our department named 'Annette Richoux.' This entire 'meeting' you have told us about. It simply cannot have happened."

"But...but..."

"Ms. Bannister, I myself have been on sabbatical for the last three months. I have not even been on campus. I most certainly did not meet with you, not the day before yesterday, nor any other time. And the article that *The New York Times* accuses me of having written? It's simply gibberish. I would never have written such a thing, nor would I have submitted it to a non-academic journal if I had."

She knew nothing to say.

She had met Daruka Narang.

And Annette Richoux.

These things existed in her mind. Narang, with his perfectly trimmed goatee. Annette, wild Annette. Her cigar.

The Blue Gator.

"Now, Ms. Bannister. At what time of day did you have this meeting?"

"About eleven."

"Did you go to the actual office of the man who saw this disk with you?"

"No."

"Or to this Ms. Richoux?"

"No. We just..."

"You just met in a deserted hallway?"

"Yes. And then we went..."

"To a deserted lecture hall."

She nodded.

All of the people around the table looked at her.

She looked at herself.

One Nina said to the second Nina:

'But if that wasn't Daruka Narang, then who…"

"Nina," Jackson was asking, "Nina, did you give this man the disk that you took from Aquatica?"

"Yes."

More glances.

Jackson's voice continued, pouring over the table like syrup.

"All right."

He rose.

"I want to make a suggestion to everyone in the room. I think it would be good if Nina and I could talk. I think we should go over to my office. I know there is a great deal of work to be done here. Steps to be taken. Mr. Robicheaux, I believe you are one of the lead attorneys for Louisiana Petroleum?"

A dark-suited man nodded:

Jackson continued.

"I hope you realize, we understand the difficulties of this situation."

"We hope so."

"But Ms. Bannister has obviously been deceived in some manner."

"I think we can say," said the attorney, "that is an understatement. She has been deceived indeed. And in a very costly way."

"You're going to want a statement…"

"We are. And we're going to want it quickly."

"Certainly. We just need some time."

"How much time?"

"A couple of hours. Nina and I just need to talk."

"That seems reasonable. All right."

There was a pause.

Sandy, somehow managing a smile, stood and said:

"Let's all go and have lunch."

It was agreed that lunchtime was at hand.

And Nina left the room with Jackson.

Jackson's office—Frank's old office—was somewhat like a womb for Nina.

It was approaching eleven o'clock in the morning, and a bright, summery, Mississippi Gulf Coast morning it was. But the office still had something dark and cool about it. There was also an aroma that she had never been able to place. Frank's office had the smell of 'establishment,'

Out of deference to Frank, his old diploma still hung on the wall behind the desk, beside Jackson's. There was the small window, which filtered everything distasteful out of streaming sunlight and allowed only inspirational illumination to enter the room, as though, rather than the cold hand of civil authority, seekers after the law found themselves in a kind of quiet chapel.

One expected organ music. Or incense.

Nina got none of these as she settled down in the old and thoroughly familiar green leather chair facing Jackson—but she got enough of the room's solace, and languished in enough of its memories, that she was able to proceed as though she were a woman to whom the world still made some sense.

Jackson sat, stared at her, heaved a sigh, started to say something, thought better of it, and instead sharpened a pencil.

This process took half a minute or so.

It also allowed him to spend another half minute contemplating the point before putting the pencil in the desk drawer.

He was looking around to find a second pencil when Nina interrupted him.

"All right. What happens now?"

He shrugged:

"Damned if I know."

Through the bottom of the small window they could see the top of a delivery truck passing. Through the top of the small window they could see the bottom of a flock of birds passing.

They watched these things for as long as was acceptable to do so.

Then Jackson said:

"Nina, what the hell happened over there?"

"In Lafayette, you mean?"

"Yes."

"I don't know."

"You have to know!"

"Nope."

"This man at the meeting just now. He is without question Daruka Narang."

"I gathered that."

"Then who did you..."

Suddenly she found herself standing, leaning on the desk, and looking down at Jackson, as though she were mad at him, which she was not.

It still, she realized as she watched herself pour out of herself, must have come across that way:

"Jackson, what am I supposed to say? I told you everything! I told everybody everything! I flew over there, and Annette Richoux met me at the airport. She took me to her little house on the edge of campus. It was no more than a one-room place, with gray paint peeling off it. She's as Cajun as oysters and alligators, and she said we were going dancing. We did, at a strange and kind of bizarre place called The Blue Gator. We danced all night, practically, until they were about to close around midnight and she went home with some guy she had picked up named 'Guidry.'"

"You're sure his name was 'Guidry?'"

"They're all named 'Guidry.'"

"Okay, so you..."

"I got a cab to take me back to her place. She wandered in about two in the morning, I guess. I'm not sure, because I was asleep when I hit the bed. I woke up at first light. We had breakfast together. Croissants and beignets. Then later in the morning we walked together to campus. We went into the geology building, found Das—found somethehellbody in a big lecture hall with a computer all set up to show the images on the screen behind the podium."

"And this man told you he was Daruka Narang?"

"Of course he did. You think he said 'Frank Smith,' and I just dreamed Daruka Narang?"

"I'm not sure what to think at this point."

"Me neither, Jackson. I just…"

At that moment, the phone on the desk rang.

It was a real phone, black and solid and recognizable as a phone and not a camera or a blender—and it rang and did not buzz, and Nina loved Jackson for holding on to it, as one might carry the faded black and white picture of a frowning, bearded, long-dead great-grandfather from somewhere on the plains of Kansas.

"Bennett here."

And for a minute or so he rumbled, growled, scowled, muttered, and nodded.

Finally he put the phone down.

"Better and better," he said, quietly.

"What?" she asked, wondering why she had let out of her head the word 'what' instead of the much more appropriate phrase, 'I want to go home now.'

But 'what' she had said, and 'what' she would have to answer to.

"More information is coming in from the people over at LP. Specifically from Narang."

"What?"

Damn it, Nina; stop that!

"'I want to go home!' is the phrase you want to hear!"

"'What!' indeed!"

"Ok, then, see what it's going to get you!"

"The house you described? The one with the peeling gray paint?"

"Yes?"

"It exists all right."

"*Of course* it exists! Do you all think I've been cracking cocaine?"

Jackson could not help smiling.

"Anyone who uses the phrase 'cracking cocaine,' Nina, has not been doing very much with either substance."

"What? Now I'm not even doing drug talk right?"

"Well, you have a few things to learn before you'll be comfortable on the street. Anyway, the house does exist. Narang knows it well. It's always been lived in by some graduate student in geological sciences. Somebody will live there for a semester or so, graduate, and kind of unofficially bequeath it to another. It's cheap and close, so somebody always wants it."

"Like Annette."

He shook his head.

"There's no Annette. The person living in that house now is named Nancy Broussard."

"Who?"

"A young woman named Nancy Broussard. She's in her final year."

"But…"

She finished her spring course work two weeks ago, according to Narang, then went home for a while. She's scheduled to be back on campus at the start of the first summer semester, June 15."

"So the house was…."

"Empty."

As was the air space following.

For some seconds or so.

Then Nina filled it with the word:

"Shit."

And then it was empty again.

She sat down after a time.

Neither she nor Jackson spoke.

The muffled sounds of Bay St. Lucy seeped into the office.

"I don't know where to begin," she found herself saying, softly.

He shook his head:

"Me neither. But…"

"Yes?"

A shake of the head:

"Every direction I go in, something hauls me back and tells me I need to go somewhere else."

She smiled.

"Yes. Me too."

"I'm asking myself," he said, "what would Frank have done?"

"Divorce me."

"You think so?"

"No. No, Frank would have found something funny in all this. He would have shaken his head and said something like, 'Nina, Nina…' and then it would have been okay. And we would have gone out crabbing."

"Yeah."

More silence for a time.

Then Jackson:

"All right. Here's where we are, as best as I can put it together. You met some people in Lafayette who claimed to be Daruka Narang and Annette Richoux. They weren't. Whoever they were, they knew the layout of the place. They knew about this graduate student house, and they knew it would be empty. They knew the geology building would also be virtually empty—at least the classrooms, the lecture halls—because of semester break."

"But why? Who would set up this masquerade and for what reason?"

"I don't know."

"And, worse…I found Edgar's cell phone in the drainage canal. It had a number on it, probably the last number he had called before he was killed."

"I know. You've told us that."

"I called that number and Narang answered."

"Well, somebody answered."

"But Jackson—surely Edgar must have known his professor's real number."

"One would think."

"But the real Narang is sitting over there in city hall right now!"

"Yes. He is that."

"And he was never called!"

"No, he wasn't."

"So somehow the call must have gone through to this—this imposter. But that doesn't make sense!"

Jackson shrugged:

"Show me something about this whole mess that does make sense."

"And the article! Writing a bogus article—which this imposter must have done—and sending it to *The New York Times*—that doesn't make sense either! Let's say the fake Narang is an opponent of Big Oil. Okay, he sends this piece in, uses my name as a source, and gets *The Times* to print it. Fine. But he must have known that the data would be almost immediately recognized as false. That a thousand technicians would almost immediately vouch for Aquatica, which apparently is the safest offshore rig in the world. Wouldn't he have expected that?"

"Yes. It seems like he would have."

"What has he accomplished?"

"Well, he's put you in a helluva position."

She was silent for a time, and then said:

"Yes, he's done that."

Jackson breathed deeply and went on:

"He's also embarrassed *The New York Times*. They're coming out with a retraction in their afternoon edition."

"They'll survive."

"They will, but…"

"What?"

"I guess I have to tell you. I found it out in the last call."

"Go ahead; hit me with it."

"Apparently Elizabeth Cohen just got fired."

"Damn."

"I know."

He rose, turned, and faced the wall behind his desk. It was to this wall that he said:

"I liked that woman. I liked the way she flew all the way down here to meet you. Went out to the cabin like that. She must have known she was taking a chance going with that story."

Nina paused for a time and then said:

"All right, she did know it, Jackson. But she did it anyway. Her job was on the line and she convinced her bosses to believe me. And some fraud. But why did she do it?"

"She wanted a Pulitzer."

"I don't think so, Jackson."

"Then why?"

"She did it, Jackson, because she honestly felt there was a chance that damned thing might blow up, and that all the academics in the world, and all the politicians, and all the do-gooders—would have just been setting up their committee meetings while the gas was seeping out of the ocean floor and up onto the deck of Aquatica. She did it because she thought it damned well had to be done. And immediately."

He turned and looked down at her.

"Which is why you did it."

She scrunched into herself a bit, sighed and said quietly:

"Yes. Since you put it like that."

Then they sat for a time, searching for something to say.

Jackson found it.

"All right, Nina. So none of this stuff makes sense. Someday we may be able to figure it out, but not now. Now the important thing is to deal with LP."

"Are they suing me?"

"No. There would be no point in that."

"Am I going to be put in jail for stealing the disk?"

A shake of the head:

"I think they realize that I could make a good case for you. You honestly thought it was Edgar's property. Also, their security people are embarrassed that they ever let you out of Aquatica with the disk."

"Dale. The Faulkner scholar."

Jackson smiled.

"Yes. He's quite a character. Maybe he knows more about William Faulkner than he knows about security. Anyway, they're not so interested in bringing their billion dollar public relations machine to bear against one retired school teacher."

"So what do they want?"

"A press conference. They want you to hold a press conference, Nina."

"How? Where?"

"I don't know. We may be able to control it somehow. Postpone it. Limit the number of reporters present. But somehow, some way, you've got to go on national TV and tell people you were wrong."

She thought for a while, then shook her head and said:

"No Willie Nelson?"

"Probably not. After *The Times* retraction—and your news conference—your picture's coming off the granola bars."

"Damn."

"And Furl may hate Big Url, but he'll probably have to do it in private."

"Well. He'll get over it."

"So. The other problem is, we've got to come up with a long term place for you to stay. There's still a crowd around your shack. Moon Rivard's people have tried to chase them off, but they seem to keep coming back."

"Wow."

"So think about it a while. We can wait a few days for the conference, put them off, say 'no comment.' A lot. Then..."

She thought for a time, then said:

"Okay. I've thought it out. I know when I want the conference. And where."

"All right. Just say."

"How many reporters are in town now?"

"A million."

"Then let's have the conference at one o'clock today."

"But, Nina..."

"In the gymnasium."

"The gymnasium? But Nina there's room for two thousand people in there!"

"I know. And as far as where I'm going to stay...I'm going home. I miss Furl. I miss my place."

"But all those people.."

"I know a way to get rid of them.

And she did.

Jackson found Nina's plan insane and told her so.

The press conference should not be held before Thursday (this was Tuesday).

They would need two full eight-hour days, during which he could prepare questions, pepper her with them, and evaluate her answers.

Also during these days, he would have time to learn the names, and reputations of the various journalists: who from NBC might ask the most difficult questions, who from CBS might be depended on to lob softballs which she might knock out of the gym, stressing all the while her patriotism and love of the land.

There might even be a way to limit the number of journalists present.

And the place...

...the place should of course be small, confined. *She* was small and confined.

Clothing. Her normal attire as principal? Or was that too formal?

Would not the jeans and sweater of a beach dweller be more appropriate?

Nina Bannister, woman of the earth?

Any lawyer worth his salt would have taken a month to prepare a client for the grilling she was certain to get.

And the length of the press conference?

The time that she would be allotted to give her opening speech?

The number of questions permitted?

And yet.

..and yet.

Nina wanted to do it in two hours. At the gymnasium.

Insane.

"All right, then, Nina. If you insist on doing this. The town is full of reporters who are hungry as rabid dogs. Two phone calls and the place is full."

"Good. Make the calls."

"That gives us two hours to eat a little lunch and let me brief you as best I may. I'll call out for some sandwiches. Then we can go into the back room and…"

"I want to eat lunch at Sergio's."

Stunned moment of shock and disbelief.

"What?"

"I want to eat lunch at Sergio's. I like their leek and potato soup. Maybe a little salad, too."

"Nina, what are you thinking about? You can't go to Sergio's!"

"Why not? I like Sergio's."

"You'll be mobbed! There'll be a hundred people around you!"

"They can get their own leek and potato soup. I'm not sharing."

"How will you get there? People are watching for my car!"

"Call me a cab."

So Jackson did so.

And so she ate lunch at Sergio's by the Sea."

Where she sat in a back booth, ate leek and potato soup, and was not noticed by anyone, even her waiter, who required several admonitions to bring the soup.

She called another cab at 12:30 and took it to the gymnasium.

It was clearly packed.

She could hardly make her way through the door.

Once she did so, she walked onto the court.

Lights were everywhere.

So were people, most of whom she had never seen.

There was a large platform that had been built in the center of the court.

Without talking to anyone or asking anyone's permission, she walked up to it and bounded the two steps that led up to the microphone.

She flipped the 'on' switch, just as she had done a hundred times as principal.

And, almost magically, she *became* principal Nina Bannister again.

The hundreds of people in the audience were her students; fifty or so hands had sprung into the air, as people recognized who she was and that she was, without introduction, about to address them.

Which she did, saying:

"I'm not going to start this until all of you quieten down. I'll say it again: we will not dismiss for lunch until you TONE IT DOWN!"

All of them did.

And she said:

"My name is Nina Bannister. I live in Bay St. Lucy. I'm sorry for what I did, and I apologize."

So saying, she walked out of a side entrance to the gym.

The cab was there, exactly where she had left it.

"The docks," she told the driver.

He took her there.

Penelope Royale was stocking *The Sea Urchin* with supplies for the next day's fishing run.

"Hey," she said, from the open door of the cab.

"------!" answered Penelope.

"I need a little help up at my shack. Can you come with me for a few minutes?"

"------! I can------if-------!"

Penelope got into the cab.

Within two minutes they were at Nina's place.

Perhaps a hundred people were milling around, kept away from the stairs by one of Moon Rivard's patrolmen, but still waving the anti-oil signs and the pictures of Furl.

Some of them had put up tents.

Nina and Penelope got out of the cab and approached the patrolman, who was standing beside his car.

"We need," said Nina, "to borrow your bullhorn."

"Here."

"Give it to Penelope. Turn it on first."

"All right."

Scrrreech of the bullhorn.

Into which Penelope brayed:

"All right you--------! You-----! You------d-----f----. I want your fat -------s--out of here right-!!!! And if you don't ------I'll ----- and ---- and-----!!! You---understand?"

A shock spread over the crowd.

The patrolman himself was white faced.

Penelope continued:

"And take those---------tents with you!"

Within two minutes, Nina's driveway was clear.

The patrolman stood like a statue by his car, unable to move.

Nina said to the cab driver:

"Could you take this lady back to her boat?"

He nodded, mechanically and said:

"Yyyess, ma'am."

"What's the fare"

Then he looked at Penelope who was getting into the cab.

Then he said:

"Nothing. Nothing at all."

Then he drove away.

CHAPTER TWELVE: CINDERELLA LEARNS OF THE BALL

Harper Lee wrote one great novel, which is, of course, *To Kill a Mockingbird*. After that—after telling the bittersweet tale of Atticus and Scout and Jem and Boo Radley and all the others—after that, she settled back to the life of a southern lady, living in the small southern town of Monroeville, Alabama.

Because of the enormous fame of *To Kill a Mockingbird* (especially following the success of the film starring Gregory Peck) hordes of people wanted to meet the great Harper Lee and talk with her. They wanted to know how she got her ideas, and who the real life inspiration for Atticus was, and many other questions of such nature.

But Monroeville protected her.

It closed its walls to the outside world.

Gawkers and would-be parasites, reporters and critics and journalists, and outright crooks were allowed into the city limits, of course, but they were given no help in locating Lee herself, who was allowed to melt back into the quiet and humble citizenry from which she had, albeit briefly, emerged.

Thus it was with Bay St. Lucy and the fabled Nina Bannister.

There was, true, a continuing flurry that lasted several days.

But it died down.

If anything remained, after forty eight hours or so, that was legendary concerning the whole matter, it was not Nina Bannister herself nor the obscure oceanside shack in which she resided—but the fabled soliloquy of Penelope

Royale, so thoroughly laced with exquisite obscenities that the very fish in the sea (those within one hundred yards or so of land, at any rate, or so went the story) were said to have flipped over on their dorsal fins and floated to land, dazed and dead by the hundreds.

Even the flowers in their boxes were withered by the rant.

No fishermen of Bay St. Lucy or sailors living in the town heard it, because none of them cared very much about the 'save our continent' movement, nor could they afford marijuana, nor did they prefer living in tents to living on ships.

But the counter-culture folk, the bearded and stoned and mosh pit crowd that actually did hear, became like the survivors of Hiroshima and Nagasaki—they lived on, but they were never the same, and they kept their eyes warily on the skies from that horrible moment on, lest a second Penelope might appear on their horizon and sear the very sky under which they had so blissfully whiled away their previous lives.

So terrible was it.

But it was not bad at all for Nina, since it gave her back her privacy and her shack and her beachfront routine…

…and her cat.

Jackson Bennett brought Furl home the following day—Wednesday—and his two girls came along to bid the animal farewell.

They had obviously brushed and petted him, and given him much love.

But he was still quite angry with Nina and showed the fact by walking straight into the bedroom as soon as he was set down upon the floor, and secreting himself beneath a cardboard box in which he occasionally liked to live. He came out of this box only twice the first day back, both times to leave small, hard, round turds in the middle of the shack's two major rooms.

After the second excretion, Nina went herself to the bedroom where she squatted down, lifted up the top flap of the cardboard box, peered down at the brooding creature beneath her, and said, quietly but sternly:

"Factum fiere, Furl, infectum non posttest."

Furl, who spoke Latin (as most cats do and would respond if addressed in that alas dead language, but never get the chance, being never spoken to in it)—and who thus understood the words 'It is impossible for a deed to be undone'—replied:

"Falsus in uno, falsus in omnimus."

(False in one, false in all.)

And he glared.

She was not about to let the matter stand as thus, and replied:

"Fac fortia, Furl, et patere."

(Do brave things, Furl, and endure.)"

But he hissed, contracted into an even tighter fur ball and said:

"Facium et mei memineries."

(I'll make you remember me.)"

Upon saying which he went straight into the living room and left another turd on the throw rug.

Other than this, though, things went remarkably well.

The world at large, at least the most sensation-seeking part of it, forgot about Aquatica and thought of it, if at all, in the same way it thought about satellites circling the earth. We can call Japan on our cell phones because they are out there, but we don't spend a great deal of our time worrying about them.

The New York Times did not cease to exist, although many right wing columnists and radio talk show hosts went on suggesting that it should.

Louisiana Petroleum did not sue Nina. Nor did they make any further effort to contact her.

The second morning after her return to the shack she rose early—it was a splendid morning, the wave foam red in first sunlight—put on her bathing suit, took her cell phone from the desk, walked down to the surf, walked out into the surf, reached waist deep water, bent back, and hurled the phone as far as she could, hoping that it would hit Germany.

It did not, keeping the Germans safe by plopping into the water some sixty feet away from her and disappearing.

Later that morning, she took a screwdriver from the tool kit that she kept under her shack, and unscrewed her small mail box.

She did not throw it into the ocean, because it was shiny and metallic and black and old (it had been her and Frank's mailbox when they lived downtown) and it looked like what it was supposed to be, a mailbox.

So she put it away in a drawer.

But, content to be unreachable by phone or mail, she felt ready to assume her old life, as well as could be expected.

True, she thought some about Sandy Cousins; about the mythic and larger than life, the cartoonish and from another era-ish Brewster Dale, about the two Narangs— one of which did not exist, but as each day passed, they faded a little deeper into her memory.

The disk was gone, but, at least in the minds of everyone but her and Hector, it had never existed in the first place.

Aquatica, for this reason, she supposed, made no effort to acquire it.

Nor did *The New York Times*, which wanted nothing more to do with the entire story.

A part of her—the amateur sleuth part—felt that some investigation should be undertaken to expose the people who had deceived her. Some Cajun red-haired woman had met her at the Lafayette airport. Some small middle Eastern man had received her in the lecture hall at the University. He had also written an article which the paper had run. He had called her to ask her permission to run it.

These things had happened.

She was not insane.

Aging a bit perhaps, but not insane.

But whose place was it to investigate these beings?

The city of Lafayette's?

The University's?

It was not really even a police matter, when one thought about it.

She had taken a trip, that much could be proven.

But after that?

Yes, perhaps Pierre could be found, and made to testify that she had been in The Blue Gator. Yes, a red-haired woman—if he could remember, having played host to so many women—had been there too, and danced.

So what?

Otherwise no one had seen these beings.

They had taken nothing, done no wrong.

And so, from time to time, as she was walking on the beach, both the unreal Narang and the ethereal Annette, would appear to her, smile, and say, hovering out over the water:

"If we shadows have offended, think but this, and all is mended. That you have but slumbered here, while these visions did appear. And this weak and idle theme, no more yielding than a dream."

And then they disappeared.

So it went for several days.

She walked on the beach each morning, went to Bagatelli's for croissants and beignets and bagels, made herself coffee, sat on the deck and drank it, and waved happily at the tourists who meandered along the beach, going from left to right in the early hours and from right to left as the sun crested, returning to their beds and breakfasts tired and dangerously sunburned.

Then one o'clock to four o'clock was spent at Elementals, where she puttered about, opening this new acquisition or that, cleaning up a bit here or there, selling something, paying a bill or so, and otherwise sitting in a quiet nook near the cash register and allowing herself to get engrossed in Maj Sjowall and Per Wahloo's *The Laughing Policeman.*

A major change in these proceedings occurred one week later when, in the late afternoon, just before she was wondering what dinner would be, dinner knocked on the door.

Or rather an invitation to dinner.

It was a beaming John Giusti, his plaid shirt bisected by two wide dark blue galoshes, and his feet clad in the combat boots he always wore in the Pelican Skeleton, his animal hospital.

"Nina! Good afternoon!"

"Good afternoon to you, John!"

"Nina, it's been more than two weeks since we…"

She cut him off:

"Yes, John. We ran together that morning in the park. You and I and Helen. And only half an hour later…"

He nodded, then said:

"You've been through a lot since then."

"Yes. It's been difficult."

"We've been keeping up with it."

"I guess everyone has."

"And we're proud of you, Nina. Whatever the real story is—well, everyone in town is on your side."

"That's good to know."

"But it just came to us: we invited you out to dinner. And we never followed up."

"Well, a lot was happening."

"Things seem to be going better now, though."

"Yes, John, they are going better."

"So why don't you come out?"

"When?"

"Now. Come with me in the rover. You haven't eaten yet, have you?"

"No."

"Then come on. Helen's doing spaghetti. We're going to have some Italian bread, and we're going to drink red wine…and we're going to sit out over the ocean and tell ghost stories. Helen loves storytelling."

"Don't worry about the short notice. I'm there."

And she was.

She could not sit in the front seat because, for various veterinarial reasons, the Labrador could not be moved. (It had something to do with his relationship to the two weasels.). She did not want to sit in the middle of the middle seat, because she did not have nor expect to have a good relationship with the weasels either.

So she scrunched against the door, used both hands to move aside an automobile part of some kind that sat, oozing oil onto the plastic covered seat—and gingerly placed it on a pancake-thin metal box that sat on the floorboard.

Then she simply listened to the animals chatter, trying once or twice to try to make small talk with John as they made their way out of Bay St. Lucy.

This did not work because of the animals: His questions and her replies, her questions and his replies, all wound up sounding something like, "RRRRaaaarghhhh arrrrghhhe rrrgggh!"

And so they gave up.

So she simply rode along and enjoyed the ride—she usually made it once or twice a month now, to visit the Giustis—over what must have been ten miles, along coastal and not-so-coastal roads that she had never explored before John had bought his place. She thought of nothing at all—except the spaghetti to come—while the yellow-pine forest wrapped itself around her.

It was getting darker. Craning her neck, she could see the stars up through the roof of pine needles. The Mississippi sky was ferocious and black, stars glittering in mute and yellow explosions.

It all remained like this for a period out of time, all changes elemental and thus of great and no importance, until they reached John Giusti's house.

"So here we are!"

"I love your place, John. It's my favorite house in the world!"

They could not see the great sea-straddling monstrosity that was John and Helen's house yet, of course. They first had to park in a driveway that looked like a deer blind, get out of the van, get the dog and weasels out of the van, and brush their way through a narrow path that led through shrubs and scrub oak, gradually descending on its way down to the sea.

But the walk was worth it, of course.

Finally, she could hear the ocean, rumbling and grating not more than a few yards over the top of the encircling trees.

But she still could not see the house.

"How did you find this?"

"A client of mine. He was a crazy architect."

"Where is he now?"

"I think he's been institutionalized."

"That's comforting."

"Here. Let's push through these last bushes and…"

"Wow!" she could not help exclaiming. As she always did when she visited John and Helen.

For there, laid out before her, was a wide, long, pier at the end of which glowed what would have been a magnificent beach house, had it been on the beach.

It was not.

It was an ocean house, perched as high above the surging waves—twenty feet or so, she judged—as her own shack was perched above the beach.

Helen stood in the doorway, beckoning.

The house, all vast glass windows, seemed to reflect a thousand images of her, the various animals around her, and the sea beneath her.

Nina started forward, feeling the pier wobble a bit, the boards swaying ever so slightly as she walked upon it.

"Nina! So good that you could come out!"

"I wouldn't have missed it!"

"Hope you like Italian!"

"Love it!"

She turned for a second. The beach was behind her now, narrow but perfectly white, dark pine forests impinging upon it, as though the trees were trying to drive the sand into the water.

Then she walked on until, John following close behind with the Labrador on the leash, she was at the door.

"Come in! Come in!"

She stepped inside.

And in so doing, she stepped outside.

For there was, strictly speaking, no inside.

There was furniture. Heavy, mahogany, leather couches, tables, chairs, rugs and things a man would have to sit on and lie on and put things on and have some woman come in from time to time and clean.

But she was still more outside than inside, the vast glass walls magnifying everything on the coast, from birds that skimmed low over the ocean to lights twinkling miles to the south in Lake Borgue, to slowly moving freighters that made their way like moving oil splotches hurled upon the clean azure evening sky and now oozing horizontally along it—to the waves, always the waves, swelling, throbbing, falling, and rising again, having vowed never to allow stillness to anything in the universe.

"We hadn't seen you since..."

"I know."

Helen was radiant, as usual, her dark eyes glittering like specks of coal which, when illumined, would have burned the color of her crimson gown.

"What a terrible day, Nina. How you've gotten through all of this…"

"Well, Helen, it isn't much more terrible than something we all had to go through earlier. And we made that. The community can make this, too. And the Ramirez family will survive. Senora Ramirez still has Hector and Sonia."

They were in the kitchen now, with soft white light coming from a fluorescent tube above the oven, and a vast glass wall to their left showing an epic film version of *The Ocean by Moonlight.*

The meal followed soon thereafter, marvelous, as she knew it would be.

A glass of red wine; another glass.

Dessert: chocolate mousse.

And then, with the ocean spread out silver beneath them and the wind making its soft moan through the yellow pines that encircled the house, they told ghost stories.

John told "Oh Whistle and I'll Come to you my Lad," and "Who's Got My Golden Arm." Nina told "Thus I refute Beelzy." Helen told "The Monkey's Paw" and then went in to get the coffee ready.

She had been gone five minutes or so when she reappeared, a concerned expression on her face.

"Nina, I don't know if I should mention this..."

"What?"

"Well?"

John stepped forward and asked:

"What is it, Helen?"

"Television."

"What about it, honey?"

"There's a broadcast on. The eight o'clock news. I've been glancing at the little portable TV just while I finished making the coffee."

"And?"

Helen took the obligatory deep breath that proceeds distasteful news.

"It's a big press conference."

"So?"

"The governor of Louisiana and the governor of Mississippi are holding a joint press conference."

"I can't think of anything more boring than..."

But Nina interrupted:

"It's Aquatica, isn't it? Has something happened out there?"

Helen was quick to cut her off:

"No! No, it's nothing like that! They're just announcing something."

"I'd like to see," said Nina, almost beside herself. "I feel close to some of those people out there, in spite of the fact that I made a fool of myself."

"You did no such thing," said John. "You were just trying to help everybody. Anyway let's go in the den. The big wall TV is in there."

Then came the marvel of walking through John and Helen's house. The walls were doors, the roofs were walls, and air seeped in from everywhere, delightfully cool, whispering out of hidden crevasses that served as ventilation ports. There were animals all around, of course, most of them dogs, but cats here or there, and slinking little reptiles that peered around crags in the wall structure or out from gurgling fissures.

Finally, they entered a smaller interior room, from which, incredibly, the Gulf of Mexico could not be seen.

They sat down in darkness and leather; John turned the lights even lower, and Helen operated the remote control stick that caused most of one wall to become life-sized images of smiling politicians.

The worst kind, thought Nina, settling in and somehow wishing for popcorn.

Another switch of the remote, and sound enveloped them.

It would have been better, Nina found herself speculating, *if they had simply stayed in the kitchen and watched the small TV.*

But here they were.

And here was a man, identified with text scrolling across the bottom of the screen, as the press secretary to the governor of Mississippi.

"All right, so much for introductions and preliminaries! And, John, down there in the front row, from *The Chicago Sun Times*, I want to say how much I like that hat you were wearing today on the golf course!"

General laughter.

Camera on John from *The Chicago Sun Times*, who was also laughing.

"I'm just kidding you, John."

More laughter.

I hate these people, thought Nina.

"But seriously, folks, it's time to get on to the more urgent and pressing matters. As all of you know, there were some pretty serious and even frightening things said last week about Louisiana Petroleum, and specifically about the installation known as Aquatica."

Silence.

Camera pans to reporters.

All of them are texting.

Camera pans back to podium.

"The statements made were false. They were completely without foundation. How such nonsense came to be printed in a newspaper with the reputation of *The New York Times*—well, that question is still being looked into, and will be for some time. There is a great deal of discussion going on in Baton Rouge and in Jackson— because the states of Louisiana and Mississippi are co-partners in the operation of Aquatica, and the mutual trust enjoyed with Louisiana Petroleum—at any rate, there is much discussion about starting hearings at the state level to ascertain ultimate blame for what was almost a complete panic."

Wonderful, thought Nina.

Where would she most enjoy being roasted by a roomful of politicians? Jackson or Baton Rouge?

And why couldn't Louisiana have made New Orleans its capital?

"Right now, though, we are here in Baton Rouge—and we have invited our neighbors from the state house in Jackson—to announce a party. And you all know the citizens of Mississippi and Louisiana luuuuuve to party!"

Huge raucous laughter.

Some moments before order can be restored.

The spaghetti, thought Nina. *The spaghetti!*"

"But to offer this invitation, I'm going to invite up here to the platform, one of the most important cogs in the machinery of Louisiana Petroleum, Dr. Sandra Cousins, who is not only one of the head engineers out at the rig Aquatica—but who is also their chief in charge of public affairs. Sandra?"

And there she was, as perky as ever. Sandra Cousins.

Beaming at the camera.

"Thank you thank you thank you, people of Mississippi and Louisiana!"

More applause.

Applause dying now.

Nina sat forward in her seat.

"What do they have you doing, Sandy?" she whispered.

"I have great honor tonight. It's an honor bestowed upon me by the executives of Louisiana Petroleum, working in conjunction with the state governments of Mississippi and Louisiana. As you know, Louisiana Petroleum is responsible for supplying energy to a great many citizens and installations of those two great states. And one of the lynchpins of our ability to do this is the Aquatica, upon which I have the honor to be based. But Aquatica is not just an 'installation;' it is a home to many of us. And a magnificent home it is. It is a factory, an ocean liner, and a magnificent hotel, all in one. Those of us honored to work on it are constantly fascinated by its state of the art equipment. And, I might add, its beyond state of the art FOOD!"

Laughter and applause.

"And that is why we feel remiss. We have been keeping the wonders of Aquatica all to ourselves. But now we want to show it off to the world!"

More applause.

"And so we, in conjunction with the major political parties of Mississippi and Louisiana, are throwing a party! A gala! If you will. We're inviting two hundred very special people—entertainers, political leaders, school teachers, college professors, scientists, writers, you name

them—to come out to the vessel Aquatica in two weeks'
time, on Saturday evening, June 28—to enjoy a tour of the
facility, plus a summer fireworks display at sea, followed
by the most sumptuous dinner y'all have ever had!
Furthermore…"

"Well, that's interesting," said Nina.

John smiled:

"You think you'll be the guest of honor?"

"I will not, definitely, be the guest of honor!"

And they all laughed.

But as time would prove, they were all to be completely
wrong.

Neither Nina nor John nor Helen were truly late night
people. She was home by nine forty-five.

By ten o'clock she had straightened up in the shack and
was thinking of going to bed.

There was a knock on the door.

She crossed the room and opened it.

Before her on her porch stood Brewster Dale.

He was dressed in a white sport coat and navy slacks.

But his hair was still wavy, and his complexion ruddy.

He smiled broadly:

"I hate so terribly to bother you at this late hour."

"No. No, it's all right."

"Your privacy is important to you, I know. But there
are some things I feel I need to tell you. You may learn
them soon anyway, but…"

"Come in."

She led the way into the living room, turning on the
light as she did so.

He followed. He did so with what seemed a mixture of
trepidation and delight, delighting that such a place as this
existed, and fearing at the same time that he might break it.
He looked everywhere, into the corners, up at the ceiling,
over at the bedroom door, down to the carpet—and all the
time his mincing steps were accompanied by two actions
Nina found noticeable: first, he held his hands tight

together just below his belt, his fingers opening and closing on the rim of a large hat.

There was no hat, but he did not seem to mind that.

Second, he kept bending and stooping, even though the top of his head was a foot and half shorter than the ceiling.

"What a delightful place you have to live in, ma'am!"

"Thank you, I like it. Will you sit down?"

But he was having none of that. His eyes were fixed on the sliding glass door that led out to the deck.

"You have access to the ocean, I believe."

"Yes. Would you like to sit on the deck?"

"It would be my greatest pleasure! I am, Ms. Bannister, landlocked, when I am not aboard The Aquatica."

"You live in…"

"In Jackson. Not an ocean around, for miles and miles."

"How sad."

"I regret it constantly. And I blame the Yankees."

"Why is it their fault?"

"Why, we always blame the Yankees. This is our nature."

"I see. Well, then. Come on, and may I offer you something? I can make coffee."

"Oh, I don't wish to impose, more than I am already."

"There is also wine, and tea, and…"

"You don't have any whiskey, I suppose."

She slid the deck door open; they walked out.

The beach lay deserted before them and the moon hung white above, its perfectly round mouth somewhat astonished to have heard the word 'whiskey.'

"Whiskey?"

"Yes, Ma'am. I only ask because it would be so much easier than coffee. I'm never certain why all people do not grasp this fact."

She pulled a chair out from the table and gestured to it; he sat, crossing his legs and sighing at the Gulf of Mexico. She thought about the matter for some moments, then said:

"I think I do have a bottle of whiskey in the pantry. I was thinking of pouring it out."

He shook his head and frowned.

"It is as Mr. Faulkner once wrote: 'Pouring out liquor is like burning books.' That line is from *Intruder in the Dust*."

For some reason, that seemed wrong to her, but no matter.

She opened the pantry door and reached high to find a nearly completely obscured bottle of Seagram's Seven.

She took it down, opened it, let the fumes escape into the air, kept a careful eye out to be sure that no live flames approached them, then found a glass to pour two inches of brown liquid into.

For herself she poured a glass of Chardonnay.

And after a moment or two more, the two of them had settled into deck chairs, the table wobbling between them, several Mississippi stars looking down.

"It is very gracious for you to receive me like this."

"Not at all."

"I must admit, I've been doing a bit of snooping into your personal history."

"I'm not sure I have very much of that."

"Oh, you do. Yes, ma'am, you have a good deal of personal history. The matter of the Robinson fortune is now lore in your town."

"That was a bizarre thing."

"And would have been even more bizarre, according to my sources, had it not been for one lady who would not give up and accept what everyone else was telling her."

"I suppose it just proves I'm stubborn."

He nodded.

"As am I, Ms. Bannister. As am I."

She smiled:

"I guess we're both children of Mississippi."

"That we are, Ms. Bannister. The name of 'Dale' has been rattling around in the northern part of our state for some generations. I feel my grandfather, and his father before him, would have been deeply disappointed in me. A common security specialist. What a fall from the plantation owners that we once were!"

"You're hardly 'common'."

"Thank you, madam. That was a gracious thing to say. I must also add that I learned more about you than your role in the Robinson affair. I learned of your years spent in teaching; and I learned of your late husband's outstanding legal reputation."

"Yes. We've been here a while, in Bay St. Lucy."

"I should say. I'm sorry that I was not able to make the acquaintance of the two of you when you were a couple. My own late wife would have taken to you immediately. And I'm sure your husband—his name, I'm told, was 'Frank?'"

"Yes."

"Well, we would have found our way onto some quail shoot, or we would have made some other kind of unrest for the community to deal with. I would have liked the man."

They were quiet for a time.

"Well," said Dale finally, after taking a sip of whiskey and savoring it for a time before swallowing it. "As much as I do love sitting here remembering…"

He looked at his watch.

…I suppose the time is growing a bit late."

"Maybe a little."

He smiled:

"Clocks slay time…time is dead as long as it is being clicked off by little wheels; only when the clock stops does time come to life. That is, I believe, from *Light in August*. Marvelous book. And quite underrated."

She knew nothing to say to that.

He continued:

"I must express to you, Ms. Bannister, "my great admiration for you. And for your actions during the past days, the past weeks. Ever since, when one thinks about it, your discovery of the young Ramirez lad."

She shook her head:

"I'm still amazed that you're not furious with me. I stole that disk. I deceived you all."

He smiled.

"You were doing what you felt needed to be done."

"I made a fool of myself."

"In the quest for truth. There are worse things that one can do, worse sins that one can commit. I'm going to take another sip, please, if you do not mind."

"Not at all."

He poured an inch more of the amber liquid into his glass, saying:

"We read in *A Rose for Emily* that 'War and drink are the two things man is never too poor to buy.' No, no, you acted bravely. And it was you, ultimately, who were deceived."

She shook her head:

"I'm still not able to make sense of that, Mr. Dale."

"Brewster, please. And I should love the privilege of calling you 'Nina.'"

"Of course. All right then, Brewster. There are, as I say, a lot of things I'm not able to make sense of. I don't know who the two people were who met me in Lafayette. And by the way, I did meet them—or rather they met me—I didn't dream the whole thing up."

"Of course, you didn't."

"And I didn't dream up Edgar's murder."

"No. Although we all wish we had dreamed that, and that it had never happened at all."

"It was two weeks ago that I found...well, anyway, it was two weeks past. And I still see his body down there."

"Of course, you do, dear lady. But you must remember what Mr. Faulkner tells us in *The Reivers.* 'The past is not dead. It isn't even past.'"

She nodded.

"Mr. Faulkner is correct about a lot of things."

"Of course, he is. But it is because of the things you have spoken of just now that I am here, stealing your whiskey, admiring your moonlight."

"What do you mean?"

"I mean, dear lady, that, drunken old reprobate whom you may take me to be, I still have a few teeth in my head, and am not completely incompetent at my job."

"No, Brewster, I never thought you were."

"Nor am I alone in my duties. The corporation is large, and there are more than one of me. We take very seriously the task of protecting the good souls who work on our installations. 'The reason for living,' as we read in *The Intruders*, 'was to get ready to stay dead a long time.' Well, one does stay dead a long time. That fact is our reason for living."

"I'm not sure I understand…"

"We have been hard at work on the matters of young Mr. Ramirez' death, Nina."

She sat forward:

"Do you know something?"

He nodded:

"Very possibly. A kind of, well, breakthrough, has been achieved."

"What kind of breakthrough? What did you learn?"

"Some very troubling things."

"About Edgar?"

"No. No, it seems now that he was doing just what you believed him to be doing. Trying to help matters."

"I'm not understanding you. If things were going wrong out on Aquatica, and Edgar knew about them…"

"Certain things, it seems *were* going wrong on Aquatica."

"But…this still isn't making any sense to me! I just watched that press conference tonight. You're inviting the whole world out to that rig in two weeks. If it isn't safe…"

"It is safe. Aquatica is safer in than The Peabody Hotel in Memphis."

"Then what did Edgar…"

"Drugs."

The word hung in the air for a while, and, never quite dissipating, finally crept to a corner of the deck, where it attempted to hide by melting into the shadows.

"What?"

"Drugs. More specifically, heroin."

Nina shook her head:

"I refuse to believe Edgar was involved in drug trafficking."

"No, no. You fail to understand. Edgar was not involved in drug trafficking. Edgar had discovered drug trafficking."

And then, finally, it began to make sense.

"He hadn't discovered some engineering malfeasance; he had discovered…"

"A smuggling operation."

"But how could such an operation have been going on?"

Dale shrugged:

"We do our best to prevent such things. But you must understand: huge amounts of materials are delivered by boat to Aquatica each day. The helicopters transport personnel. But foodstuffs, replacement parts, drilling equipment—all of these things are brought out to the vessel, and taken into shore from the vessel—by boats. More than a hundred crates of various materials are transferred each way, on any given working day."

"So it would be easy…"

"Why don't we play a guessing game, Nina?" he interrupted.

She looked at him, then said:

"All right."

He smiled and continued:

"How much high-grade heroine is estimated by the Food and Drug Administration to enter the United States' borders illegally, coming from countries all over the world, each month of the year?"

"I don't know."

"One point four million pounds."

She was stunned, and said:

"I'm stunned."

He drained his whisky, seemed to want more, seemed to decide against it, and said:

"And well might you be. It is a war, and we are losing badly. But we fight our hardest. Security at border checkpoints is very tight. It is not so tight, though, on the personnel flying in and out of Aquatica each day. We subject all of our people to rigorous background checks. We flatter ourselves that Aquatica is staffed by the best and the brightest. But the possibility of a packet of something being offloaded from one of the supply boats, slipped into the duffel bag of a newly hired roustabout heading into Bay St. Lucy—or any village along the Gulf Coast—well, this possibility not only exists, but exists as a highly lucrative source of bonus money."

"And you think Edgar may have discovered such an operation?"

"That is the theory with which we are now working."

"But the disk! All those figures…"

"When you opened the disk, you saw figures, is that correct?"

"Yes."

"And that was as far as you went. You did not search the entire disk?"

Suddenly it began to be clear to her.

"No," she said, softly. "No, we didn't."

"Because what you saw was a kind of computerized mask, Nina. A casual observer would have taken that disk as a backup source for purely engineering data. But a more thorough search of it would have revealed…"

"…Names."

He nodded.

"Precisely."

"The person Edgar called that night…"

"Was undoubtedly someone he felt he could trust, in revealing what he knew."

"But who he really called…"

"Was a smuggler. Perhaps the head of the operation."

"And he killed Edgar."

"Most probably."

"And the person I called…"

"You called the same person."

"The meeting in Lafayette…"

"Was a kind of wild goose chase, designed to do two things: first, to GET THAT DISC, which the smugglers needed at all cost. Second, to create a kind of smokescreen, making you and Ms. Cohen, I suppose, what one might refer to as—well, fall guys."

"Or fall girls."

"Or fall women, if we are to behave as enlightened feminists."

"Yes. We want to get the language right."

"The story in *The Times*, the entire scandal…it masked completely the operations of the smugglers, who, some two weeks ago, must have felt that they were on the verge of being discovered."

"They were on the verge. Edgar had discovered them."

'Unfortunately, he seems to have trusted the wrong man."

They sat for a time. Finally Nina said:

"We are closing in. That is all I can say at this time."
"But you now know who these people are?"

"Annette Richoux…"

"There is almost certainly no such person. Nor is there any actual professor of geology resembling the small goatee-wearing man you met in the lecture hall."

"But do you know who they are?"

"Again, I am not at liberty to say at this time. Still, there is one question that I must put to you, dear Nina. And I must do so with your safety in mind. Forgive me if I seem distrustful."

"Of course."

"Is there even the slightest possibility that you and young Hector Ramirez might have made a copy of that disk?"

She shook her head:

"No. I didn't. And Hector never really had it. He couldn't have."

Dale seemed to sigh.

"That is very good news. Because if the smugglers thought there was such a disk, and that you still had it…"

"I understand. No. No, there isn't."

"Then all I can advise you to do is wait patiently. I and my colleagues may work slowly, but we are not inefficient. I believe I can promise you that Mr. Ramirez' family will receive justice. The murderer of their son will be located, and probably within the next few weeks. The entire deception perpetrated against you—and against Ms. Cohen—will be unraveled."

Nina breathed deeply and said:

"I don't know what to say."

"You don't have to say anything. But I do have one or two further bits of what I hope will be good news for you."

"All right."

"The first concerns your, well, partner in crime, Ms. Cohen."

"Yes?"

"You may have heard that she was released from *The New York Times*."

"Yes."

"This was a decision made by the newspaper. It was not done because of any pressure brought by Louisiana Petroleum."

"All right. But the problem is, she's still fired."

"No. She is not."

"What?"

Dale smiled:

"We are not a vindictive corporation, Nina. We hold no grudges for what has happened. We are, however, led by certain executives who wield a good bit of persuasive power. People who belong to golf clubs, etc., and who collect favors, so that they may give favors in return."

"Are you saying…"

"One of the 'favors' we have called in—from a retired but still influential managing editor of the newspaper, is the re-hiring of Ms. Cohen. She is, we have been able to ascertain, a first-rate journalist with an impeccable record. She was taken in, as were you. As were, when one thinks of it, all of us. This thing needs to be put behind us; and there is no need for her to remain the victim."

This called, Nina felt, for another glass of Chardonnay, which she happily poured herself, while saying:

"That is excellent news! We seem to keep wanting to villainize you folks out at Aquatica; and you keep on making it impossible."

"I hope that is true, and that it remains true. But in order for us to make absolutely certain that it does remain true, there is one more urgent request that I must make of you, on behalf of Aquatica, and of Louisiana Petroleum."

"What? What request?"

He reached into his jacket pocket and pulled out a card.

It was postcard size, laminated, and gold-embossed.

It read:

"To Nina Bannister:

Louisiana Petroleum requests your presence at a gala celebration to be held on board the vessel Aquatica, on the evening of Saturday, June 28, at eight p.m. Transportation to and from Aquatica will be provided. Formal attire, please. RSVP"

For a time she could only stare at the card.

Then she said:

"I would have thought myself the last person you would have wanted."

He shook his head.

"Precisely the opposite is true. I believe you remember Ms. Cousins?"

"Sandy? Of course!"

"She was instrumental in planning this gala. And as the guest list was being prepared, with all of its film stars and athletes and celebrities, she remained insistent: the first name on the list will be, must be, that of Nina Bannister."

"I can't believe it."

"Indeed you should and must believe it. We want you to be our guest, Nina. Both you and Ms. Cohen. This nightmare is over."

She was speechless.

Liz was rehired.

She herself, would be undisgraced.

Champagne would be flowing.

The world was beginning to make sense again.

And Cinderella was going to the ball!

CHAPTER THIRTEEN: PREPARATIONS

The week preceding June 28 was a memorable one in Bay St. Lucy.

The tourists talked about the same things they always talked about: swimming in the surf and crabbing on the jetty and fishing from the pier.

But the residents talked about the upcoming great and wonderful Aquatica party, which, much like the great and wonderful Oz, was hard to imagine and harder still not to think about.

Every edition of *The Bay City Gazette* contained a new addition to the guest list. Monday a rock star agreed to come, Tuesday the star running back of The New Orleans Saints, Wednesday, three members of the Mississippi legislature (they did not generate as much interest as the musician or the athlete), Wednesday evening...

...etc., etc., etc.

And as interest in the party grew, so did Nina's activity list.

She spent Monday afternoon at a tea held by Alanna Delafosse in the rose garden of the Auberge des Arts.

Tuesday morning she went shopping, trying to find something appropriate for a fairy tale evening.

Tuesday afternoon she went to Bay St. Lucy's AT&T store to buy a new cell phone.

Wednesday morning she had brunch at Gerard Park, under a gazebo, with Paul and Macy Cox, back for a week's visit from their new home in Jackson.

Wednesday evening she had dinner with several people at Edie Towler's beautiful house on the north side of town.

All of these events were designed as part of kind of a 'let's forgive Nina' for making a fool of herself' week, but also as a genuine celebration. For the town had tolerated bearded activists and marijuana smokers; but it more badly needed Aquatica.

Aquatica supplied residents.

And money.

A great deal of money.

Bay St. Lucy needed big oil, as did the entire states of Mississippi and Louisiana.

And big oil was not sufficient in and of itself.

What was needed was SAFE big oil.

The coming gala seemed to promise every assurance of that.

The two hundred or so celebrities planning to attend might just as well, in the words of Brewster Dale, have been spending an evening at The Peabody in Memphis, or The Monteleone in New Orleans, or on The Queen Elizabeth.

...or, Nina occasionally mused despite herself, on The Titanic.

But that was ridiculous.

Why think things like that?

And so things rocked on until Saturday morning, the big day.

She tried to go through her weekend routine as best she could, but somehow she could not avoid feeling excited. She bought a black, bejeweled gown, for which she had paid decidedly too much at Sarah's Fine Fashions. She could feel cold champagne on her taste buds. And the helicopter ride!

How often did one get to look at the sea from a state of the art helicopter?

And, of course, there were the celebrities.

Movie stars!

Running backs!

Politicians!

(Well, forget them for the moment and go back to thinking of:

Movie stars!

Running backs!

And it was in this sort of mind set she found herself, when, at 3 p.m. (she was to be at the airport at six thirty, all dressed and sparkling and ready) her new cell phone rang.

She flipped it open and heard:

"I'm at the long pier."

"Good," she replied.

"Where do I get bait?"

"Turn around and look behind you. About fifty yards from the pier entrance, there's a shop that says 'Kate's Baits.' There are several bait shops near the pier, but that's probably the best one. It's where I go when I fish off the pier."

"What do I use for bait?"

"What are you trying to catch?"

"Fish."

"Squid."

"What?"

"Squid."

"You've got to be kidding me—that's disgusting!"

"Well, you could use chocolate cake if it sounds better, but you won't catch anything. Oh, and by the way…"

"Yes?"

"Who are you?"

"What?"

"Who the hell are you?"

"Liz of course. Who the hell did you think I was?"

"Wasn't sure."

"Well who else would be calling you?"

"Now that I think about it, nobody. Not a soul in the world, other than Elizabeth Cohen."

"So why don't you come down here to the pier and join me? You can teach me how to fish. Then we can go out to the Aquatica party together. Oh, and you don't have any whiskey do you?"

"No, I gave it all to a security guard."

"That doesn't make any sense."

"I know, but it seemed the thing to do at the time."

"Well, no matter. There's somewhere in town that sells whiskey isn't there?"

"There's no place in town that doesn't."

"Sounds like my kind of place. Anyway, I'm supposed to write a story about this shindig, and I want to be good and drunk when I do it."

"Don't worry about it. The philosophy here is "Pouring out whiskey is like burning books.""

"I love it. Who said that, besides you?"

"Faulkner, in *Intrud*..no, in *Light in August*. Why did I think *Intruder in the Dust*?"

"Damned if I know. But we don't have too much time for this fishing, or for the getting drunk. So get your ass down here!"

And Nina did.

She drove to the pier, parked her Vespa, and looked out. Sure enough, there was Liz Cohen as far out as possible, waving and smiling.

One minute later, the two women were embracing, a flock of seagulls screeching over them, and long green waves of ocean washing around the pier posts beneath them.

"Hey girl!" said Liz, finally, as the embrace loosened.

"Hey yourself."

Liz wore only a white t-shirt and jeans. She had accumulated a store of various fishing supplies that lay harmlessly (at least to the fish) at her feet.

"Liz, when did you get to Bay St. Lucy?"

"Late this morning."

"Where are you staying?"

"Some B&B. I don't remember the name of it."

"Why didn't you call me? You could have stayed with me."

"Are you kidding? The last time I had anything to do with you, I got fired."

"Yes, but you're rehired now, aren't you?"

"Damned straight How'd you know?"

"A guy from LP told me. Apparently the corporation doesn't want any hard feelings. This guy said that they hired you back because a retired managing editor spoke up for you, as kind of payback for a favor LP had done him."

Liz nodded:

"A managing editor did speak up for me. Old fart. And it might have had something to do with encouragement from LP."

She shrugged:

"Or it might have been because I've been sleeping with the guy, off and on, for a couple of years."

"Well," said Nina, thoughtfully, "if you want to take the cynical view."

"I'm a reporter. I'm paid to do that. So how do you fish?"

"Let's take a look. What have you got here?"

"Pole and stuff."

"That's a rod and reel."

"Yeah, like I said."

"Come on. Let me help you fix up this rig. Where's the bait?"

"I think it's in this sack."

"You think?"

"I didn't have the guts to look at it."

"Aren't you supposed to be a hardened journalist? Don't you cover combat, and all of that?"

"Yeah, but that's just war. This is squid."

"Here. Watch."

In some minutes, Nina had found the end of the fishing line, attached bobber, sinker, and hook, and opened the package of squid.

"That is," said Liz, "the most disgusting thing I've ever seen."

"Okay, I'll bait it for you."

"I can't believe you're not throwing up."

"I'm a child of the coast."

"I'm a child of the Bronx, and I couldn't do what you're doing."

"There, it's ready. Now pick up the rod."

"Like this?"

"Perfect. There, see that little curved metal rod just above the reel?"

"Yeah."

"That's the bail."

"The what?"

"The bail."

"Bail is to get prisoners out of jail."

"This bail is to catch fish. Flip it."

Liz did so.

"All right, now put your finger on the reel, so that you're pressing down on the line."

"Like this?"

"Exactly like that. Rear back and cast. When the rod is sticking straight up, let up on your finger."

"Okay, here goes!"

Swish.

"Perfect!"

"Hey, I did it."

And she had done it.

The tall red bobber was jerking in the waves, some thirty feet from the end of the pier.

They watched it for a time as, caught in the slow incoming tidal currents, it gradually worked its way toward them.

"So how long," asked Liz, "do we have to do this?"

Nina looked at her, noting almost complete misery.

"As long as it takes, Liz."

"Until what?"

"You catch a fish."

"Oh."

"And by the way, I wanted to tell you…I'm sorry."

"For what?"

"Almost getting you fired."

Liz shrugged.

"Wasn't' your fault. I've been a reporter for a lot of years. Good reputation, all that crap. I fell for that scam like a midway rube."

"Well, I did too."

"You're a school teacher. People lie to you all the time and you can't do anything about it. But me—I'm supposed to know better."

"Thanks."

'You're welcome. By the way, what does it mean when it goes under like that?"

"It means you've got a bite."

"Oh, hell."

"It's not too bad. It happens sometime when you go fishing."

"You didn't warn me."

"Slipped my mind."

"So what do I…"

"Jerk hard on the rod."

"Like this? I…oh, my God, it's pulling back at the other end!"

"Yes, it's trained to do that."

"Maybe I should just let go of the rod."

"That would solve the problem. The other option though is to start reeling in."

"Like this?"

"Hey, you're a natural."

"So what do you think we've caught?"

"Shark, maybe."

"You're kidding, right?"

"People catch sharks."

"Maybe if I just let go of the rod…"

"No!"

The fish, whatever it was, was getting closer.

"So, how big are the sharks around here? Like twenty feet, like the one in Jaws?"

"The sharks around this pier are maybe three feet, like the one in *Finding Nemo*. Now, out at Aquatica—there you might get some big ones."

"Great Whites?"

"They're rare in the gulf. But from what I can understand, there are the occasional sightings."

"I just don't want to...hey, there he is!"

"Keep reeling. Hold the rod pointed higher!"

"What is that?"

"Whitefish. Maybe a foot long. Nice fish, Liz!"

Liz, giddy as a school girl, hauled the flipping fish over the rail of the pier and let it land at their feet.

"What will we do with it?"

"Are you kidding? We'll take it back to my place and put it in the fridge. Tomorrow we'll have it for dinner. We would have it tonight, but we're eating out in style."

"Damned straight we are! Tomorrow though I'm supposed to be flying back to New York."

"I wouldn't hear of it, Liz. One night at least you've got to spend with me."

"You got room?"

"No, but I'll get Scotch."

"You're beginning to tempt me."

"And somebody's got to show you Bay St. Lucy."

"Well..."

"Beside, they're not going to fire you; you're sleeping with the damned ex-managing editor."

"There is that."

And so, fish dangling between them, the two women walked back off the pier, toward Nina's Vespa.

Within fifteen minutes—the drive would only have taken five minutes, but they had stopped at a liquor store to buy Scotch—they were back at Nina's, the whitefish dutifully stored in the refrigerator, the glasses of Chardonnay and Scotch sitting before them, and the ocean sky in the East turning a strange lemon color.

"What does that mean?"

Nina shook her head.

"Maybe nothing. Maybe a line of squalls though. We might have rain tonight on good old Aquatica."

"Oh, great."

"It probably won't be anything that bad."

"That's what my first husband told me about marriage."

Nina thought about comments relevant to that, decided there probably weren't any, and sipped her wine.

She seemed to be drinking a lot of wine these days, but then life was forcing her to do so.

And it was difficult to argue with life, wasn't it?

Yes, it certainly was.

"So, Liz, you're keeping on with *The Times*?"

"Well, they're offering me my old position back."

"But?"

"I don't know. I may not take it."

"Why not?"

She shook her head:

"Confidence."

"What do you mean?"

"If I could be fooled like that one time."

"Surely everybody makes mistakes."

"I never had. Never one like that, anyway."

"But what would you do?"

Another shrug.

"Maybe come to Bay St. Lucy Maybe live with you. How would that be? We could be sea rats together. I like it down here. You need a roommate?"

Nina smiled.

"I could stand a roommate."

"People would call us lesbians. That might be a kick. I'm not a lesbian though, so—I mean, who do you do it with if you live here?"

"I don't do it with anybody."

"Who would *I* do it with, is what I'm asking."

"Fishermen."

"That's all?"

"How many professions do you need?"

"Well, I…"

And there was a knock at the door.

The two women looked at each other.

"You expecting anybody?"

Nina, getting to her feet, shook her head.

"No, I'm not. But folks seem to drop by here lots these days."

"Maybe," said Liz, "it's Willie Nelson."

Nina shook her head as she passed through the living room, and said over her shoulder:

"I think Willie has decided to pass on us."

Then she opened the door.

Standing before her was an entirely nondescript woman, a woman of above average height, who seemed remarkable for nothing at all, except for the fact that she was wearing sunglasses, a beige scarf over her head, and a London Fog trench coat.

It was at least eighty degrees, and, if rain was possible for later in the evening, it was far off right now.

"I'm sorry to bother you. Are you Nina Bannister?"

A soft, shy voice. No accent.

"Yes, I am."

"I had read about you, and…I wonder if I might come in?"

Educated. Polite. Shy and unassuming.

"Of course. Please."

Nina stepped aside and let the woman pass into the living room.

"Just go through and out to the deck. A friend of mine and I were having a drink."

"I am disturbing you! I'm so sorry!"

"No, it's all right. Just go on out to the deck."

When they both had reached the sliding glass door, Nina said:

"This is my friend, Liz Cohen."

Liz rose.

"Hi!"

"Hello, Ms. Cohen. You are the lady who wrote the story about Aquatica for *The Times*."

"Yes, I am."

"Sit down," said Nina.

"Thank you."

"Would you care for a drink?"

A shake of the well-covered head.

"No, thank you. I really can't stay. It's just …"

They were all three seated now.

"It's just that…well, I have been keeping up with Ms. Cohen's story. And the retraction. And…"

Liz sat forward.

"And what? What is it?"

The woman bit her lip.

She was obviously nervous.

"I..I think I know something…that I should tell you both."

"What?" asked Nina.

The woman was silent for a time.

She seemed to be making up her mind.

Finally, she continued, in a voice both somber and penitent.

"It's the Tool Master."

Both of them said, simultaneously:

"What?"

"The Tool Master. It's so strange. I don't even know who he is. I've never seen him. But his codename is simply 'the Tool Master'."

"All right," said Liz, "so there's somebody who calls himself the Tool Master. What does that…"

"He coordinates all of our activities. It's all for the money, you know. None of us has any feelings politically at all. But we're very talented. And we can be any number of people. There are acting jobs far removed from the stage."

She sat for a while.

The tide was coming in.

The sky in the East looked ever more lemon.

Squalls certainly.

"The security people have been deceived, you should know, into thinking drugs are involved."

Nina remembered her conversation with Brewster Dale.

"Okay," she said. "But what do you mean by 'deceived'?"

There might have been a smile on that face.

If there had been, though, the sunglasses would have hidden it.

"It has nothing to do with drugs."

"What?" asked Liz. "What are you talking about? And who are you?"

"I've forgotten. I was somebody once. But now I've forgotten."

Nina leaned toward the woman and said:

"Are you all right? Should we call someone?"

A nod.

"Oh I think you should definitely call someone. Yes, no doubt about that. But as for me, I was all right once. Then I lost my conscience and became…well, less than all right. The people dying. All the people dying…"

"What people?" asked Liz.

"Doesn't matter. Except I can't stand by and see it happen any more. They will find me of course. They find everyone who tries to leave. And they will find me, too."

"Who will?"

"It doesn't matter. At least not to the two of you."

Nina:

"We just don't…"

The woman interrupted her:

"Do you know anything about cement?"

Silence for a time.

Then Liz said:

"No. Nothing."

"All right. Here:"

A sheet of paper upon which had been typed:

"Segment 642C tube #4. Then check 789D tube number 2."

"That's where it is; that's where they put it."

"Put what?"

But the woman ignored the question and simply asked Nina:

"Do you have a computer?"

"Yes."

"Could you bring it out here?"

"Certainly."

Nina went into the shack, unplugged her laptop computer, and brought it out to the deck.

"Could you put it over on that far rail?"

Nina did so.

"Now, Google the word, *Cemex*."

Again, Nina did so.

"What does it say?"

"Cemex," Nina read from the computer screen," is one of the most commonly used brands of cement. It's especially useful in…"

"That's all right. You get the idea. Now…"

So saying, the woman stood bolt upright and ripped off her scarf.

Revealing a mane of bright red hair.

She ripped off her sunglasses too and said:

"It's nice to see you again, Ma Cher! I'd ask your friend there for a cigar—I do love cigars, those little ones—but I think she's a cigarette smoker."

For a time Nina was too stunned to speak.

Finally, she stammered out:

"Annette. You're Annette Richoux!"

And the woman laughed.

"Not by a longshot, Honey. Not in a thousand years. Annette is just a little place in my life I happened to be passin' through. But I tell you what. If you want to do something important, stop worrying about that Annette bitch, and about that weasel with a goatee you saw over in Lafayette, cause you ain't never gonna see him either. Not ever. He don't exist no more. None of us do for more than a week at a time. And then we're somebody else."

"But how…"

"Naw, if you want to do something important— something damned important—look up something else on that computer of yours."

"What?"

"You've already looked up CEMEX. Now look up SEMTEX. Sounds close, doesn't it?"

"Is," asked Nina, "SEMTEX a less expensive brand of cement?"

The woman threw back her head and brayed:

"Haw! No, my chere, it's a more expensive brand of cement! Helluva lot more! But more effective, too. Now, I've got some materials down in my van that will tell you all about the difference between SEMTEX and CEMEX. But why don't the two of you get a jump on the process by just looking up SEMTEX. I'll be back in a few seconds."

So saying, she strode off the porch and into the living room.

"Is that," Liz asked, "the woman who met you?"

"Yes."

"Then what the hell..."

"I don't know, Liz. But let's look up SEMTEX."

They bent together over the computer.

As they did so they head a car door slam.

Then they heard the motor start.

Then they heard the car pull away.

"Where did she..."

"She's gone," said Liz, quietly.

"But I want to..."

"She's gone...whoever she is...and we'll never see her again."

They were silent for a time.

Then they looked at the computer screen.

Which said:

"SEMTEX is a brand of plastic explosive widely used for industrial purposes. Also known as C-4 or 'plastique,' it..."

Plastic explosive

Plastic

Explosive.

Liz bowed her head, and, as though praying, said:

"Oh my God."

And then again:

"Oh my God! They're going to blow up Aquatica."

And then again:

"Tonight. At eight o'clock. With all the world watching."

And one final time:

"They're going to blow up Aquatica."

CHAPTER FOURTEEN: THE MANY USES OF PLASTIC

They sat in silence for some seconds.

"So what is this plastique, Liz?"

"It's bad stuff. I got to know about it in Iraq. Lot of missing legs because of plastique. It's kind of the weapon of choice in roadside bombings. You only need a tiny amount. Use just a bit more and you're blowing up buildings."

"Or oil rigs."

"Yes."

More silence.

"Do you believe this woman, Nina?"

'Yes."

'Why?"

"Can we not believe her?"

"No."

"So what do we do?"

"I have no idea."

"Call the police?"

"The Bay St. Lucy Police?"

"We're back to Moon Rivard, and that's crazy."

"State police? FBI?"

"I'm always in this position," said Nina, softly. "I think I know something. And it's important. And nobody will listen to me. You can't call your paper, I guess."

Liz half smiled.

"Right. Call *The New York Times*, who have just rehired me after I filed a crazy story about Aquatica, with another crazy story about Aquatica."

"So how many assistant managers have you slept with?"

"Not enough."

"OK. I have one contact that I always trust. I have my new little phone here. I'll try him."

She called Jackson Bennett's office; no answer. Jackson Bennett's home; Sonia answered:

'Bennett residence."

"Sonia?"

"Ms. Bannister?"

"Yes. Sonia, is Jackson at home?"

"No, ma'am, he isn't. He's one of the guests at the big gala on the oil rig. He left an hour ago. I think they wanted to fly him out a little early, because there was some legal problem between the company and Bay St. Lucy. I guess he should be on the helicopter now."

Nina felt her heart fall.

She was silent for a time.

Finally, Sonia said:

'It's really exciting, isn't it?"

"Yes," Nina answered, quietly, envisioning Jackson getting off the helicopter.

All of them, all the guests, getting off the helicopters.

Drinking champagne.

Having a good time.

Seven o'clock.

Seven thirty.

Somehow she knew eight o'clock would be the time.

She knew this.

"Thank you, Sonia."

"Sure. Shall I take a message?"

A message, she found herself thinking.

Jackson, you've just stepped onto a time bomb.

And I know this, and I know when the bomb is going off.

And I can't do a damn thing about it, because most people already think I'm crazy.

"No, Sonia. No message."

And she clicked the phone closed.

So they sat for a moment or so more.

Then Nina:

"Okay, so let's go to the airport. We've got to tell somebody about this."

"You want to take my rental car?"

"Let's do it."

And they did.

Ten minutes later they were navigating the streets of Bay St. Lucy, watching the huge beige helicopters land at the airport a mile in front of them.

"It's brilliant, when you think about it," said Liz, gripping the wheel hard.

"I don't know. I'm still confused."

"Well, they're not. Whoever 'they' happen to be."

"So explain all of this to me."

"From what the woman told us, I would say we're dealing with a highly professional group that works for some international terrorist organization."

"Which organization?"

"I don't know. There are a lot of them. But they're often tracked by the FBI, and they have difficulty getting access to planes or buildings. So other organizations spring up to help them. The terrorists pay these organization huge amounts of money. And the organizations, in turn—being comprised of faceless people with no criminal records—"

"Blow up buildings."

"Or they blow up Aquatica. What a terrorist coup this will be, Nina. And we helped them put it together."

"I still don't see…"

"I know, and I'm only beginning to. But let's say there's a team of pros out there, working on the rig. Somehow they've gotten hired, despite Aquatica's security."

"Well, that's conceivable. Brewster Dale, would-be Faulkner expert and security man. What a joke. They've gotten him to believe—him as well as the people working for him—that this whole thing has to do with drugs. Which we know now is ridiculous, and at most a cover up for what's really happening."

"Okay, so they've gotten through Mr. Dale. From what I know of these rigs—and I've had a little experience with them—the drilling tubes have to be lined with cement. Some of the spillage problems in other rigs have happened because the company used a lower grade cement than is recommended. Also, sometimes water gets mixed with the cement, and the resulting mixture—impure and too soft— has to be chipped away. A guy has to be physically lowered into the tube to do this."

"So if the guy is one of these…"

"…these ghosts, for want of a better word."

"Good," said Nina. "These ghosts, then. If he's working for them…"

"He simply attaches, somehow, a small packet of plastique in the well wall and plasters it over with cement."

"How large a packet?"

Liz merely shrugged.

"I've seen four ounces destroy a building."

'Oh my God."

"Yeah."

"How does the plastique get set off?"

"A detonator of some kind. It can be very simply rigged. If they know what they're doing…"

"And they seem to."

"Yes, they do. At any rate, you can detonate the explosive with a cell phone. That's how it's usually done in Afghanistan."

"But wouldn't you have to be close by?"

"Within half a mile."

"So what are we saying? One of them is out there now."

"Probably," said Liz, "The leader. The woman you knew as Annette referred to him as 'the tool master.'"

Nina nodded.

"I know the tool master. Tom Holder. He's got a kind of cockney accent."

"For the time being. Actually, he probably is no more British than 'Annette' was Cajun."

"So our job," Nina continued, "is somehow to get out to Aquatica and unmask this guy."

"Yes."

"But Liz, what did you mean about our being 'used' in all of this?"

"Don't you see? The way everything worked out—it turned out perfectly for them."

"Go on."

"Edgar found out about the plastique. I don't know how. Maybe those bewildering numbers on the disk were the answer all the time. Maybe, chemical engineer that he was, he could get a reading back from the 'cement' that was being put in, that didn't match the viscosity reading of actual cement. At any rate, he figured out what was going on, and he may have also figured out that a team of..."

"Ghosts," said Nina, quietly.

"Yes, ghosts, were responsible for setting up the whole scheme, getting the plastique on board Aquatica, plotting the explosion."

Nina continued:

"He was terrified though, because he didn't know which people out there he could trust."

"Right. There was only one man he actually did think he could trust."

"And that was Holder, Liz. The tool master is, I think they said, the second highest-ranking man on board—but the one most likely to understand about cement and its application."

"Right."

"So Edgar flew into town. He wanted to get off the vessel, maybe not sure if the gang was onto him or not. He called Holder, who had also flown in, probably on a separate helicopter flight, and set up a meeting in the early morning hours."

"The meeting took place," said Liz. "And exactly where it took place we'll never know."

"But Holder—of all of these people, if truth be known—was and is a professional assassin."

Liz shook her head:

"Edgar never had a chance."

"All right, but then..."

"Then comes the beautiful part, Nina, if you want to look at it that way. Edgar, you have to understand, had been calling Holder off and on during the night. On one of these calls he might have said that he didn't understand the readings. Might have suggested to Holder that the two of them get in touch with the brilliant professor Daruka Narang."

"So when I called Holder..."

"He was probably shocked to get the call. But he's not dumb. And immediately it came to him. He imitated an Indian accent..."

"...we know these people can imitate any accent..."

"...pretended to be Narang, and suggested you fly to Lafayette."

"Why didn't he just meet me in Bay St. Lucy?"

Liz shook her head:

"No, no, it wouldn't have worked. You were already suspicious of anybody working for LP so you wouldn't have given the disk to Holder himself. And a professor of Narang's rank was probably not going to go flying off around the country to look at some phantom disk."

"So I went to Lafayette. And met two ghosts."

"Whom, like the fake Annette said, we'll probably never see again."

"And once you did that, Nina, everything fell into place for them."

"They got the disk."

"Which was their first priority. But once they had the disk, they had the chance to take what could have been a monstrous, disastrous, terrorist attack and make it infinitely worse."

"The fake Narang..."

"...or somebody, we'll never know who."

"Wrote a story so horrific, with such urgent overtones, that you would have to write it, and *The Times* would have to print it."

"And, of course, I would write it and vouch for it, because I had the word of …"

"Me."

"You. The solid and dependable Nina Bannister, solver of the Robinson Case and the Reddington murder."

"The data couldn't be false, at least in your mind, because I had gotten it directly from Aquatica's computers."

"So *The Times* printed it, and all hell broke loose."

"Now," Nina continued, "let me be sure I understand this. The ghost team knew, first, that the environmentalists would demonstrate all over the country, insisting that big oil rigs were inherently dangerous and should be shut down. But the ghosts also knew that engineers and scientists would descend on Aquatica…"

"…looking not for the subtle marks of plastique being somewhere hidden by cement…"

"…but for the problems," Nina continued, "outlined in *The Times* story."

"Which were fake problems to begin with."

"So Aquatica would get a clean bill of health, in the spotlight of world attention."

Liz nodded:

"And so Aquatica would also do something very stupid."

"Like plan this gala."

"Making them the most juicy terrorist target in the history of the world."

Nina thought for a time, then said, quietly:

"It gets worse and worse, the more you think about it."

"Yes it does, Nina, yes it does. Before, the attack was going to kill a hundred and twenty or so innocent oil workers. Innocent…"

"But anonymous."

"Now…"

Nina nodded and said:

"Now it's going to kill political leaders, celebrities…"

"The cream of the coast—and of the country."

"We're just delivering them all up for the slaughter. Not only that—"

Liz interrupted:

"Not only that, but I'm just beginning to realize: the explosion will be so massive that no one will be able to pinpoint plastique as its cause. And, if no terrorist group claims responsibility…"

"Which none probably will…"

"The whole disaster," said Liz, " the destruction of all these lives plus the entire ecosystem of the gulf coast, will go down simply as a horrible affirmation that *The Times* story was right."

"No oil rig will ever be trusted again."

Liz:

"Because this is the safest one ever built."

Nina:

"And it turned out to be nothing but one huge floating hydrogen bomb."

"Our oil industry will be destroyed."

"My God," Nina whispered.

It seemed the only reasonable thing to say.

They parked as near the terminal as was possible, given the chaos that was going on around them. It was only six o'clock, but transport helicopters, some belonging to the Aquatica fleet, some privately owned, were hovering everywhere, ready to take formally-dressed guests out to the rig.

"What is our plan?" asked Nina, slamming the door and squinting into the late afternoon sunlight.

"We tell them we're invited out to Aquatica for the party. I think I can make them believe that."

"It's true."

"Well, that puts me at a disadvantage. But I'll have to chance it."

"Then?"

"Then we find the drill master, who, I guess, is the head man out there."

"His name is Phil Bennington. I've met him twice; he's a nice guy."

"Okay, we somehow get to him."

"All right."

"Then we just tell him the truth. His second in command is a highly-paid operative, a kind of ruthless international spy, working for some terrorist organization. This man and a group of a several others, having deceived the Aquatica security measures, have secreted a certain amount of plastic explosive in the vessel's well linings, and they plan to blow up the entire rig in approximately two hours."

"And how do we know this?"

"A strange woman just came by and told us. Then she disappeared."

"So that's our plan?"

"That's our plan."

"And you think they're going to believe us?"

Liz shook her head.

They were approaching the terminal.

"They would have believed us."

"Back when we had credibility, you mean."

"Yeah, then."

"Well, we don't have any credibility now, Liz. We have absolutely no credibility."

Liz stopped and glared at her, almost shouting:

"And so what? So damned what? Do you have a better plan? This is an utterly fantastic story! We've already told one utterly fantastic story and been revealed as complete idiots. So now we're going to come at them with another story, even more absurd? Nina, no one out on Aquatica is going to believe us; but no one here is either. No one anywhere is…"

"Until the damned thing," Nina said quietly, "blows up."

Liz nodded:

"And then it will be a little late, won't it? So if my plan seems a little rough around the edges, I'm sorry. But unless you have something better…"

"No, I don't."

They were both quiet for a time.

Then Nina said, almost whispering:

"If you want to dance with the girls at the county fair, you must first go to the county fair."

Liz stared at her:

"What?"

"If you want…"

"Yeah, yeah, I heard you. What is that, something you people say in the South?"

'I don't know. I just…"

Liz shook her head in disgust and walked on, saying:

"Maybe I don't want to live here after all. County fair indeed."

They walked into the terminal.

One of the gates was being used as a boarding area for Aquatica passengers.

"All right," said Liz as they approached the smiling young man seated at the desk. "One thing we know. One thing we can depend on. We have been invited to this thing. They will take us out there. What we do when we get there is anybody's guess. But county fair or not, kiss the girls or whatever, they will take us out there, that much we know."

Liz stepped up to the counter:

"I'm Liz Cohen and this is Nina Bannister. We want to be taken out to Aquatica. We're on the guest list for tonight."

The young man looked over a list that sat on the desk in front of him:

"I…I…ah, here you are. I'm sorry, but you're slated to go on the seven o'clock helicopter."

"We're what?"

"You're booked on the seven o'clock helicopter. Were you not informed of that?"

"No, we...Nina?"

"Yes?"

"I haven't been reachable for a few days. Did you..."

The man behind the desk smiled:

"The flight schedule was mailed to you two days ago, ma'am."

"Nina?"

Nina could feel herself blushing.

"I've been throwing away all my mail for the last week or so."

Liz stared at her.

"Great."

"I'm sorry."

Then Liz turned back to the counter attendant.

"Listen, we've got to get out there."

"I'm sorry, ma'am, but the rules are very strict. So many people are going. We can't just do first come, first served. And space on the 'copter is limited. And by the way, ladies..."

He looked at them, and seemed embarrassed:

"You do realize that formal dress is required for the occasion."

"Formal..."

Liz was, Nina could tell, losing her temper.

"'The occasion,' you jerk, is going to be a great deal different than you imagine it—or any damned body imagines it—if you don't get us on one of those helicopters!"

"I'm sorry but..."

"WE'VE GOT TO GET OUT THERE, DAMMIT! THE WHOLE THING IS GOING TO EXPLODE. YOU HAVE TO LISTEN TO US."

The young man was, in fact, listening, as were most of the people who were waiting to board, and most of all the other people in the airport.

Liz took a deep breath then, and said:

"I'm sorry."

"That was perhaps," Nina whispered, "ill-timed."

"Yeah," replied Liz, "yeah, sometimes I lose my temper a little."

The young man was making a telephone call.

"I'll have someone from security come," he said, quietly.

Someone from security came.

He was, in fact, a Mississippi State Trooper.

This, thought Nina, *is not good.*

"What seems to be the problem?" growled the huge man in the Smokey the Bear hat.

The boy behind the desk answered:

"These ladies feel there is to be an explosion out at Aquatica."

"A what?"

"An explosion."

And from that, simply all hell broke loose, with more and more policemen showing up, and Liz getting madder and madder, and finally calls to LP headquarters being made, and more finally still—in about twenty minutes—a limousine pulling up to the terminal and one of the LP lawyers whom Nina had seen at her first LP meeting one week ago, got out.

He entered the terminal, stared hard at Nina and Liz, and almost shouted:

"You two!"

And that was not good either.

"What in hell are the two of you trying to pull here?"

"I know," said Liz, "that…"

"Haven't the two of you caused enough trouble already? Everybody involved in this mess has been more than gracious to you! I and several other colleagues had insisted that you both be brought up for criminal charges! We were voted down, and you were shown every possible courtesy, even up to being invited out to the rig tonight. And now you show up here like this? With another wild story? Do you think this is funny? Is this your way of making a name for yourselves? Are you just trying to create scandals at everyone else's expense? Do you know how damaging these ridiculous accusations can be?"

"Listen," Liz insisted, "if you'll just let us…"

She was interrupted by the attorney, who said to the nearest state policeman:

"Will you please escort these women back to wherever it is they came from?"

'Yes, Sir."

Then, to both of them:

"If you ever have anything to do with this corporation again—either of you—I will have you jailed, and believe me, I can do it."

He turned and left.

The two women were then summarily escorted out to Liz's rental car.

They were escorted back to Nina's shack.

Once there, they were left in the front seat of the car while their cortege of police escort vehicles pulled away.

Liz was silent.

"Okay," said Nina. "We tried your plan. Now we'll try mine. I have a way to get us out to Aquatica. Maybe the only way. And once there—I'll find our tool man for us. Now come on."

She led the way to her Vespa.

It was a strange phenomenon, but things were coming together for Nina Bannister. This mistake, that bit of incongruity—it was all beginning to make sense.

She felt a strange kind of confidence as she puttered through Bay St. Lucy that she had not felt before, since Edgar's death.

And the first thing she knew, was that the two of them, she and Liz, had a stop to make before going back to Aquatica.

They made the stop.

And within two minutes of that stop she was talking to Hector Ramirez in the front yard of the Ramirez home.

"My brother is gone," he said, the sad almond eyes reflecting the darkness that was creeping over the city. "My brother is gone, and they are having a big party."

"I know, Hector."

"They believe he was selling drugs."

"Some of them believe that."

"It is not true."

"I know it isn't."

"You go out there tonight? Everybody drink champagne?"

"I go out there. I go out there right now. But no, Hector. No champagne for me."

He looked at her.

"Why do you go?"

"I think I know something, Hector."

"About Edgar?"

"Yes."

"About what happened to him?"

"Yes. But Hector, I need your help."

"Of course I help."

"The phone. Edgar's phone. You remember I brought it back to you that night?"

"Yes, I remember."

"You still have it?"

"I have. I keep in my room."

"Excellent. And you haven't called anybody with it, or received any calls?"

"No, ma'am."

"Then please go and get it for me."

"Do you think…"

"I don't know exactly what to think, Hector."

He walked toward the house, but turned at the door, and said:

"But I know what to think."

"Yes? What?"

"I think nobody get over on Ms. Bannister."

Then he entered the house.

Within a minute, he was back with the cell phone.

He handed it to her, and she left with Liz.

Five minutes later, they were at the far end of the wharf, where Penelope's boat *The Sea Urchin* was moored.

Penelope, to her great relief, was sitting in the boat, eating a small carton of fried chicken.

"Penelope," she said. "I want to hire you for tonight."

Penelope put down the red and white box, looked up, and said:

"Where are we going?"

It was a strange thing. Penelope spoke only in obscenities.

Unless business was being discussed.

Specifically, the business of fishing.

"Where are we going?"

"You know of the Aquatica?"

"Sure I do."

"Can you get out to her?"

She nodded:

"I go out there every now and then. Ten miles or so. I've got her coordinates plotted into my navigation system."

"How long would it take to get out there?"

"Maybe an hour and a half."

"Okay. It's five thirty now. We should get there at seven. That should work. Why do you go out there?"

"Sharks. They vent a ton or so of garbage off that rig every week or so. Lots of sharks."

"You fish for them?"

She shook her head:

"Naw, I just like to go out there at night and shoot at them."

"You go out to Aquatica and shoot sharks with a pistol?"

"It's fun."

"Don't they mind?"

"I go at night. They never know I'm there."

"And you do this with fishing parties?"

"Nope. Just by myself."

Liz, hearing all of this, shook her head and said:

"God, I like this woman."

Nina nodded:

"The two of you have a lot in common. Penn, there's something I have to tell you before we go."

"All right."

"The rig is filled with explosives. It may blow up."

Penelope nodded, thoughtfully, then said:

"We'll need more beer."

"That's possible."

"And the two of you?"

"Yes?" answered Nina.

"There's a locker over there about fifty yards up the quay. I use it to store stuff. Take these keys, if you will, and open it."

"What are we looking for?"

"A forty-five automatic."

"We're not going to be shooting any sharks tonight, Penn."

Penelope simply shook her head:

"I get these feelings sometimes. I'm getting them now."

"What kind of feelings?"

"Just…there are things to shoot besides sharks.

Yes, there are, Penn. Yes, there are."

She and Liz went to the lockers, while Penelope went half a mile or so in the other direction to buy beer.

They opened the locker and took out of it a big black oil-glistened automatic, which Liz examined, thoroughly, cocking and uncocking it, checking its chamber.

"Loaded, well oiled, and ready," she said, quietly.

"You know how to use one of these?"

She nodded.

"Combat zone coverage."

"Afghanistan?"

"Flushing."

In five minutes, they were back in the boat.

"Never doubt that a small group of dedicated women," began Nina, "can change the world."

"Indeed," added Liz, "that's the only thing that ever has."

"All right, ladies," said Penelope, starting the boat's engines, "let's go fishing."

CHAPTER FIFTEEN: BACK TO AQUATICA

There was a small chop for the first two miles out, but otherwise the sea was calm. Nina and Liz sat on cushions in the bow of the rectangular craft, while Penelope steered from the back.

"I think," said Nina over the roar of the outboards, "that we must have missed something all along."

"What?"

"I can't pin it down. It's just...what he said..."

"What who said?"

"It's not important. Or maybe it is. I've just got to piece it together in my mind."

She then turned and shouted back to Penelope:

"Penn, do you think they'll let us board?"

Penelope shook her head and answered.

"Either they'll have to let one of us come up, or they'll have to send somebody down."

"Why?"

"We'll be out of gas by then."

"What?"

"Yeah, I've only taken on enough gas to get us out there. Rule of the sea, though; they have to help us."

No one had anything to say to that.

The boat plowed on.

At the five-mile mark the skies began to darken.

At seven miles it began to rain.

Penelope reached under a tarpaulin to get slickers out. The three of them put on the rain gear, and, at that point, something moved under a second tarpaulin.

"What was that?" asked Liz.

"I don't know," Penelope answered, but..."

Before she could finish, the tarpaulin seemed to rise by itself.

It then slid off to one side, revealing Hector Ramirez.

"Hector!" shouted Nina.

"Oh my God!" shouted Liz.

"----!" shouted Penelope, forgetting, for a moment, her rule about avoiding obscenities while fishing.

"Hector what are you doing here?"

"I know you are going out to the boat, to do something important. Something that is to do with Edgar."

"But you can't…"

"So I follow you tonight on my bike. I know you do not see me. When you leave the boat…"

"For beer and guns," whispered Nina, remembering the five minute interlude when *The Sea Urchin* was empty.

"…when you leave, I sneak on."

"You got something over," Nina said quietly, "on Ms. Bannister."

"We have to take him back," said Liz.

"We can't, Liz. We don't have time. We're going to get there at seven as it is. If we double back now…"

'Okay, okay, I understand."

"--------!'"

"It's all right, Penn. We don't have a choice."

Finally Hector spoke:

"Sometimes, Senora…"

"I know. I know."

Then she smiled:

"Sometimes a man is needed."

And they sailed on.

They reached Aquatica at ten minutes before seven.

The massive rig loomed even larger than Nina had remembered, since they came up below it now, and not from above, as she had done before.

The rain was harder now, but it had not become completely dark, and they could be seen easily by teams of orange-clad men lining the rail.

"Ahoy below! Who are you?"

"*Sea Urchin!*" shouted Penelope in reply. "We have some people who need to come aboard!"

"Can't allow that! No security check!"

Damn, thought Nina. *Maybe this is not going to work, after all.*

"Get Sandy Cousins!" she shouted as loud as possible. "Get Phil Bennington. I know both of them!"

"Who are you?"

"I'm Nina Bannister."

This caused a furor among the men who had heard it. Some laughed, some cursed, some gestured.

"It's nice," said Nina, quietly, "to be famous."

"What do you want out here, ma'am? Do you still think we're going to blow up?"

Laughter.

If only you knew, thought Nina.

She could see now that there were helicopters hovering everywhere, some waiting while others landed to disgorge white dinner-jacketed men and gown-clad women.

"The best and the brightest," said Liz.

"Nina!"

She looked up, at the rail directly above them.

Thank God.

Sandy Cousins.

"Nina, what in hell is going on?"

"We need to come up!"

"We got a call from the airport. One of the lawyers says you're..."

"I know, I know. It's all kind of crazy, Sandy."

"We're not supposed to let you on board!"

"Sandy, you've got to trust me! You've got to trust all of us!"

"I don't have the power to..."

And then Phil Bennington appeared beside her at the rail, saying:

"I do have the power. It may cost me my job later on, but...all right. Come on up. We'll send the platform down

for you. You can moor your craft on the side of Aquatica.
Then you can ride the platform on up."

"Thank you! Thank you so much!"

"I have no idea what's going on here, but…well, I don't
propose to leave three women and a young boy in a
driving rain in the middle of the Gulf of Mexico."

And in this way, Nina, Liz, Hector, and Penelope were
taken aboard the Aquatica.

A little over an hour, if they were correct, before the
vessel blew up.

Within a matter of minutes, they had been dried off,
offered coffee, and led through smiling crowds ever farther
toward the bowels of the rig.

"We need to go," said Nina," to the control room."

"That's impossible," said Phil Bennington. "We're
breaking security right now, by even having you on
board."

"All right. Where can we go?"

"Nina," said Sandy. "You've got to tell us. What's
happening here? They said you were making some awful
row at the airport, talking about explosions again. Are you
both crazy? Haven't we been all through this?"

"Just find us a room, Sandy. And get your Tool Master
there."

"Tom? Tom Holder?"

"Yes. And you probably want the head of security, too.
He needs to hear this. Get Brewster Dale in the room."

"But I don't know where they…"

"I'm not insane, Sandy. Neither is Liz here. There's
something you've got to hear. And you've got to hear it
soon."

Sandy nodded reluctantly and said:

"All right. I'll try."

And she did.

The room was small but well insulated. It contained a
round table.

Within five minutes, the people Nina had named were seated around the table.

They could have been seated at a board room in the Bay St. Lucy town hall.

At twelve o'clock, Phil Bennington. Two o'clock, Tom Holder. Four o'clock, Brewster Dale. Six o'clock, Liz Cohen. Eight o'clock, Nina.

Penelope and Hector were somewhere else, being fed and shown the hospitality of Aquatica.

There was a clock on the wall behind Bennington.

Seven thirty.

"All right, Ms. Bannister. Ms. Cohen. We've pretty much done as you asked. The people you wanted are all here."

"And," said Brewster Dale, his face even ruddier than ever, "it has been done at great expense to my good name. Why, they're going to have my head back in Lafayette for even allowing you two to be brought up on board. Why, you can't go around shouting 'bomb' like that! Not in a crowded airport. And certainly not on Aquatica!"

"Yeh," interjected Holder, leaning forward. "All the blokes think you're both crazy! Talkin' about a bomb that way! That's a thing we don't joke about, bombs!"

"But," said Nina, quietly, "there is a bomb."

Silence in the room.

"I think," said Bennington, starting to rise, "we've all had about…"

"Do you know," she continued, "what semtex is?"

More silence.

A dreadful kind of silence.

Except for the ticking of the clock.

Seven thirty-five

Finally, Holder.

The Tool Master.

"Aye, lass. Every driller knows what semtex is."

"It's in your drilling tubes."

Sandy:

"What?"

"There is plastique in your drilling tubes."

Bennington:

"That's impossible."

Nina:

"From your central control panels, can you check the density of the cement in each tube?"

Holder:

"Yes. Of course we can. We have to be able to…"

"Check segment 642C tube number 4. Then check 789D tube number 2."

Everyone in the room was looking at her now.

Finally, someone asked:

"How do you know all this?"

She ignored the question and said, simply:

"You have maybe half an hour to check those tubes. Then they're going to blow up."

Holder looked at Bennington and said:

"I'll go and do it, Chief, if you want me to."

But Nina interrupted:

"Not so fast. Just wait a second. Tool Master."

And, as she finished speaking, she reached into her purse, put her hand around Edgar's phone, flipped it open, and pressed the 'call' button.

Silence.

Then a buzz.

From the coat pocket of Brewster Dale.

Now everyone was looking at him.

Including Nina.

"Answer your phone," she said, quietly.

Buzz.

Buzz.

The staring continued. Dale showed no expression at all. Finally, Phil Bennington asked:

"What's going on here?"

"Your Tool Master," Nina said quietly, "is not your Tool Master."

Bennington:

"You're not making any sense."

Nina continued to look at Dale:

"All your quotations were wrong."

Sandy leaned forward, but Nina ignored her, saying:

"Pouring whisky is like burning books," is not from *Intruder in the Dust*. It's from *The Hamlet*. All the rest of them are wrong, too."

Finally, Dale bowed, slightly:

"My compliments, Madam."

She shook her head.

"It bothered me a little bit while you were making all those mistakes. The quotes were always accurate, but you had them coming from the wrong books. At first, I just thought, oh let it go, he's an amateur scholar. Then finally I realized: no lover of Faulkner would have a character from *The Sound and the Fury* saying something that only the narrator from *A Rose for Emily* could possibly have said. Or misquoted Flem Snopes, who speaks in a voice all his own. Or failed to give credit to Boon Hoggenbeck for saying "Unless you're ashamed of yourself now and then, you're not honest."

"Again. My compliments."

"You never read Faulkner at all. You couldn't have. You just went to Wikipedia and memorized ten or so quotes. I did it myself today. They're right there on the screen. The problem is, Wikipedia doesn't attribute the quotations. It doesn't say where they came from. So you just found a list of Faulkner's novels—there's one of those in Wikipedia too—and memorized them. Then you put a novel with a quote. Just at random."

She shook her head:

"I don't know what your name really is. But, whoever you are, did you really think you could misquote William Faulkner to a high school English teacher—IN MISSISSIPPI?"

The man who had pretended to be Brewster Dale shook his head.

"I apparently underestimated you, Ms. Bannister."

Nina shook her head.

"You underestimated Faulkner. You might try reading him sometime."

"I shall. I certainly shall."

A recording was playing on Nina's cell phone:

"The number you have called is not available. Your call has been forwarded to an automatic message system…"

Etc. etc., etc.

"You may hang up, or…."

"I'm going to leave you a message," she said.

Then into her phone:

"You killed Edgar. He thought you were a security officer. We all did. In fact, somewhere back there in time there probably was a Brewster Dale. And he probably did like Faulkner. And he probably did work in security, even maybe for Louisiana Petroleum. But he's dead now, isn't he?"

And then, magically, the southern accent of the man sitting across from her disappeared. The gracious glint in the laughing eyes hardened. And the back stiffened as the man in the white sport jacket leaned forward slightly and said:

"Yes. That man is dead. He was, unfortunately, in the wrong place. And at the wrong time."

Tom Holder leaned forward also:

"I'd like to bleedin' know what's going on here! You're talkin' to me about bloody semtex.."

"It's exactly where I said it was," Nina continued. "And it's going to blow up in…."

She looked at her watch.

"Fourteen and a half minutes."

"My God," said Phil Bennington, "we've got to get it out of there!"

Nina shook her head:

"No you don't. Not right now, anyway."

Then she looked back at the man who had been known as Brewster Dale:

"It's not going to blow up," she said, "until you detonate it, is it? That's how plastique works. It gets detonated by a remote control device. "

The man nodded:

"You're a very perceptive woman."

"Just a little slow. Like Edgar was. How did you kill him?"

"That hardly matters now, does it?"

"No. No, and I pretty much know anyway. He thought you really were a security officer. You met him somewhere in Bay St. Lucy. You got him to drink something, maybe a little coffee from a thermos. The drug you put in it made him groggy, but he was still able to swallow the whiskey you poured down him against his will. Once he had passed out you took him to the coulee and put him in it, face down in the water. He must have drowned in a minute or so."

"An admirable sleuth you are. I did wonder though: how were you able to penetrate our little ruse?"

"Annette Richoux came by and told us."

"Did she now?"

"No. But somebody who had pretended to be Annette Richoux did."

"How naughty of her."

"She'll be dead too, in a week or so, I guess."

"Well, disloyalty always has its price."

"As does blowing up Aquatica. Who's paying you? And how much?"

The figure smiled an ice smile and said:

"Oh, that would be telling. And we don't tell. But alas, *tempus fugit*. Time flies. I must have leave to check the full message you left me."

So saying, he opened his sport jacket pocket, reached in, and pulled out a smart phone, which he laid on the table in front of him.

"That's the detonator, isn't it?" asked Nina.

"Just another 'app.' Camera, detonator…it's a useful device. I have another useful device though…"

He reached into the other side of the jacket...

...and produced a small, black, oil-shiny handgun, which he levelled at Bennington.

"I'm now in the rather difficult position of dealing with the five of you."

"You are going to leave Aquatica on the next helicopter, aren't you?" asked Nina, surprised at how calm she was, given that a gun was being levelled at her.

That had never happened before.

Surprising.

The Robinson Affair. The Reddington murder.

No gun being levelled at her.

But there it was, nevertheless, the end of its barrel a small metallic circle moving slowly around the table as the man holding it got slowly to his feet.

"Yes. It is unfortunate. But I must miss the gala."

"The rest of your 'crew,' the ones who helped you plant this stuff...they're already gone."

"The ebb and flow of talent. Some are already out of the country. It's a shame. They won't be able to see the explosion. And quite a sight it will be."

He was now backing toward the door of the room.

"So what," asked Sandy, ashen-faced, "are you going to do with us? Just leave us here while you go flying off?"

The man shook his head.

"No. That would not be the best course of action."

"He's going," said Nina, again astonished at her own calmness, "to shoot us."

"No!" Sandy screamed.

"How are you going to get away with that?" said Bennington.

A shrug.

"There will be five shots. Please don't worry; every shot will be perfectly on target. None of you will know what hit you. Then Brewster Dale will run out onto the deck, calling for help. While help runs into the room going one way, he will be making his way against the current of humanity, going the other way."

"Then you," said Nina, "will make your way down to the landing pad, commandeer a helicopter while the pilot is not in the craft…"

"I am, it is true, a man of many skills, helicoptering being one of them."

"How far from Aquatica will you be when you press the detonator switch? Just curious, you understand."

"I would say half a mile should do it," came the chilling reply.

There was silence of an instant.

The gun came up.

"Then, sadly, I must…"

"I have one thing to ask," said Liz, who had not spoken.

The figure in the door looked at her:

"Then ask."

"Can I light a cigarette and at least have one drag? Even prisoners about to be executed have that right."

He nodded.

Be quick about it.

"All right."

She reached into her purse.

From which she pulled the forty-five automatic, cocking it as she laid it on the table pointing directly at the man standing in the doorway.

"I have," she said, quietly, "a forty-five automatic. You have a thirty eight."

Silence for a time.

"My gun is bigger than your gun."

Another pause.

Then Holder:

"Shoot the bleeding son of a bitch! Do it! Shoot him!"

Nina shook her head:

"Don't shoot, Liz!"

Liz was ice cold.

The combat journalist.

"Why not, Nina? It will make a big splatter. But we can clean it up."

Nina continued to shake her head:

"He's got that detonator in his hand."

What? Had Brewster Dale smiled?

"Yes, I do. And my finger is on the detonator button."

"Shoot the bloke! Shoot him!"

"Don't, Liz," Nina supplicated. "We can't let him push that thing."

Bennington rose.

"Look, we have to be able to make some kind of a deal. You forget this scheme, and we let you go!"

"Oh, I shall go. But the 'scheme,' as you put it, must regrettably be carried out. Otherwise a great many people would lose patience with me completely."

"But think of what's going to happen here!"

"A great deal is going to happen here, Dr. Bennington."

"The oil from this explosion will literally destroy the Gulf of Mexico!"

"Yes, but there are other bodies of water in the world."

"Shoot him! Shoot him now!"

"Don't, Liz!"

"I'm going to leave now. I'm going to back out of this door, then descend the stairs to the main deck. If anyone tries to stop me, I shall press this button and blow up Aquatica."

"You'd be killing yourself, too," said Nina, rising, as was everyone else in the room.

"Unfortunately, yes."

"You wouldn't dare do it."

"Can you be certain of that? Go ahead, Ms. Cohen, pull the trigger. Then say goodbye to your life, and your world!"

He backed out through the door. They, as though hypnotized, followed him.

It was a bizarre parade of people.

A stalemate.

He could not shoot them; Liz could not shoot him.

And outside there was the chaos of two hundred guests, one hundred and twenty or so workers, all drinking plastic glasses full of champagne and milling around each other, the celebrities and athletes signing autographs on everything in sight, everyone taking shelter under metal roofs and covers from the spattering rain, which seemed to be intensifying.

The parade made its way down a rain slickened stairway.

Nina could see a helicopter on the landing pad below, its two great fore and aft rotors revolving slowly.

A voice at her shoulder:

"What the------ is----g---------the-------!"

Penelope.

Penelope!

"We can't let that man get onto that helicopter," she whispered. "We've got to stop him somehow."

"---------?"

"Yes."

"---------?"

"No."

"Okay."

And Penelope was gone, slipped off down a smaller stairway, and vanished into the rain-slickened shadows.

One step after another.

The man with the detonator now on the main deck of Aquatica; Liz ten feet away from him, her forty five pointed at his chest. Then Holder; then Sandy...

No one seeing them.

The helicopter, empty, having just disgorged a final load of celebrities, its pilot swigging a plastic bottle of mineral water forty feet away.

Phil Bennington stepped forward:

"Please. For God's sake, don't do this!"

His plea was followed merely by a shake of the gunman's head.

"Give me the damned gun!" Holder bellowed at Liz. "I'll shoot him if you don't have the guts to do it!"

Liz simply shook her head.

And the parade continued.

Ten feet from the helicopter.

Five feet.

"I regret that I must now bid all of you a good night."

"All right," shouted Bennington, stepping forward still more and gesturing to the lifeboats, which Nina remembered from her earlier trip out to Aquatica. "Let's make a deal! We let you get on the helicopter! We let you take off. You agree to give us ten minutes before you push that thing. In ten minutes, we can fill these six lifeboats and get them launched."

The nearest lifeboat was only a few feet from Nina. She peered down into its darkened interior, which looked not too different from the interior of the helicopter. *Strange*, she found herself thinking. The thing still looked like a monstrously long okra plant, purple in color, and heavily plated to withstand the fifty-foot plunge into the sea.

It was built, they had told her, to go through burning oil slicks.

But tonight…

Could it withstand the explosion that might be coming? Instinctively, she put her hand on what seemed to be the door leading into the thing, while Barrington implored again:

"Give us ten minutes! We'll let you go, if you'll give us ten minutes!"

Holder shook his head, bellowing:

"Don't make deals with that SOB! If you let him get on that 'copter, he'll blow us up!"

The man who was now at the point of entering the helicopter nodded:

"All right. You have your ten minutes. I shall circle the craft for that length of time, then fly shoreward. As many people as can be gotten off Aquatica…will be saved. Some of you, at least, will live to tell the story."

"Ok. We'll take you at your word."

"Excellent!"

And even as the man smiled, even as he climbed into the helicopter, Nina knew that he was lying.

He was going to give them nothing.

No time at all.

He was going to fly one half mile away.

And then he was going to do the job he and his 'crew' had been paid to do.

He was going to blow up Aquatica.

And nothing could prevent that.

She was going to die.

They were all going to die.

And the Gulf Coast was going to die.

He was on the copter now, in the pilot's seat.

The rotors began to spin faster, as the engine roared.

All she could think of was Frank.

Maybe I'm going to see you now, Frank.

Maybe we'll be walking along the beach together, as we always did.

And it will be a beach in heaven.

A clean beach.

In heaven.

Strange. She wasn't even trembling, as the helicopter lifted off.

She was just watching, like a spectator at an athletic event.

The helicopter rose slowly, a foot off the pad. Two feet.

And then it happened. It came from out of nowhere. A gigantic, black crate seemed to come crashing down out of the heavens. It was as though an asteroid had fallen to earth, slanting, its path straight for the helicopter.

"Watch out! Watch out!" screamed several crew members at once, as they looked on, horrified.

CRASH!

The crate swung mightily against the hovering copter, as the wrenching screams of metal on twisted metal drowned out the overmatched piping screams of sprinting, orange-clad men, who sounded like terrified birds watching the thing that many of them worked their hardest, during loadings and unloadings, to prevent.

A crane accident.

The helicopter, Nina saw, had been knocked out of the air and was lying at a forty-five degree angle on the edge of the deck, black smoke pouring from its forward engine, a gaping hole in its side.

"She's gonna go over! Get the pilot out! Get him out!"

And crew members were indeed running across the circular yellow landing pad, slipping on its rain-soaked tarmac.

They had almost reached the door when one of them, looking up and behind him, screamed again:

"Watch out!"

For the asteroid was falling again.

And again the huge black metal crate came crashing out of the sky, the bloated pendulum of some gigantic seismic grandfather clock, falling terribly against the rotored-craft below, which, with another agonized screeching of metal against twisted metal, heaved and gave up and toppled over the side and into the black, surging ocean.

"Man overboard! Man overboard!"

Water from the crash into the ocean sprayed up over Nina and soaked her, as, looking up and behind her she saw the crane operator, who smiled down at her.

Penelope!

Penelope whose lips were mouthing some pitiless obscenity.

But who was, nevertheless, smiling broadly.

"Good job, Penn," Nina whispered.

She felt an unutterable sense of relief.

It was to last perhaps two seconds.

And after those two seconds she became aware of two things, simultaneously: first, a group of Aquatica workers were sprinting toward her, shouting, "Get away! Clear away! The life boat's going down!"

Second, the interior of the lifeboat had begun to flash red and then yellow, then black, red and yellow, as if it had been the inside of a circus chamber of horrors, or a border bordello.

Now a loud buzzing noise filled the air...

..and now an automated voice bellowing in her ear from some amplification system that must have been installed in the life boat itself:

"BOAT LAUNCH IN TEN SECONDS! BOAT LAUNCH IN EIGHT SECONDS!"

"Get away from there! The boat is going down!"

She looked down.

The helicopter, like a black, massive, shining sea creature, was sinking into the ocean. But a figure had escaped from the cockpit and was thrashing in the water.

The Tool Master—for what else could she call him?— had not drowned.

Damn! she found herself thinking.

BOAT LAUNCH IN...

"Get away from there!"

No.

She could not 'get away from there.'

Because the man who was swimming away from the drowning helicopter would, almost certainly, make it onto the lifeboat.

The lifeboat which was, as she had been told earlier by Sandy Cousins, programmed to be shot through oil slicked water at high speeds, at least for a mile.

At that distance he could still blow up the craft.

He would be rescued of course.

Brewster Dale, sole survivor, left to tell the tale.

She could not let that happen.

"Get away! It's going down!"

BOAT LAUNCH IN TWO SECONDS!

She threw herself inside.

"Get out of there!! It's..."

And at that moment, the lifeboat exploded away into the water.

She was hurtled forward in the craft, which fell sickeningly and forever as she tumbled like a pool ball, thrown first one direction and then another. She may have lost consciousness for an instant; but when she regained awareness she was sitting folded between two rows of seats, her forehead bleeding, her wrist aching, and her brain filled with the flashing of garish lights and the braying of horns that seemed to come from super animated World War II movies:

RAAA DAAA! RAA DAA! RAADAAA!

For a few instants she was not able to move at all.

Finally, she crawled to an upright position and looked around. She was alone on the lifeboat which was rocking heavily in churning waters.

Around her, the ocean was ablaze with lights, all pouring down off the decks of Aquatica.

The rails were lined with people, all shouting down at her.

And now, she could make out what the boats' PA system was braying:

"Jettison in one minute. Jettison in fifty five seconds…"

The lifeboat, then, was not programmed to be instantly shot away from Aquatica; instead it was programmed to stay by the craft to pick up any people who might be swimming toward it.

And there…

THERE!

There was a person swimming toward it.

White hair, ruddy face, riding high in the water…

Hands swimming expertly…

One of those hands was holding the detonator.

And he was no more than fifteen feet from her.

He would reach the life boat where she was in only a few seconds.

He would clamber aboard.

He would kill her.

Then the boat would be jettisoned.

Then he would be two hundred yards from Aquatica.

Then he would press the button.

Then the explosion.

She looked over the side again.

He saw her now, and was smiling at her as he swam.

When, from the deck of the ship, another voice rang out:

"Man overboard! Man overboard!"

She looked up. A body came hurtling down off the deck...

SPLASH!

Spray inundated her.

She wiped her face with her sleeve, which, like the deck beneath her and the seats beside her, were drenched.

Then she looked overboard again.

Two figures, not ten feet from the side of the lifeboat, were locked in combat. Both were flailing madly at the water and then at each other, their shouts and curses muffled and gasping as they tried to grasp and escape, breathe and kick, claw and survive.

One of the figures was the Tool Master, snarling, red-faced still, his big hands clenching and unclenching, his grasp seemingly unbreakable, the detonator still held firmly above water.

The other was smaller, darker, and far more slender.

Hector Ramirez.

Hector was losing.

He was under the water now.

And now the other, free of the boy, began swimming in powerful strokes again toward the lifeboat.

"Ahhaguu!"

Hector lunged up out of the water and flailed at him, both fists flying, those sad eyes ablaze now, his whole body writhing:

"DAMN YOU!" shouted the tool man, pulling an arm up and out of the water, ready to deliver a final blow.

But as he did so, the detonator slipped from his hand.

He might as well have thrown it like a baseball player, so perfectly centered did it land, clattering, on the deck of the lifeboat not two feet from Nina's feet.

She stared at it.

It glowed blue and yellow and green, lying half in rainwater, its screen like a miniature pinball machine.

"Don't go off," she prayed.

"DROWN, DAMN YOU!"

She looked right.

There was only one figure now.

The Tool Master was alone in the water, swimming toward her, and glaring at her.

Ten feet away.

Eight feet away.

Hector was gone, his body, she knew, sinking.

But the detonator was here, with her.

She picked it up, reared her arm back...

"NO," screamed the figure in the water, "NO! DON'T THROW IT!"

She stared through rain-filmed eyes at the figure swimming toward her, and then shouted:

"Go to hell, you bastard! Here goes your precious detonator!"

And she prepared to heave it as far as she could...

...but before she could do so, something huge and gray erupted from the surface beside her; it convulsed, shook its mammoth body, and bared a gaping hole filled with teeth.

"AAAAHHHGGGH!"

There was time for one scream.

Then the shark and what had been Brewster Dale were gone, disappeared, nothing remaining of them but black, rain-pelted ocean and a small pool of blood.

"Help! Help me!"

She looked again.

Hector.

Hector!

He was swimming manfully, gasping, choking..

...but closing the distance.

"Come on, Hector! Come on!"

And make it he did.

She reached over the side and grabbed his collar.

Within ten seconds, they were huddled together, shivering, crying on each other's shoulders, and laughing.

"The shark, Hector. The shark just..."

He nodded.

"I know. I see."

"It could have gotten you!"

"No. It had to take that man, the shark. It had to take that man. He killed Edgar. And we could do nothing. But when he tried to kill the sea...well, the sea killed him, instead."

She nodded, then said:

"But you, the way you dived in...sometimes a man is needed, Hector. Sometimes a man is needed."

For the first time, she saw a smile in his sad, olive eyes, and he said:

"And sometimes, Senora...sometimes a woman."

EPILOGUE

The Blue Gator was just as Nina remembered it. Peering through the garish yellow light, she saw the crumbling garden, vines overhanging bare rafters, tables scattered here and there, some with tablecloths, some bare and reflecting in their green metal tops the half moon that peered mockingly through the places in the roof that were not roof. The garden was a jungle of furniture and vine-tangles that seemed to keep opening out from itself, passing a bench here and there, and overhearing patches of conversation.

"Non, c'est…c'est bien trop…"

"Oui, je crois bien que…"

French. English. Cajun. Creole…yes, just as it had been those strange weeks ago…

.. when she was here with a woman who did not exist.

Now she had come back to celebrate. She, Liz, Hector, Penelope—all of the heroes who had saved the Aquatica, and a great deal more.

They had been feted all day, had met the top officials of Louisiana Petroleum and had been offered an evening anywhere in town—at the company's expense, of course.

Nina had chosen The Blue Gator.

Now they all were seated at a large table in the back, the gang from Aquatica—Sandy, Phil Bennington, Tom Holder—interspersed with them, everyone drinking Abita Beer, everyone anxious for the dancing to start.

But, dancing notwithstanding, the conversation kept coming back to those last minutes on Aquatica.

"How did you learn to operate a crane, Penelope?" Nina asked.

"I---. Then I ---. But I can operate any kind of ---machine! Also, it's great---fun to destroy things. Especially that ---helicopter!"

A mixture of laughter from those who had heard Penelope before, and those who were experiencing these obscenities for the first time.

Tom Holder to Liz:

"I kept telling you to bleedin' shoot, Ms. Cohen."

"Liz."

"Okay, Liz. I kept telling you to bleedin' shoot. Thank God, you didn't."

Liz shrugged.

"Maybe I should have. Maybe he wouldn't have had a chance to press the button."

Holder:

"Yeh, but maybe he would have."

Liz nodded, then leaned over and whispered in Nina's ear:

"He's such a hunk. I want him. Tonight."

Nina smiled:

"The Blue Gator has that effect."

Upon hearing which Liz merely shook her head:

"Blue Gator be damned. I'd want him in a Dairy Queen. So I may be a bit late coming back to the hotel room tonight. Like maybe eight o'clock in the morning."

"Suit yourself, girl. You earned a night on the town. I'll never forget your sitting there, hard as steel, not moving an inch, that huge forty-five automatic just resting on the table: and that great line, "My gun is bigger than your gun.""

"Well. It was."

"So what about *The Times*? You going back to work for them?"

Liz shook her head:

"Don't know. Have to think about that one for a while."

"My invitation is still open, you know."

"I'm thinking about that too. It's just that, right now, I'm thinking mainly about the Tool Master. I want to see his..."

"Don't say it."

"Okay. Let's just say that I'll let you know later about my plans."

"Got it."

Phil Bennington interrupted:

"Sorry to break in on your conversation," he said, "but the music is going to start soon, and I want to propose a toast, to the one man here who can't drink one."

General laughter around the table.

"Here's to Hector Ramirez. The bravest young man I've ever seen."

Applause, shouting.

Bennington:

"You dove twenty feet into the ocean and wrestled a professional assassin to a draw, Hector."

Hector shook his head:

"Not really. He was so much stronger than me. I just held him up for a little bit."

"A little bit," said Nina, "was all it took."

"Yeah, Senora. And then the shark did the rest."

Silence for a moment.

Then Nina to Phil:

"They still don't know who he was?"

A shake of the head:

"They don't know who any of them were. But the FBI is very grateful, Ms. Cohen, that you're agreeing to keep this quiet."

Liz nodded:

"I don't want to write another story I know nothing about."

"We're glad you feel that way. Somehow, Aquatica's security simply melted. The real Brewster Dale, we have learned, was, in fact, murdered over fourteen months ago. This man killed him, and simply 'became' him. Dale was a perfect target. A widower, coming off one job, having applied for the position at Aquatica—no one in our corporation had really met him."

"And Annette?" asked Nina.

Again, a shake of the head.

"That woman could be anywhere now."

"Or nowhere."

Bennington:

"That's right. I wouldn't want to cross this bunch. And she did so."

To which, Nina replied:

"And we're all lucky she did. A spark of conscience. That was all that saved us."

Liz:

"Well, not quite all. Your seeing through the Faulkner scam didn't hurt."

Nina simply shook her head in disgust:

"The very idea. He might just as well have misquoted the gospels to a Baptist preacher."

General laughter.

"The bottom line," Sandy said, "is that LP owes all of you a great deal. And any time you want to…"

She was interrupted by a general movement toward the dance floor.

"Come on, blokes," said Holder. "Let's go up there."

They rose and made their way through the garden.

The floor itself looked just as Nina had remembered it:

The single melancholy saxophone player, the scattered musicians, the scratching fiddle, the bass…

…and of course, the box accordion.

Then the chiming clock:.

Bong. Bong…

And The Red Stick Ramblers, belting it out:

"GEAUX GEAUX GEAUX de GEAUX GEAUX GEAUX!

MEAUX MEAUX MEAUX de MEAUX MEAUX MEAUX!

The music pounded and throbbed, and, once more, as it had for decades or more, the Cajun dance floor filled.

Liz and Tom disappeared into it; then Sandy and Phil; then Hector; then Penelope...

Then:

"May I?"

And, precisely as had happened before, a man—a different man, but a man nonetheless—was standing just in front of Nina with his arm outstretched.

He looked...

Oh, hell, what did it matter how he looked?

"Do you wish to dance, Miss?"

"Sure."

She took his hand,

And once again, all bad things, all evil deeds, disappeared.

OH OH OH, de OH OH OH!

"You a good dancer, Miss!"

"Thank you!" she shouted to the six faces closest to her.

All of them, as they had before, smiled back.

THE END

ABOUT THE AUTHORS

Pam Britton (T'Gracie) Reese is an Assistant Professor in the Communication Science and Disorders Department at Indiana/Purdue University at Fort Wayne. Previously, she worked as a speech pathologist in schools in private practice. She was also a supervisor in communication disorders at Ohio University. She likes nothing better, professionally, than helping small, silent two-year-old boys start talking. She has also published books about autism with LinguiSystems for the last 15 years. *The Circle of Autism* was previously published on-line at ken*again e-magazine

Joe Reese is a novelist, playwright, storyteller, and college teacher. He has published four novels, several plays, and a number of stories and articles. When he is not teaching (English and German), he enjoys visiting elementary schools, where he tells stories from his Katie Dee novels and talks to students about writing. He and his wife Pam have three children: Kate, Matthew, and Sam.